The Secret of Whitewitch Mountain

R P R IRVINE

ISBN-13: 978-1534999855
ISBN-10: 153499985X

DEDICATION

In memory of Marnie & Douglas
Who always encouraged me to use my imagination.

Chapters

Ordania

1 A CLOSE ENCOUNTER WITH THE DISTANT PAST.

'Next stop Ardroil!' shouted the bus driver of the W4 bus from Uig to Stornoway as it trundled along the hilly coastline of Lewis. Despite the *dreich* weather as it is known in Scotland, the scenery from the bus window was truly breathtaking. Even under the dark, damp clouds visitors to this remote island off the west coast of Scotland could not fail to marvel at its rugged beauty. However, the two elderly passengers on the bus barely took notice. They could be forgiven for not admiring the scenery for they had used this bus route for many years and between them they had spent almost one hundred and sixty years on the island. Brighid and Ealasaid were best friends and they were making their weekly Saturday afternoon trip to their favourite coffee shop. They were seated towards the front of the bus and enjoying a gossip on the way to Lochcroistean.

'Do you remember Catriona Macgregor who used to live in the croft just down the road from us?' asked Ealasaid.

'Which Catriona Macgregor do you mean? There were three of them in the same house,' replied Brighid.

'The one who got married to the man from North Uist and went to live in Stornoway. I think she's the youngest. Well, did you know that she just had triplets?' said Ealasaid.

'No, I did not. Triplets you say? Oh my! That'll keep her busy,' replied Brighid.

'Well, that's not all. I've heard that the strange husband of hers from Uist has been away at sea for almost a year, so goodness knows how the triplets came about,' said Ealasaid.

'Tut, tut. I always said that no good would come of that couple marrying so young and then him taking to the seas for such a long time. She should have stayed back in the croft with her seanag, at least then she'd have some help with three babies. That'll teach her to run away to Stornoway,' said Brighid shaking her head.

Just then the W4 bus reached the stop of Timsgarry and pulled up at the side of the road.

'Oh, Brighid. The bus is stopping. I wonder who this is getting on?' said Ealasaid. Both ladies were surprised as the bus hardly ever stopped at Timsgarry when they made their weekly jaunt to Lochcroistean.

Both ladies stopped talking, leaned their heads to the side and stared at the door of the bus. Moments later the door opened allowing an elderly lady and a young girl to step on. They noticed immediately that the young girl was blind as despite being at least fifteen years of age, the old lady held her arm and then helped her place her hand on to the rail inside the bus whilst she fumbled about in the pockets of a rather large raincoat. Eventually, the elderly lady withdrew a few coins from one of the pockets.

'Feasgar math! Aird Uig please!' said the elderly lady and she dropped the coins into the slot, took hold of the young girls arm again and began to make her way over to the seats.

'Where shall we sit Gran?' said the young girl.

'It's only one stop, so we'll just sit at the front,' said the elderly lady. She guided the young girl into the seats directly opposite where Brighid and Ealasaid were seated and staring in silence.

'Feasgar math,' said the elderly lady and she smiled at Brighid and Ealasaid before taking her seat next to her granddaughter.

'F… feasgar math!' replied both ladies at the same time, eventually finding their tongues.

Shortly after that the bus pulled away and continued along the road in the direction of Aird Uig, which is where the elderly lady and her blind granddaughter were heading.

Brighid found that she could not stop herself from staring. Her eyes followed the strange looking lady from the moment she stepped onto the bus until she took her seat adjacent to them.

'I think she's got glitter in her hair. Look, it's sparkling under her hat,' whispered Brighid. As she said this, she gently nudged Ealasaid who looked over at the old lady and sure enough there were several strands of wispy, silver hair sticking out from under her hat that sparkled and twinkled.

'Do you think she's from Glasgow?' whispered Ealasaid.

'No, she's most likely from Edinburgh with hair like that,' whispered Brighid.

Sensing she was being watched, the elderly lady turned her head and smiled at Brighid and Ealasaid.

'Terrible weather isn't it?' said the elderly lady with the sparkling hair and she smiled again.

There was a short silence before Brighid eventually spoke. 'Yes, indeed it is awful but I believe it's to be dry tomorrow. Have you travelled far?' asked Brighid.

'Oh, yes we have travelled quite far. I'd forgotten just how exhausting it is to travel. Thankfully we've not got much further to go. In fact, this is our stop coming up. Latha math leat,' said the elderly lady.

'Next stop Aird Uig!' shouted the bus driver as the W4 bus pulled up at the side of the road. The elderly lady with the sparkling hair stood up and took her granddaughter by the arm, smiled once more at Ealasaid and Brighid and left the bus.

'Where do you think they are going?' said Ealasaid.

'I wouldn't be surprised if they're heading to Ailsa Carmichael's house. She lives down near the beach and they say she hasn't come out of her house for almost three years but there are always lots of queer folk coming and going,' said Brighid.

'Ailsa Carmichael? Oh, yes I remember her. She was always travelling off to faraway places and bringing odd people back. Indeed she is a strange one but that's what happens when you marry a man from the city,' said Ealasaid.

Moments later the bus pulled away with the surprised faces of Ealasaid and Brighid pressed against the window, desperate to know where the strange lady and her blind granddaughter were heading.

'I hope those old dears aren't too disappointed. I think they were hoping for a little more information from me,' said the blind girl's grandma, who if you haven't already guessed was actually Queen Valda of Ordania in disguise now that she was on earth. She waved at the bus and then turned to her granddaughter.

'Right Eden, I mean Emily, let's go and see the family. They'll be wondering where we've got to. I said we'd be there ages ago,' said the grandmother. They began to make their way along the path that took them closer to the beach.

'Shouldn't you have a different name while you are on earth just like us Grandma?' asked Emily.

'Actually, I do have one but I haven't used it in a very long time. Ailsa Carmichael gave it to me years ago,' said the grandmother.

'So, what is your earth name then?' asked Emily.

'It's Veronica Bartholomew or Vronnie for short,' said the grandmother. 'Anyway, I'm Granny Bartholomew to you whilst we are on earth,' smiled the grandmother. She stopped talking as soon as she caught sight of Uig sands.

'Ah, there's a pretty sight. What a beautiful beach,' said Granny Bartholomew.

'Oh! I'm sorry dear. That was thoughtless of me.' She suddenly remembered that her granddaughter was blind.

'It's fine Gran, don't worry. Although, I do wish I could see the beach with my own eyes. Anna said that it is one of the most beautiful beaches she has ever seen,' said Emily.

'Just take a moment to stop and listen, smell the fresh sea air and in a moment or two you should be able to see what the beach looks like. Let your imagination be your eyes,' said Granny Bartholomew as they stopped and turned towards the sea.

Emily did exactly as her grandmother said and listened carefully to the waves as they crashed against the shore. Overhead she could hear the same bird call over and over again; '*kittee-wa-aaake, kitte-wa-aaake*'. She breathed deeply once more and noticed how clear and pure the air was, just like in Ordania. Moments later a smile spread across Emily's face.

'Oh, yes Gran. I can see it now. It really is beautiful, just like Anna said it was,' said Emily and then she and her grandmother continued along the path until they came to a small row of cottages on the right.

'I feel really strange Grandma. Ever since we passed through the portal, I feel ….well, I feel kind of heavy. It's hard to explain,' said Emily.

'That is because your powers have been temporarily switched off. Remember the spell binds your powers automatically as soon as you arrive on earth,' said Granny Bartholomew. 'That is why you feel *heavy* as you describe it.'

'Oh, so does that means I'm no longer a sorceress then?' asked Emily.

'No dear, you will always be a sorceress but for the time being, until we return to Ordania your powers are dormant. It's best that way, at least until you have reached adulthood and are able to control your powers more. We don't want any mishaps whilst we are here.

Ah, here we are. The cottage of Ailsa Carmichael, your old nanny,' said Granny Bartholomew. She pushed open the gate and led her granddaughter up the short garden path. Just as she reached forward to unlatch the front door, it flew open and the familiar faces of Emily's twin brother and younger sister appeared.

'Emily, Granny, you're finally here!' shouted Anna. She ran forwards and hugged both her grandmother and big sister.

'Gran and Emily have arrived,' shouted Aaron. It wasn't long before the short hallway became quite crowded as Granny Bartholomew and Emily were enthusiastically hugged by members of their family.

'Mum, what took you so long? We thought you were lost,' smiled Mr. Bartholomew and then he kissed his mother on the cheek.

'Lost? When have you ever known me to get lost? Delayed perhaps, but never lost. The strangest of things happened. For some reason the portal has moved from the beach right down the road and it is now in the middle of a thicket beside Ardroil. When we first stepped out, we had no idea where we were. We walked out onto the road and found a bus stop,' said Granny Bartholomew.

'You on a bus? I'd love to see that,' laughed Mr. Bartholomew.

'I bet that has given the locals something to talk about,' said Mrs. Bartholomew as she took her mother-in-law's raincoat and hat and hung them in the hall cupboard.

'Is Ailsa here?' asked Granny Bartholomew.

'Yes, she's in the front room waiting to see you,' replied Mrs. Bartholomew.

Ailsa Carmichael was an old friend of Granny Bartholomew and was originally from the Isle of Lewis but for the past three earth years she had lived in the magical land of Ordania. Three years on earth is the equivalent to seventy two years in Ordania and Ailsa Carmichael had recently celebrated her one hundredth and second birthday. This was the first time she had been back on earth since she had left three years previously at the age of thirty three.

'Oh my, you are a young thing again,' said Granny Bartholomew when she walked into the front room and discovered that her old friend Ailsa was now only thirty six years old.

'Hello Vronnie, yes can you believe it? At this rate I'll live forever. It's strange to be young again, although one hundred and two isn't really that old for an Ordanian. I've lost count of how old you are,' smiled Ailsa. She was seated near to the window beside Granny Bartholomew's eldest grandson, Quentin.

'Aren't you going to give your Grandma a hug?' said Granny Bartholomew to Quentin who stood up immediately to offer his grandmother his seat.

'Hi Gran, it's great to see you,' smiled Quentin and he hugged his grandmother.

That evening the family ate together merrily in the now rather crowded cottage. It was mid-October and the children's parents had decided to spend the half term break in Scotland, rather than return to Ordania so that the children could enjoy a carefree break and hopefully spend time outdoors getting lots of fresh air before they returned to the classroom.

Although it now seemed a lifetime ago, the summer holidays of that year had been anything but quiet and peaceful for the royal children of Ordania, especially for Emily who had been blinded after an encounter with a terrible sea monster. Their parents were determined that this time nothing would stop them all from having a simple, quiet family holiday together. They certainly didn't want any more mishaps and thought that they were in the perfect place for it. After all, what could possibly go wrong on the tiny remote island of Lewis in the Western Hebrides?

'It's great to have everyone together again,' said Mrs Bartholomew. She had missed her daughter Emily who had remained in Ordania when the rest of the family returned to Scotland back in August.

'What has been happening at Williamsburgh High?' asked Emily.

'Oh nothing much as usual. Everyone was asking where you were when we first went back to school,' said Aaron. Although he didn't want to admit it, he had really missed his twin sister.

'There's only so long I can pretend that I am in Australia. Katie and Chloe write to me all the time. Gran made a time portal especially that links Ordania with Australia and we sometimes go there just to send parcels and postcards. It makes it look much more authentic,' said Emily.

'You've been to Australia?' asked Anna. 'I've always wanted to go there.'

'Yes, we've been to Brisbane loads and the Great Barrier Reef and made friends with a giant sea-turtle. I love it there,' replied Emily.

'Oh and you'll never guess what else?' said Aaron as he winked across the table at his brother Quentin.

'What?' asked Emily.

'Anna has a boyfriend,' said Aaron.

'I do not have a boyfriend. We're just friends,' said Anna.

'Who is it?' asked Emily.

'Who do you think? Angus Macpherson of course, who else would it be,' said Aaron and he stuck out his lips and made a loud kissing noise.

'Emily, how old are you now in Ordanian years?' said Quentin, trying to quickly change the topic as he could see his youngest sister getting really annoyed.

'Well, it has almost been four Ordanian years since I was last here, so by rights I should be older than you Quentin. However thanks to a special gift from Grandma Lucinda, I haven't really aged at all,' said Emily. She showed them a beautiful necklace that she had around her neck. It had a large blue ethereal stone hanging from it.

'Wow! That's amazing. If you wear it too much you'll outlive us all,' said Aaron remembering what he had learned about the precious stone from the Everlasting Cave on the Ethereal Isle, known to rejuvenate people and prolong life.

'I'll only wear it until you all move back to Ordania permanently, that way I won't get too old. Grandma Lucinda also used crushed blue crystals when she healed me after the accident, so I am probably now guaranteed to live forever. It would be weird if you all arrived home in your late teens and I was almost a pensioner,' laughed Emily.

That night the children slept in the front room of Ailsa Carmichael's cottage on make-shift beds. They sat up until late in the night talking and telling each other stories. They enjoyed being back together again and they talked of their next trip to Ordania. They wondered what sort of adventures lay in store for them. Quentin was secretly disappointed not to have returned to his homeland for the October break. He longed for another adventure and could not wait until he moved to Ordania permanently but his parents insisted he had to pass his exams at school. Quentin had tried to argue the point that he didn't need to go to school anymore but his parents and grandparents told him that to be a successful sorcerer and king, he needed to have a wealth of knowledge.

The next day the family enjoyed exploring the island of Lewis. They collected shells on the beaches, visited old crofts and imagined what life was like on the island in years gone by. Most impressive of all was their visit to mystical Callanish, site of the ancient standing stones.

'This is amazing, what are these stones?' asked Aaron as he stared around in wonder at the ancient stone structures, some of which dated as far back as 3000BC.

'Why don't you put your ear to one and find out?' said Emily who was already hugging one of the stones. The children copied their sister and threw their arms around a stone each, closed their eyes and pressed their ear against them.

Quentin was the first to experience a strange sensation. At first it felt as if the ground had started to spin and then he began to hear voices. They were voices from the distant past and they were calling out his name, not his earth name but his Ordanian name. Quentin listened harder until he could just make out what one of them was saying.

'We know who you are Prince of the Stars. Shine your light and help us be free of the dark,' said one of the voices.

'Who are you?' said Quentin.

When he spoke his parents and grandmother who were standing nearby turned around to see who Quentin was talking to and saw that he was still hugging the stone. Suddenly, the voice of Granny Bartholomew interrupted Quentin's concentration when she shouted across at him.

'Quentin, step away from the stone now please,' said Granny Bartholomew. She noticed that her grandson now had a bright blue glow around his body. Quentin did not respond, instead he continued to hug the standing stone with his eyes closed and his ear pressed firmly against it.

'What's happening to him?' asked Mrs. Bartholomew.

'It's the spirit within the stone. It has communicated with Quentin and I think that it has awoken his powers,' said Granny Bartholomew.

'Quentin must hide before someone sees him. What will they think if they see a young boy glowing brightly like that? He'll be on the front page of every newspaper, especially when we are standing in a place as sacred as this,' said Granny Bartholomew. Just then the strange blue glow became much brighter and a beam of blue light shot right up into the air.

Mrs. Bartholomew ran over towards her son and just as she reached out to touch him, Granny Bartholomew shouted; 'No! Don't touch him. It's too dangerous.'

However, it was too late. Mrs. Bartholomew's hand had already made contact with her son's shoulder. There was a bright flash and everyone fell backwards.

A great silence followed and the strange, blue glow that had appeared around Quentin disappeared.

The family lay on the ground stunned for a few moments. Granny Bartholomew was the first to find her feet and look around.

'Oh dear, you'll never guess what has happened?'

'What is it Mum?' asked Mr. Bartholomew who was now sitting upright and rubbing a sore elbow.

'I think you'll find we have gone back in time, how far exactly I don't yet know,' replied Granny Bartholomew.

All members of the family had now found their feet and they looked around cautiously. The sky overhead was heavy but to the west there were breaks in the cloud that revealed a burning sky of orange and gold, suggesting it was sunset. No one spoke for several minutes and then they heard someone approach.

'Quick, hide behind the stones,' said Granny Bartholomew. All seven members of the family quickly ran behind the stone that was nearest them. No sooner had they slipped behind the standing stones, than a group of hooded figures marched into the centre of the stone circle. There were men and women amongst them and they were all dressed in long, woolen cloaks under which they wore simple tunics tied around the waist with leather belts. Some of them carried long swords and on their heads they wore hats made from linen. They gathered in a circle and lifted their hands and eyes to the sky. Those who had swords withdrew them and then raised them high above their heads. Suddenly a brilliant flash of lightening shot out of the sky and struck the ground in the middle of the circle creating an enormous hole that glowed brightly.

The Bartholomew family secretly watched the strange spectacle unfold in front of them as they continued to hide behind the standing stones. Quentin happened to glance up to the sky again and noticed that there was now a break in the clouds displaying hundreds of brightly shining stars.

Suddenly the light from the enormous hole in the ground grew brighter until it lit up everyone and everything in the surrounding area, including the standing stones.

'There is someone or something coming out of the ground,' whispered Aaron. He was standing beside his twin sister, Emily and was describing to her everything that was taking place.

The rest of the family peered cautiously around the stones and sure enough out of the hole in the ground rose what looked like a giant, seated on an enormous throne. He wore great robes of the finest materials and magnificent jewelry hung around his neck. His hair and beard were long and silver and upon his head he wore a golden helmet decorated with wings on each side. In his right hand he held an enormous spear. On each of his broad shoulders sat two ravens and by his feet were terrible looking wolves that snapped and snarled at the group of worshippers. It was only when he lifted his head to look upon the group gathered before him that the Bartholomew family noticed he only had one eye.

'Oh dear. We certainly have gone back in time, by at least two thousand years I think,' whispered Granny Bartholomew who was standing next to Quentin.

When the grandmother turned to face her grandson, she noticed that he had started to glow again. This was something that he had no control over, especially now that his magical powers had been restored.

Eventually the bright blue light could be seen shining from behind the standing stone where Quentin and his grandmother were hiding and it didn't take long before it caught the attention of the group of worshippers. When the men and women dressed in hooded cloaks turned towards the standing stone that was now bright blue, they gasped loudly and then fell to their knees.

Suddenly the ravens took off and flew towards the spot where Quentin and Granny Bartholomew were hiding. It didn't take the birds long to discover the hidden family and when they did they called out to their master. The one-eyed giant stood up from his throne and pointed his spear at the standing stone where Quentin and Granny Bartholomew were hiding. A huge bolt of lightning shot out from the spear and made its way towards them. Quentin found himself being lifted off the ground and was soon suspended in mid-air above the heads of the worshippers. There was yet another blinding flash that made everyone look away temporarily. When they looked back, the one-eyed giant and his group of worshippers had completely vanished leaving the Bartholomew family alone once again. Everyone was still crouched behind the standing stones, except for Quentin who was lying face down on the grass in front of them.

Mrs. Bartholomew was the first to run forward and check on her son.

'Quentin, are you alright?' shouted Mrs. Bartholomew and she knelt down beside her son and gently turned him over. The rest of the family joined her and moments later Quentin opened his eyes to find his entire family staring down at him.

'W…What happened?' said Quentin as he sat upright and rubbed his eyes.

'I am not entirely sure, but I think we underestimated just how powerful these stones are. This is a very mystical place that has been here for thousands of years. There was some sort of connection between your power and the power of the stones. I don't quite understand it myself. Anyway, I think we should get away from here for we have attracted some unwanted attention,' said Granny Bartholomew.

The family looked round and noticed that a small group of onlookers had gathered on the far side of the field and they were watching the Bartholomew family with great interest. Shortly afterwards, the family left Callanish and made their way back to Ailsa's cottage where the adults discussed in detail the bizarre events of the afternoon.

'Well, it would seem that Quentin's powers have been fully restored which normally wouldn't be a problem, only his powers are so strong it will be hard for him to look *normal* as he goes about his business here on earth. The star-like glow that often shines from his body will look most unusual walking around on the island and there is no predicting when it will happen,' said Granny Bartholomew.

'He can't stay indoors all week. That was the whole point of us coming here in the first place. I want the children to get lots of fresh air. Can't you cast another spell to bind his powers?' asked Mrs. Bartholomew.

'I'm afraid I have already tried but it doesn't seem to work. Whatever happened back at Callanish seems to have overridden my spell. He encountered a very powerful force this afternoon and it seemed to recognise the fact that your son is a very powerful sorcerer,' said Granny Bartholomew.

'Well, we will have to do something. Quentin can't be glowing from head to foot when he returns to school next week,' said Mrs Bartholomew.

'I shall take him back to Ordania first thing tomorrow morning. We won't be gone long. I am hoping that when we exit earth and then re-enter, the binding spell will take effect again. However, I should warn you that as he and his brother and sisters get older, it will become more difficult to bind their powers,' said Granny Bartholomew.

'Yes, I am fully aware of that but please, before that happens can't we just have one last holiday as a family? I could do without any excitement for a while,' said Mrs. Bartholomew.

2 NEWS BY OWL

That night a terrible storm that had been brewing over the Atlantic Ocean finally arrived on Lewis forcing everyone and everything indoors. As the children sat in the front room of the cottage they listened to the wind as it screamed its way through the eves and rattled the window panes.

'Shall we sneak outside so that we can see the storm,' said Anna.

'Are you mad? Why would you want to do that?' asked Quentin.

'I remember a time when you were terrified of storms,' said Emily.

'Yes, well I love storms now. They give me energy,' said Anna.

'That might be the case when you are in Ordania but in case you had forgotten you are on earth just now and that means you are powerless. It's far too dangerous to go outside at the moment,' added Aaron.

'Who's powerless?' asked Anna. She closed her eyes, lifted her hands, turning her palms upwards. Suddenly, various objects around the room and pieces of furniture began to lift and float through the air, including her older brother Aaron.

'Whoa! What's going on?' shouted Aaron as his head hit the ceiling light.

'It looks like I'm not the only one whose powers were restored today. You kept that one quiet Anna,' said Quentin.

'Well, I wasn't going to say anything but since you're showing off, take that!' said Aaron and he pointed towards his little sister. Seconds later she too shot up from the floor where she had been sitting and started to spin round in the air.

'Stop it Aaron. You're being mean,' squealed Anna.

'That's what you get for making me float through the air. I'll put you down if you put me down first,' said Aaron.

By now every chair, vase, table, cushion and lamp in the room had floated up the ceiling. Quentin was worried that if either Anna or Aaron broke their spells, all of the objects would coming crashing back down to the floor.

'Be careful with the furniture. We don't want to trash Nanny Carmichael's home,' said Quentin. No sooner had he spoken than Aaron and Anna pointed at each other again. Anna instantly stopped spinning, then both she and Aaron started to fall.

Quentin reacted instantly and just in the nick of time he shouted *na caraich*. Suddenly everything in the room froze in mid-air, including Aaron and Anna.

'It's a good job you've got fast reflexes,' smiled Emily. 'I might as well tell you, I have my powers back too.' She waved her hand gently in the air and returned the furniture back to their original positions; however Aaron and Anna were left frozen in mid-air.

'I think we'll just leave those two where they are,' smiled Quentin. They are much less trouble that way.

Just then the door that led into the front room flew open and Granny Bartholomew walked in.

'What's all the shouting about in here?' asked Granny Bartholomew. There was no need for Quentin or Emily to answer for as soon she entered the room she saw Aaron and Anna suspended and frozen in mid-air.

'Quentin, I'm surprised at you. Remember what I told you about using magic unnecessarily and especially when we are outside of Ordania.

'Grandma, it was actually Anna and Aaron who started it. Quentin only stopped them from destroying Nanny Carmichael's front room,' said Emily.

'*Dùisgibh,*' whispered Granny Bartholomew and she waved her hand in the air. Suddenly Aaron and Anna began to stir. Then, slowly but surely they started to descend until they were seated comfortably on the floor. Both Aaron and Anna looked somewhat bewildered at first, they were unsure what had actually happened.

'It would seem that our visit to Callanish this afternoon has broken the binding spell and your powers have now been restored. I must ask you all to be very careful whilst we are here on earth. Under no circumstances must you use any more magic. I warn you that if you do, no good will come of it and you'll end up in all sorts of trouble,' said Granny Bartholomew. She then told her grandchildren to get to bed for it was now very late.

The children said goodnight to their grandmother and promised that they would be careful. Once Granny Bartholomew had closed the door, the children climbed back into their makeshift beds. They were all very tired and decided that they would go to sleep immediately. Aaron turned out the light and shortly afterwards they settled down in the darkened room. The only light came from the glowing embers in the fireplace. As Quentin lay in his bed, he stared at what was left of the fire. He listened to it crackle and watched as its fading light cast a strange, orange shadow around the room. Aaron and Anna fell asleep almost as soon as their heads hit the pillows.

'Quentin, what are you thinking about?' whispered Emily.

'How did you know that I was even awake?' whispered Quentin.

'I could tell by your breathing, plus I can almost hear your busy brain buzzing with thoughts,' answered Emily.

Since Emily had lost her eyesight, her other senses had become so much sharper and in many ways it was as if she could see, hear and smell even better than before. She certainly did not seem in any way disadvantaged by the fact that she was now blind.

'I'm just wondering what is happening back home in Ordania just now. I'd love to be lying in my bed and staring up at Starrydell at the moment,' whispered Quentin.

The ceiling above Quentin's room back in Ordania was enchanted. When you looked up you could see thousands of stars burning brightly. They were the stars of Ordanian sorcerers past and present.

'You'll be back in Ordania soon enough and I'm sure there will be lots of adventures,' whispered Emily.

'You're lucky, you get to live there all of the time now and you don't ever have to go back to school,' whispered Quentin. Just after he said it, he was worried that he was perhaps being insensitive. The only reason his sister had remained in Ordania was because she had lost her eyesight. Their grandmother had been teaching her how to use her magical powers as her eyes.

'Oh, I'm sorry Emily. That really was thoughtless and stupid of me to say that you are lucky after all you have been through,' added Quentin.

Emily smiled and told him not to worry. She said that there were many people who were far worse off than her, then they whispered goodnight to each other and closed their eyes.

Several minutes later, just as Quentin was about to doze off, a loud noise sounded against the window making Emily and Quentin sit upright in their beds.

'Did you hear that?' whispered Emily.

'Yes, it sounded like someone tapping the window,' answered Quentin.

Seconds later the same noise came again, only this time it was much louder. Aaron and Anna began to stir from their sleep.

'Wha … What's that noise?' came a muffled voice from Aaron's pillow.

Quentin got up to investigate and made his way across the room. When he reached the window, he pulled back the curtains and was most surprised to find an owl sitting on the window ledge and staring at him through the glass.

At first Quentin said nothing and simply stared back at the huge saucer-like eyes that blinked at him.

'Oh Athelea, is that really you?' squealed Anna with delight. She too was now fully awake and looking over Quentin's shoulder at the beautiful owl.

Anna ran to the window and pushed her older brother out of the way, she was so excited to see her watcher who had arrived from Ordania in the form of an owl. Athelea was a creature from the ancient forests called a tàcharan which to you or I is a shape shifter. Athelea could change into many different shapes and forms including birds, flying horses and human beings.

Anna unlatched the window and pushed it open to allow the owl to enter the room.

'Good evening Your Royal Highnesses,' said Athelea in her strange owl voice.

'Athelea, it's great to see you. What brings you here?' asked Anna excitedly.

'I am sorry to disturb you. I was hoping to speak with your Grandmother,' continued Athelea.

Seconds later she changed into her human form. Soon the room was filled with an exceptionally tall and beautiful woman with long shiny, brown hair, tanned skin and the most striking green eyes.

'I can't stay long, I just came to bring some very urgent news to your grandmother and parents,' said Athelea.

'Has something happened in Ordania?' asked Quentin.

'No, everything is fine in Ordania. It's the land of Westerlyn where there are problems and I know that your grandmother would want to know,' replied Athelea.

'Whatever is the matter? What has happened in Westerlyn?' asked Emily.

Emily had spent a fair bit of time in the land of Westerlyn that lay to the north east of Ordania and had many friends there. She was understandably concerned to hear that something untoward had happened. She thought that whatever it was, it must be serious to make Athelea travel all the way to earth in order to let her grandmother and parents know.

'I'm sorry Your Highness, please forgive me. I don't mean to be rude but I really should speak with your grandmother and parents first. I also didn't realise the time; I am sorry for waking you up.

'That's okay Athelea. I understand. We'll go and fetch Gran. She won't be asleep, she always reads until very late,' replied Emily.

However, there was no need for anyone to go and fetch Granny Bartholomew or their parents, for as soon as Emily spoke the door swung open and in they walked.

'Children, you are all making far too much noise in here. It's now very late and we need to sleep …. Oh!' said Mrs. Bartholomew and she stopped and stared at the tàcharan standing in the middle of Ailsa Carmichael's front room.

'Athelea? What brings you here?' said Granny Bartholomew.

'Forgive me for arriving so late Your Majesty. I did not mean to wake the children but I bring very important news that I really must share with you,' said Athelea.

Although in earth time, only 2 days had passed since the Queen had left Ordania and arrived on the Isle of Lewis, in Ordanian time this equated to more than one month and quite a lot had happened in that time.

'Perhaps we should go through to the kitchen were we can talk in private and leave the children to sleep,' suggested Mrs. Bartholomew.

'Please don't keep us in the dark. Why can't we listen to what Athelea has to say?' protested Anna.

The truth was the children's parents were worried that whatever it was Athelea had to tell them, if the children heard about it they would most likely try to get involved. However, experience had also taught Mr. and Mrs. Bartholomew that it was near impossible to keep a secret from their children and if they tried, it would only make them more curious. The children would stop at nothing in order to try and find out what was going on, especially if it sounded like a possible adventure.

Mr. and Mrs. Bartholomew looked at each other nervously. They had hoped that their week-long holiday on the Isle of Lewis would be carefree.

'Okay children, you can listen but I warn you that whatever news Athelea brings, it does not concern any of you and under no circumstances must you get involved,' said Mr. Bartholomew.

'Okay Athelea, please tell us what has happened?' said Granny Bartholomew.

Word has reached the great Ordanian forests that the people of

Westerlyn are under attack. I heard it on the wind and through the trees. Trees from the border between Westerlyn and Ordania began to whisper and finally it reached Belwald and Northwald in Ordania. I came as soon as I could to share this with you. The Westerlyn Warriors are struggling to protect their towns and villages from attack. Many Snee Menesker have already been killed and their homes destroyed,' said Athelea.

'This foe you speak of must be strong if the Westerlyn Warriors are struggling for they make a formidable army. What more do you know of the attackers?' said Granny Bartholomew.

'Well, I do know that they come in huge numbers and they are incredibly large and ferocious. I must say, I have never heard of a creature called eis jätte before but that is what the trees are saying,' explained Athelea.

'Eis jätte did you say? Oh my goodness, I've only ever heard of them in folklore. Eis jätte have not wandered the frozen plains of Westerlyn since before the last big freeze,' said Granny Bartholomew.

'What are they exactly?' asked Emily. She was now very concerned for the safety of her friends who lived in the land of Westerlyn.

'Eis-jätte were or are giant, carnivorous, bear-like creatures that stand at least thirty feet tall. As your grandmother says, they were thought to have become extinct following the last big freeze,' said Mr. Bartholomew.

'Well, that's just it. It turns out they've simply been frozen and buried deep in the ice. There has been an unusual warm spell in Westerlyn recently which has caused a lot of the ice and snow to recede. These frozen monsters are now awake once again and they are incredibly hungry and grumpy after having been in a frozen stupor for centuries. Apparently they'll stop at nothing and are eating and killing everything in their path. There are just far too many of them for the

Snee Menesker of Westerlyn to cope with. Many of the villages are remote and cut off, therefore the Westerlyn Warriors can't reach them in time. It's only a matter of days before the first pack of eis jätte reach the gates of Westercourt,' said Athelea.

'Oh we must go there immediately and do something to help them. My friends Henrik and Megriit live on a small farm in a very remote part of Westerlyn. I really need to see if they are okay. They will have no way of defending themselves against these terrible monsters,' said Emily.

'Try not to worry my dear. Your parents and I will return to Ordania and from there we will lead an army to Westerlyn. I have not forgotten how kind Henrik and Megriit were to you and how they saved your life. I will go to their home in person to make sure they are okay,' said Granny Bartholomew.

'But Gran, it's very difficult to find. It is very far from Westercourt. Surely I should go and help them? I always promised that I'd go back one day,' said Emily.

'My dear, I'll find their house, don't you worry about that. You must stay here with your brothers and sister and enjoy the rest of your holiday. Your parents and I are more than capable of taking care of this,' said Granny Bartholomew.

'No way, you can't expect us to just stay here? We insist on coming too,' said Aaron.

'Look, I know you want to help and I am sure that you would all be very useful but for the time being we need you to stay here. Once we get back to Ordania and organise the army, we will call for you. We really need to assess the gravity of the situation first of all, although it does sound already as if it is serious enough. Trust me, we will call for you but in the meantime we need you to wait here with Nanny Carmichael.

Until now the only person who hadn't said anything was Quentin. He had been standing in the background listening to all that was being said. Although he hadn't told anyone, he had been having the same recurring dream for several weeks now. In the dream Quentin had seen a frozen land with a clear blue sky that made a striking contrast against the white snow and ice. The frozen ground sparkled and glistened in the bright sunshine. Then Quentin would hear a terrible roar, followed by screams and then he would watch as the white snow on the ground turned dark red.

Having listened to Athelea's story, everything made sense now. Quentin had also listened to his parents and grandmother plead with him and his siblings to remain on the Isle of Lewis whilst they returned to Ordania to help the people of Westerlyn. Quentin said nothing because he did not want to make promises that he would or could not keep. He knew deep down that his recurring dream meant that he had a role to play in helping the people of Westerlyn in exactly the same way they helped the people of Ordania during the War of the Wolves.

3 MEDDLING WITH MAGIC

When the children got up late the following morning and made their way through to the kitchen where Nanny Carmichael had prepared breakfast, they were most disappointed to discover that their grandmother and parents had already left for Ordania.

'I can't believe they left without taking us,' said Anna sounding very disappointed.

'I'm sure your parents will send for you in a few days. In the meantime you should try to enjoy yourselves. It won't be too long before you have to go back to school. Why don't you explore the island today? The sun is shining outside,' said Nanny Carmichael. She placed a large plate of hot buttered toast in the middle of the kitchen table.

'If you like, I can make you a nice picnic and you can take it down to Uig sands,' said Nanny Carmichael.

The children thanked her. They did not want to appear rude since she had very kindly let them stay in her home. They decided to go out and explore the island. At the very least they would head down towards the beach and perhaps a little further along the road.

'Can you remember the spot where you and Gran arrived the other day?' whispered Aaron to his twin sister.

'I'm blind you numbskull, of course I don't remember,' whispered Emily.

'Oh, of course, sorry sis. I am a numbskull!' replied Aaron.

'Although I do know that it was beside a place called Timsgarry and the number 4 bus takes you there. It was only a couple of stops from Uig,' added Emily.

'What are you two whispering about?' asked Quentin.

'We'll tell you after breakfast,' smiled Aaron and he winked at his older brother.

After breakfast the children got themselves ready and it wasn't long before they said goodbye to Nanny Carmichael who had presented them with a picnic shortly before they stepped outside the front door of her croft.

'The weather should remain dry and sunny all day, so you can stay out for as long as you wish but please be back home before it gets dark. Shall we say four thirty at the latest? Will that be long enough for you to explore?' said Nanny Carmichael.

'Yes, that will be plenty of time. Thanks again for the picnic,' said Quentin. The children headed out the garden gate and began to make their way along the footpath that led to the main road. Once they were out of sight of the croft, Aaron and Emily decided to share with Quentin and Anna their plan to try and locate the time portal that would take them all back to Ordania.

'I'm not so sure if that's a good idea Aaron,' said Quentin. 'Mum, Dad and Gran will be furious if we all just turn up out of the blue without being invited.

'Don't be daft. They only made us stay behind because they don't want us to get caught up in any sort of trouble. They really ought to stop treating us like babies and let us do what we were born to do and that is use our magical powers to help the people of Ordania or in this case the people of Westerlyn.

'What about Nanny Carmichael? Won't she be worried about us if we don't turn up at the house when it gets dark?' said Anna.

'Anna's right, it wouldn't be fair to worry her. She'd end up coming out in the dark to look for us,' said Quentin.

'Let's just go and see if we can find the time portal first of all and then we can decide what to do,' said Aaron.

The children continued along the path that led them away from the beach. Eventually they reached the main road where they crossed over to the bus stop.

'How frequent are the buses?' asked Anna.

'Let's look at the timetable and find out,' suggested Quentin.

They carefully studied the timetable that was pinned to the bus stop and were able to work out that the next bus would be along in about fifteen minutes.

'We might as well sit down while we wait,' said Aaron and he plonked himself down on his backpack by the side of the road. He was soon joined by Quentin, Emily and Anna as they waited patiently for the number 4 bus to arrive.

Fifteen minutes later there was still no sign of the bus. After twenty five minutes the children stood up and began to pace up and down.

'Are you sure you read the bus timetable correctly?' asked Emily.

'Yes, the bus should have been here ten minutes ago,' said Aaron.

'We should have walked. If we had, we would have been there by now,' said Quentin.

Everyone agreed that it made sense to start walking and so they brushed themselves down, put on their backpacks and began to follow Quentin along the road. No sooner had they started to walk than they heard the sound of a vehicle approaching. They turned around and saw the number 4 bus coming trundling along the road. The children quickly ran back to the bus stop and waved their arms frantically to get the driver's attention.

Moments later Quentin, Aaron, Emily and Anna boarded the number 4 bus and took their seats. There were only a few locals on board including two individuals, who had she been able to see, would have been quite familiar to Emily. Best friends Brighid and Ealasaid were in their usual seats on left hand side of the bus. They had been on the bus the very day Emily and her grandmother had arrived from Ordania. They recognised Emily immediately as soon as she stepped on.

'Brighid, look it's the blind girl who was with the strange old lady the other day,' said Ealasaid. As she spoke she nudged Brighid hard in the ribs.

'Oh, Ealasaid, not so hard. I'll be black and blue. Yes, you are right. It is her and it looks like there's an entire family,' replied Brighid as she rubbed her ribs.

Ever since they had seen Granny Bartholomew and Emily board the bus, both Brighid and Ealasaid had travelled up and down the road daily in the hope of spotting them again. Sometimes they had taken the bus two or three times. They had made a point of getting off at Aird Uig and going to the local post office in the hope of retrieving some information from Mrs. McNeil who worked there.

She had told them that Ailsa Carmichael did have quite a few visitors staying in her cottage at the moment but she had no idea who they were. She had assumed they were relatives of her late husband who came from the mainland.

Both Brighid and Ealasaid were desperate to find out more about the mysterious family and had therefore made it their mission that week to reveal the identity of Ailsa Carmichael's visitors.

They could not quite believe their luck when Emily stepped onto the bus along with her siblings.

When the bus reached Timsgarry and the children stood up to get off, both Brighid and Ealasaid shot up out of their seats, grabbed their handbags, straightened their hats and followed the children off the bus.

'This isn't your stop ladies!' shouted the bus driver when he saw Brighid and Ealasaid getting off.

'Oh, we know that. It's such a fine day we thought we'd walk a bit. Brighid could do with the exercise. *Tioraidh*,' said Ealasaid and she smiled at the driver.

The children hadn't noticed the two old ladies who had stepped off the bus behind them, they were far too eager and excited about the prospect of finding the time portal which could take them straight home to Ordania.

'I remember we walked through some trees and bushes. The grass was quite high and very rough. Gran took me by the hand but I still tripped a few times on the roots of thick shrubs,' said Emily.

The other three scanned the area to look for a stretch of land that resembled what Emily was describing. There were very few trees around and so it didn't take them long to identify what they thought must be the spot on the other side of the road.

'Come on, let's cross over and investigate the group of trees over there,' said Aaron. The grass was indeed tall and it wasn't easy to walk through it. It was the kind of rough grass that you often find growing near sandy beaches.

Once they were inside the small group of trees Quentin, Aaron and Anna scanned the area for any signs of a portal. They had seen portals before and they were usually bright in colour, therefore quite hard to miss. However, after ten minutes of searching they found nothing and came to the conclusion that either the portal had moved again or their grandmother, knowing that they might try and find it, had closed it behind her when she left for Ordania.

'This is so frustrating. I really need to get back to help Henrik and Megriit. With every hour that passes here, an entire day passes in Westerlyn. I cannot afford to waste any more time,' said Emily.

'What do you suggest we do? If only we knew how to create a portal,' said Aaron.

'I'm sure I could create one,' said Anna.

'You? Don't make me laugh. What do you know about creating time portals?' laughed Aaron.

'I know a damn sight more than you Aaron,' replied Anna, clearly irritated by her brother.

'Okay, go on then. Let us see the formidable sorceress at work?' smiled Aaron.

'I can create a portal but if you think I am going to create one here just so that you can jump in and get back to Ordania before me, you can think again. Why don't you create your own and we will see who gets back to Ordania first?' said Anna.

'It's a deal and I bet we have to come looking for you, no doubt you'll end up in some crazy place,' laughed Aaron.

'That's enough you too. You can't go messing around with magic. Gran warned us about that,' said Quentin but it was no use. Anna had already stormed off further into the trees, just enough so that she was out of sight. She closed her eyes and began to whisper magical words.

As soon as Aaron saw what his little sister was doing, he smiled and began to do the same.

'I can't wait to see the look on her face when she arrives home at Castle Draccwyne and finds me already standing there waiting. She'll be so annoyed,' laughed Aaron. He too turned his back on his brother and sister, closed his eyes and began to chant.

'Look, stop it now you two. This really isn't helpful,' shouted Quentin but neither Anna nor Aaron were now listening.

'Don't worry Quentin. I don't think it will work. They aren't doing it properly, I know because I was with Gran when she created the portal that brought us here and I heard every word she said,' said Emily.

'Well, whatever you do, don't go creating one and travelling by yourself. That would be too dangerous,' said Quentin.

'I can't wait here any longer. I'd never forgive myself if something happened to Henrik and Megriit and I knew that I had delayed in going there to help,' said Emily.

Quentin walked over to the spot where Anna was standing. He tried once more to convince his youngest sister to stop messing around. As soon as Quentin's back was turned, sensing that he was walking away, Emily quickly lifted both hands in the air and whispered *'s fheàrr an saoghal ionnsachadh na a sheachnadh, Ordania!*

There was a sudden flash of white and Quentin turned back just in time to see Emily step into a hole that had appeared in the ground at her feet.

'Emily, No!' shouted Quentin and he ran back over to the spot but it was too late. The portal had already closed by the time he got there.

'I can't believe this. Aaron, Anna stop this nonsense now. We need to find Emily quickly,' shouted Quentin. However, when he turned back and looked over to where Anna was standing, he saw the same bright, swirling mist appear on the ground in front of his youngest sister.

'Anna, don't dare step into that portal. You have no idea what you are doing,' roared Quentin.

'Ha-ha, see you later Aaron. I'll be home before you,' shouted Anna and before Quentin could reach her she jumped right into the hole of bright, swirling colours.

Quentin raced after her but just as before, as soon as he reached the spot the portal completely vanished taking Anna with it.

'I can't believe this. What a silly girl,' shouted Quentin out loud.

'Aaron, come over here quickly. Please stop this nonsense. I need your help,' said Quentin, but no reply came from Aaron.

Quentin looked back over to the spot where his brother had been standing only a few moments previously and noticed that he too had disappeared.

'This is terrible. What will Mum, Dad and Gran say when they find out that they have all disappeared through portals. What if they end up in the wrong place?' thought Quentin to himself.

He now realised that he was alone amongst the small group of trees by the side of the road, or at least he thought he was alone. As he stood and looked at the ground around his feet he failed to notice the faces of two old dears who were standing behind a bush. They had observed everything that had happened.

Quentin turned to walk away and started to head back towards the road. He quickly decided that he would return to the house first of all, explain everything to Nanny Carmichael and then work out how he would get back to Ordania.

Unfortunately, for Quentin he failed to notice something on the ground to his left as he began to make his way out of the trees. It was partially hidden behind some thick bushes. A strange, brightly coloured mist had appeared amongst the dead leaves. It was in fact the portal that the children had been looking for, the very portal that Granny Bartholomew had used earlier that day to return to Ordania.

She had indeed hidden it, for she knew her grandchildren would try to follow. However, for some reason it had reappeared, probably something to do with the magic that had just been used by Emily, Aaron and Anna to create new portals. Quentin did not see it and walked right by. He continued on his way until he stepped out of the trees and found his feet on the tarmac.

As Quentin started to make his way along the side of the road, he had to stop momentarily and move to one side when a car travelling at top speed flew right past him. Little did Quentin know, the car engine had muffled the sound of two ladies screaming. Ealasaid and Brighid had waited until Quentin had left the cover of the trees for they were too scared to move in case they were caught hiding behind the bush. They were also half terrified by what they had just witnessed. Brighid was desperate to get out from the trees for she was being eaten alive by midges and she had torn her good tights. Desperate to leave their hiding place, both ladies quickly stepped backwards. However as soon as they moved, they felt the ground beneath them give way and suddenly they were falling through the air at a terrifying speed. Both Ealasaid and Brighid had fallen into Granny Bartholomew's secret portal.

By the time Quentin arrived back at Nanny Carmichael's house and explained to her what had happened, it was starting to get dark. Quentin still had no idea how he would get back to Ordania or even contact his parents.

Sensing how worried he was, Nanny Carmichael told Quentin to sit down with her so that they could go through what options they had.

'I don't see that we have any options,' said Quentin. 'I could try and create another portal just like Emily, Aaron and Anna but what if it doesn't work properly and I end up somewhere else entirely. That won't help anyone at all. Gran said that creating a time portal is not straight forward and it takes great skill, experience and practice'.

'You have always been the sensible one. Even when you were a very young boy, you always did the right thing, unlike Aaron and Anna. I must say that I'm surprised by Emily. It's not like her to be so impulsive,' said Nanny Carmichael.

'I think she just panicked and was really worried about her friends in Westerlyn. She wasn't thinking clearly,' said Quentin.

'Well, one of the options is to go back to the area where the portal was or is. I am pretty sure that it will still be there. Your grandmother will no doubt have hidden it. Perhaps you can use a revealing spell to find out where it is exactly?' suggested Nanny Carmichael.

'Yes, that is a possibility and although we are not allowed to use magic, given the circumstances I think I'll be allowed. I assumed that Gran had closed the portal but I suppose it makes sense to keep it open, otherwise my parents wouldn't be able to get back here quickly and easily,' said Quentin.

'There is also the second option, which I think might be the best. Since we can't be sure if your brother and sisters are actually in Ordania, first of all we should use your grandmother's magic spy glass,' said Nanny Carmichael.

'My grandmother's magic spy glass? What is that exactly?' asked Quentin.

'Your grandmother left in such a hurry she forgot some of her things. If you go into the bedroom where she slept, you'll find a small sphere-like object sitting on the bedside table. We can use it in order to see where your brother and sisters are. Your grandmother won't mind, it is an emergency after all,' said Nanny Carmichael.

Quentin walked through to the bedroom where his grandmother had been staying and sure enough, sitting on the bedside table were several items that belonged to her. One of them was a glass ball. Quentin picked it up to examine it more closely and discovered that when you looked inside you could see the perfect summer sky with white fluffy clouds. Quentin carried the small glass object back to the sitting room where Nanny Carmichael was waiting and carefully placed it on the table.

'Now what do we do?' asked Quentin.

'Well, it's very easy. I've seen your grandmother use it many times before. All you have to do is hold it in both hands, close your eyes and picture the person you want to see. Once you have a clear picture of the person in your mind, whisper *faigh for air* and then say the person's name. You must then hold the glass ball up to the light and look into it. It's really that simple,' said Nanny Carmichael.

Quentin picked up the glass object and did exactly as Nanny Carmichael said. He decided that he should try and look for his youngest sister first. With any luck he would see her, along with the twins already at home in Ordania.

Quentin closed his eyes and pictured his youngest sister. Since she was most likely to be in Ordania or so he thought, he decided to use her Ordanian name. He lifted the glass ball towards the window and whispered *faigh for air bana-phrionnsa Luna*. At first he saw nothing and then the blue summer sky inside the ball began to cloud over. Next, thick clouds began to gather and swirl as if a great storm was brewing.

'Can you see anything yet?' asked Nanny Carmichael.

'No, not really. It just looks cloudy and dark....wait, it's starting to clear again,' said Quentin.

After thirty seconds or so, Quentin could see what looked like a small town square in front of a church. There were crowds of people gathered around and they seemed to be shouting and waving their fists angrily in the air. Quentin also noticed that many of the people were dressed in strange clothes and many of them looked very poor.

There were several children wearing nothing more than rags and their faces were almost as muddy as the filthy ground upon which they stood.

'Well? What can you see?' asked Nanny Carmichael.

'I'm not really sure what I'm looking at to be honest. It doesn't look like Ordania and I can't see any sign of my sister,' said Quentin.

'Let me have a quick look,' said Nanny Carmichael and she walked over to where Quentin was standing by the window. It was now growing dark and becoming quite difficult to see through the magic spy glass. Nanny Carmichael carefully took the magical object from Quentin and held it up in the fading light.

'*O mo chreach, 's e Dùn Èideann a th' ann,*' said Nanny Carmichael. She recognised almost instantly that the town inside the spy glass was in fact Edinburgh, the Scottish capital city and judging by the clothes worn by the people, it looked like medieval Edinburgh.

'Why is the spy glass showing us the streets of Edinburgh several hundred years ago?' wondered Quentin, now more confused than ever.

He then asked Nanny Carmichael if he could have another look. When Quentin looked again he immediately caught sight of his sister. She was being chased by an angry mob of men, woman and children. They were shouting at her and shaking their fists. One of the men carried a pitch fork and he waved it threateningly in the air.

Luna began to run which was not easy on such slimy, muddy ground and she slipped a few times. The mob roared loudly and began to chase after her down a long, winding street which Quentin now recognised to be the High Street or Royal Mile in Edinburgh's old town.

'Oh dear. My sister is in real trouble. It seems she has time travelled to Edinburgh and it must be at least three or four hundred years ago,' said Quentin.

'That's what I was afraid of when I saw St. Giles and the crowd gathered outside what was once the Old Tollbooth. I could tell straight away that it was Edinburgh in the past. Oh my, your sister has got herself into a right pickle,' said Nanny Carmichael.

'I need to help her but I don't know what to do,' said Quentin, beginning to panic.

'Right, there is only one option now and that is your grandfather's clock,' said Nanny Carmichael.

'My grandfather's clock? I'm sorry but I'm not quite sure what you mean,' said Quentin.

'Haven't you heard about your grandfather's special clock? It's the one that is standing out in the hallway,' said Nanny Carmichael.

'Oh, that old clock? I didn't even think it worked,' said Quentin.

'Well, it depends on your definition of '*work*'. I suppose if you want it to tell you the time here on earth, then it wouldn't be that much use,' said Nanny Carmichael.

'I really don't understand. What else would you use a clock for?' asked Quentin. He was becoming more confused by the minute.

'Oh, I'm sorry. I had assumed you already knew about the traveller's clocks, but clearly not,' said Nanny Carmichael. She then went on to explain to Quentin all that she knew about the magical traveller's clocks which had been crafted especially by the younger brother of Quentin's grandfather, Great Uncle Georg.

As a young man, Quentin's Great Uncle Georg was very skilled in the art of making enchanted traveller's clocks and the one that now stood in Ailsa Carmichael's hallway had been a special wedding gift to King

Andris and Queen Valda. It was one of twelve special traveller's clocks that Uncle Georg had made. This one was the largest and grandest of the clocks. The rest were kept at Easthall, Uncle Georg's home in Ordania.

'Come through and take a look,' said Nanny Carmichael. Quentin followed her through to the hallway to where the beautiful wooden clock was standing. Quentin had noticed it before with its bright, shiny wood and tiny carvings of animals. He had always admired it each time he visited Nanny Carmichael's home but he had no idea that it was from Ordania and that it was magical. When he looked more closely, he could see that many of the carvings were in fact Ordanian animals. It stood tall and proud at almost seven feet in Nanny Carmichael's hallway.

'How exactly does it work?' asked Quentin.

'Well if you look carefully, you will see that this clock doesn't just have two hands, but four. Each hand is a different length. In order to time travel, all you have to do is move the hands until they point at the year to which you want to travel. For example if you wanted to go back to the year 1950, you would move the longest hand so that it is pointing to 1, the second longest must then point to 9, the third longest must point to 5 and finally the shortest hand must point to 0. You then open the front door and turn the large key four times, state your destination and hop inside,' said Nanny Carmichael.

'Have you used it before?' asked Quentin.

'Yes, but not for some time. Your grandparents lent the clock to me so that I could travel back in time to see my husband. I found it hard when he died and so they thought this would help. At first I did think it was a great idea and then I used up all of my four chances. I forgot to mention that each person can only use it up to four times. In a way I'm glad that I can no longer use it because it was actually making me feel sadder. Although I enjoyed going back and seeing my husband talking and laughing, I always knew that it was for a limited time and that I would have to leave him again. It has been a while since I last used it but I'm sure it will still work,' said Nanny Carmichael.

'Oh, I've just thought of another problem. We don't know the exact year Luna is in,' said Quentin.

'Ah, good point. Quick, grab the spy glass again. There isn't much time left,' said Nanny Carmichael.

It was almost dark and since the spy glass only worked in natural daylight, they had no time to lose.

'Do exactly as before and when the scene appears, ask the spyglass to tell you the exact year,' said Nanny Carmichael as she shoved the glass object back into Quentin's hand.

Quentin did exactly as he was told and moments later he could see his sister again. This time she was hiding from the angry mob in a tiny courtyard, just off the Royal Mile in Edinburgh's old town. Quentin could sense her panic and wondered why she wasn't using her powers to protect herself. He then asked the spyglass to show him the year in which his sister had arrived. After a few seconds the glass clouded over once more and when it finally cleared, the numbers 1-6-3-2 appeared.

'She's in the year 1632. I must head there now,' shouted Quentin and he ran back through to the hallway to where his grandfather's clock was standing.

'Wait, before you go I need to tell you that you only have a very limited time at your destination. Plus, the further back in time you go, the shorter that time will be. If you are travelling back to 1632, I reckon you'll have less than half an hour to find your sister before you are whisked back here by the traveller's clock,' said Nanny Carmichael.

'In that case I'd better take my watch with me,' said Quentin and he ran to the bedroom to fetch it.

'There is just one more thing that you need to remember before you go,' continued Nanny Carmichael.

'And what is that?' asked Quentin, now eager to get going.

'You do not leave here as Quentin Bartholomew, you must travel as Prince Qadir Rosencratz, the Starry Prince,' said Nanny Carmichael and she smiled.

'Of course. I'm just not used to using that name when I am on earth but it makes sense,' said Quentin. He then moved all four hands on the clock until they pointed to 1, 6, 3 and 2. Once he was satisfied that the hands were pointing to the correct year, he opened the wooden door on the front of the clock and looked inside. It was surprisingly spacious but it was dark and he couldn't really see much. Suddenly a breeze picked up and blew from inside the clock causing several letters to blow off the hallway table and onto the floor.

'Reach inside and you will find the handle on the left. You must turn it four times,' said Nanny Carmichael.

Moments later, Qadir began to turn what was an enormous key and with each turn, his grandfather's clock began to creak and groan loudly.

After the fourth turn Qadir shouted; '*Dùn Èideann*' and then stepped inside the clock. Once inside, the breeze strengthened and soon his ears began to fill with the sound of howling wind.

'*Mar sin leat an-dràsta! Bithibh air ur faiceall,*' said Nanny Carmichael and she waved.

'*Tioraidh!*' replied Qadir and then he smiled before closing the door, encircling himself in complete darkness. The Prince paused momentarily, held his breath and waited to see what would happen next. Suddenly he felt quite dizzy when the air around him began to spin. 'Here goes!' whispered Qadir quietly and then he closed his eyes and braced himself.

4 THE TRUTH ABOUT THE PAST

'Well done me!' said Asmund as he looked around him. He found himself standing deep in the heart of an ancient forest and by the look of things, his first attempt at creating a time portal which would take him back to Ordania appeared to have worked. You might of course be wondering how Asmund knew this for he could in fact have been in any forest, anywhere on earth or indeed in another realm. However, Asmund knew as soon as he opened his eyes and breathed in the fresh air that he was in Ordania. There was a familiar feeling of magic around and everywhere he looked he saw woodland creatures that were native to his homeland. The birds and animals were caught by surprise when Asmund appeared suddenly and silently and they had little time to run and hide. Several firebirds took off in fright from the forest floor and found refuge in the leafy boughs above. They gave a startling display of red and gold as they flapped their wings before disappearing into the thick, green foliage. A family of long-eared conills was quietly nibbling away on young shoots and roots when the larger male spotted Asmund. It made a strange noise which sounded like a bark before thumping the floor of the forest to warn the other conills. Asmund watched as the large family bounced away, deep into the forest and out of sight.

Suddenly the bird song seemed to stop and an eerie silence filled the forest. Asmund felt as if he was being watched by invisible eyes. However, the silence was short lived when in the distance he thought he heard someone cry out. Although Asmund could not be sure what it was, he knew that it wasn't an animal. What he heard definitely sounded like a man shouting, although he could not make out the words.

Asmund began to move in the direction of the noise. He wondered if it might be his older brother, Qadir who had perhaps just arrived from earth.

'If that's Qadir then I'd better move fast and get back to Castle Draccwyne. I'll be really annoyed if he gets there before me,' thought Asmund.

The next time Asmund heard the voice cry out, he thought it sounded much closer. He also noticed that the trees had started to thin suggesting he might be close to the edge of the forest.

'Once I get out of this forest I will be able to see more clearly and get my bearings,' thought Asmund.

He considered shouting out his brother's name but then thought better of it.

'I don't want Qadir to know that I am still here in the forest otherwise he'll race back to Castle Draccwyne and beat me and I can't have that,' thought Asmund to himself.

He looked straight ahead and saw a clearing in the trees where the sun was beating down. As he began to make his way towards it, he heard a blood curdling scream that almost made him jump out of his skin.

As if the scream wasn't frightening enough, (Asmund wasn't easily scared!) another sound followed that was even more terrifying; it was the snarl of a large beast, followed by a series of chilling howls.

'Landga wolves? How can they possibly be in Ordania?' thought Asmund. His heart began to pound.

Landga wolves had of course been banished many years ago thanks to the new protection spell which prevented any evil being from crossing over into Ordania. The War of the Wolves had been won thanks to Qadir and his family.

Suddenly Asmund caught sight of someone moving amongst the trees to his left and so he quickly hid himself behind an oak tree. He remained perfectly still for several minutes and then slowly peered around the trunk to get a better look. What he saw surprised him, for standing in the clearing was an Ordanian soldier. He was dressed in full armour and judging by the cuts and bruises on his face, he had just been in a battle. The man seemed exhausted and was trying to catch his breath. Asmund guessed that he had been running from a landga wolf which was probably a good idea since he appeared to have lost his weapons. The soldier peered around the clearing nervously and with great caution.

Asmund continued to watch, unsure whether or not he should try to catch the soldier's attention and ask him to explain what was going on.

'Surely we would have heard about it if landga wolves had re-entered Ordania? Mum and Dad wouldn't keep that a secret from us,' thought Asmund.

Just as Asmund was about to try and catch the attention of the soldier, there was a rustle in the trees to the left of the clearing. The soldier looked terrified and just as he turned to run, an enormous, dark shape leapt out from the trees and landed on top of him.

There was no mistaking what this creature was, it stood on four enormous paws with terrible claws that tore up the earth when it ran. Its large, muscular back was covered in thick, coarse hair and its eyes were cold and cruel. The landga wolf pinned the soldier to the ground and widened its terrible jaws. Drool dripped from the beast's mouth and the terrified soldier began to scream and kick but to little avail. He was no match for the powerful landga wolf that stood almost six feet tall and had the strength of at least three fully grown men.

The soldier closed his eyes and prepared himself for death however he was unaware that he and the evil wolf were not alone in the heart of the ancient forest. Asmund was of course watching from his hiding place and just as the great wolf brought down its terrible teeth and tried to make contact with the soldier's neck, Asmund leapt out from his hiding place and charged.

The landga wolf swung its huge head round to look at the Prince. It's not clear who was more startled, the wolf or the poor soldier but both looked at Asmund in surprise as he flew through the air towards them.

'*Teine,*' shouted Asmund and he pointed at the landga wolf. Suddenly the wolf's thick mane burst into flames and the creature screamed loudly before rolling onto its back in an attempt to put out the fire.

'*Sgiath!*' roared Asmund and he pointed at the landga wolf again. This time the great beast was lifted up off the ground and sent flying through the air. Seconds later it crashed against the trunk of a tree on the far side of the clearing, then fell down in a crumpled heap on the forest floor.

The soldier sat himself upright, shocked by what he had seen. At first he was speechless and it took several moments before Asmund broke the silence.

'Are you injured?' asked Asmund.

The soldier shook his head and then he thanked Asmund for saving his life.

'Who are you?' stuttered the soldier. He was still shocked by everything that had happened.

'I am Prince Asmund Rosencratz and I have just returned to Ordania. Can you please explain to me what is going on?' asked Asmund.

'Prince Asmund Rosencratz? Are you related to King Andris Rosencratz?' said the soldier.

'King Andris was my grandfather,' replied Asmund.

'King Andris is your grandfather? Forgive me, I don't mean to be rude but that just isn't possible. King Andris does not have any grandchildren, at least not yet anyway. Neither of his sons are married. Prince Espin is only about fourteen years old. In fact I would say that he is about your age. As for His Royal Highness Prince Adair, he is only seventeen,' said the soldier.

Asmund was confused as nothing the soldier said made any sense. He wondered if the soldier had lost his senses or perhaps had suffered a blow to the head.

'You speak of King Andris as if he were still alive,' said Asmund.

'Well, of course he is still alive. He is our King and he is out there on the battlefield now leading one of the bloodiest battles we have ever seen in Ordania.

'Are you telling me the truth?' asked Asmund.

'Yes, of course I am. If you make your way over there to the edge of the forest you will be able to see for yourself,' said the soldier and he pointed to the trees on the right side of the clearing. In the distance Asmund could hear the sound of a lone war horn.

'What year is this?' asked Asmund.

'The year? Why it's the year 3010 of course,' replied the soldier.

'The year 3010? But that's the year of the Great Civil War that we read about in Ms. Tanck's history lesson. How can I possibly be in the year 3010?' thought Asmund.

'He thanked the soldier and began to make his way towards the edge of the clearing. 'Wait, please tell me who you are?' shouted the soldier who was still sitting on the ground in the middle of the clearing.

'I already told you, I am Asmund Rosencratz, Prince of the Mountain High and from what you have just told me, it appears that I am from the future,' said Asmund.

The soldier looked at Asmund in complete bewilderment as the Prince made his way back into the trees. Soon he had entered the thick forest again and his eyes had to readjust to the dark. However, in the distance he could see more daylight and so he pushed on until the trees began to thin out once more. By the time he reached the last few trees on the edge of the forest, the sound of clashing metal filled the air. He hadn't appreciated the fact that the trees had filtered much of the sound but as soon as Asmund stepped out from the forest he was almost deafened by the roar from the enormous battle that he found underway in the valley below him.

Asmund gasped when he saw the huge army of landga wolves and blood sucking grotta ghoul as they swarmed the green mountainside and attacked the Ordanian soldiers from every angle. The war horn sounded again and when Asmund looked round to the left, he saw a magnificent sight. A flying stallion swooped down on the army and upon its back sat a magnificent king. Although he was dressed in battle gear, his long, golden hair was still visible beneath his helm.

Asmund knew instantly who this king was, it was his own grandfather only he looked much younger. Asmund watched in wonder as the valiant King Andris effortlessly crushed several landga wolves and grotta ghoul. Suddenly, Asmund's attention was drawn back to the right hand side of the battlefield when he saw another winged horse fly though the air and then land on the grass. The armour clad warrior upon its back was difficult to identify at first, however when he withdrew his sword and cut off the head of a grotta ghoul, Asmund was certain who this mysterious warrior was. He recognised the blade that cut through the enemy as easily as a knife cuts through butter. It was an enchanted blade and Asmund had seen it many times before. In fact, he had been told that one day he would own the blade for it belonged to his father, Prince Adair Rosencratz.

Asmund swelled with pride as he watched his grandfather and father take on the formidable army and then his heart stopped momentarily when another familiar shape emerged from the crowd. It was another landga wolf, only it was much larger and darker and it wore heavy battle armour. Asmund recognised Abnocta Mirus, the leader of all landga wolves whom his older brother Qadir had slain. He watched as the enormous wolf leapt through the air and landed on top of his grandfather. Abnocta killed the flying horse with one strike from his terrible paw however King Andris was far too quick for him and the powerful sorcerer King spun round in the air. The King brought down his mighty sword and struck Abnocta's armour with full force, knocking the great wolf to the ground. However, Abnocta did not stay down for long and soon the giant wolf was on his paws again and trying to attack the King. Moments later there was a terrible scream when the King's sword struck Abnocta once more, only this time the edge of the blade made contact with the wolf's eye. Asmund watched as the landga wolf leader retreated from the battlefield in agony.

It was then that Asmund saw someone else whom he eventually recognised for he had only ever seen him in paintings. At first Asmund was shocked for he thought that he was looking at himself. On the far right of the battlefield a young lad had arrived wearing a set of armour that was clearly too big for him. He stopped momentarily to remove his helm and adjust the strap. It was Prince Espen, the younger brother of Prince Adair and youngest son of King Andris and Queen Valda. Asmund remembered the tragic story that his father and history teacher had told him of how Prince Espen had died at the age of fourteen. He had wanted to join his father and older brother in the battle but was told by his parents that he was too young. They had then made him stay in the castle whilst his older brother and father went off to war.

Prince Espen was desperate to prove to his parents and to the people of Ordania that he was more than ready to be a warrior. After all, he was one of the most powerful sorcerers ever to have been born and so he used his magic to free himself from the castle and made his way to the battlefield.

'I need to do something to stop him. This is my only chance to prevent Espen from dying,' thought Asmund. However,

Asmund had no time to think or do anything for seconds later, before Prince Espen had even set foot onto the battlefield, the strangest of things happened. What can only be described as a strange, black mist suddenly appeared in the air around him. It seemed to choke Espen and seconds later he fell to the ground unconscious. Asmund began to run down the mountainside towards the spot where he lay. However, he was quite far away and before he had travelled any great distance, he watched as a large, winged beast swooped down, grabbed Prince Espen and carried him up and away from the scene of the battle. Asmund continued to watch on helplessly as the winged beast headed north over the Esterway Mountains.

'So, Uncle Espen didn't die on the battlefield after all. I wonder where that creature has taken him?' thought Asmund.

5 Eden and the Mammohofs

Eden had forgotten just how disorientating it is when travelling through a time portal and it took a while before she stopped feeling dizzy and was able to find her bearings again. Although her feet were now firmly on the ground, when she tried to walk forwards, she found it quite difficult. With each step, her feet sank down into deep snow, although Eden did not realise it was snow at first. She felt a sudden chill in the air and thought how silent the world around her had become. Since she lost her eyesight, her ability to hear had improved significantly and she was therefore usually able to pick up the slightest sound but there was now nothing to hear; no birds on the wing, no scuttling beetle in the grass, simply an empty silence in a vast open space. Eden shivered as she continued to try and find her bearings. She began to wish that she had brought a warm jacket. The air was indeed icy cold and certainly not what one would expect during the month of October in Ordania. Eden crouched down to touch the ground and was surprised when her fingertips touched crisp, fresh snow.

'I don't think I am in Ordania at all but I am not on earth either,' thought Eden. She listened again carefully but the deep snow had created a thick blanket that covered the landscape, silencing every sound.

Luckily Eden's grandmother had been teaching Eden how to use her magical powers in order to see the world around her. Although she hadn't quite mastered it yet, on several occasions she had been able to see images in her head and when she described them, her grandmother confirmed that she had been quite accurate.

'A land of snow? The only land of snow that I am familiar with is Westerlyn which is where I want to be. Could I be in Westerlyn already?' thought Eden to herself.

'Maybe it is just wishful thinking that I am already in Westerlyn, although I really don't know where else I could be with so much ice and snow around,' whispered Eden to herself and then she shivered again.

Eden was unsure what to do next. It was growing colder by the minute and she began to feel flakes of snow fall on her hair and face. In order to get warm, she pictured herself wearing warmer clothes and then lifted her hands up to the snowy sky and shouted *seasgair*. Seconds later Eden was dressed in warm boots, a heavy winter coat, scarf and gloves and her favourite fur hat.

'Oh, that feels so much better. I can actually think straight now that I am a bit warmer,' thought Eden.

'Great Spirit of this frozen land, please can you tell me where I am?'

Eden shouted out the words loudly and clearly. Her voice echoed around the vast, open plain but there was no response and so she tried again.

Great Spirit of this frozen land. I am Princess Eden Rosencratz of Ordania. I have no eyes to see with, please can you guide me?'

Eden stood quietly for a few moments, trying to decide what to do for the best. She had no idea which direction she should take and even if she did, she had no way of knowing how long it would take for her to reach the nearest civilisation. She considered using her magic to conjure up some form of transport but that would only be useful if she knew the direction in which she was heading.

Suddenly Eden's thoughts were disturbed when she heard a rumbling noise in the distance and was worried that it could be an avalanche. There was a vibration that travelled from the ground right up through her feet and into her body.

'What is this? An earthquake?' thought Eden.

The snow was now falling thick and fast and the temperature

continued to drop. Eden knew that she had to do something and so she concentrated again and began to search her soul as most sorcerers do when they are unsure what to do in what is potentially a crisis situation.

'May the powers within me be my eyes. Help me to see the cause of all this noise. Give me a clear vision of this land in which I find myself,' said Eden. When she lifted her head, although her eyes remained closed, she finally had a vision in her mind of the mysterious world around her. As she looked ahead into the thick, falling snow, she saw a dark mass moving towards her.

She concentrated hard in order to identify who or what was approaching.

'Is it a herd of animals? An army of some sort?' thought Eden. Suddenly she heard what sounded like many elephants trumpeting.

'Elephants in the snow? How odd,' thought Eden.

She thought that she should move to avoid being trampled and so she lifted herself high up off the ground until she hovered several feet in the air. In order to see better, she used her powers to temporarily stop the snow from falling. She knew that she couldn't do this for too long as using such magic would exhaust her energy very quickly.

The snow stopped almost instantly and finally Eden was able to get a clearer picture of the great army that was now passing directly beneath.

In many ways they did resemble elephants, although they ran upright on two exceptionally long and sturdy legs. Their bodies were covered in thick, red hair. She thought their heavy coats resembled those of the highland cattle she often saw when she visited the north of Scotland. They had large ears like those of elephants and on the front of their faces they had a trunk-like nose as well as two short tusks.

Although perhaps nowhere near as long as the trunk of an elephant, the noise that came out certainly sounded exactly the same as that of a charging bull elephant that you would find on the African continent. They had enormous padded feet with a thick, tough skin, perfectly adapted for moving across a vast terrain of ice and snow.

Eden noticed that many of them carried great bows and strapped to their large, hairy backs were pouches packed full of arrows. Towards the front of the great army were two distinctly larger males. One of them in particular looked tough and rather mean. Eden could not help but notice that both his ears were terribly torn and ragged and he had several hooped earrings in each one. He gave the impression that he had perhaps been in many fights.

Eden watched on with great interest as the largest of the strange elephant-like people came to an abrupt stop, almost causing the army behind to crash into one another. The one with the hooped earrings lifted his trunk-like nose into the air and trumpeted loudly. It was then that Eden heard them speak for the first time.

'Look Iglis! It has stopped snowing above us and yet if you look around it is still snowing everywhere else,' said the giant elephant-like man. His voice sounded rather gruff and croaky.

Iglis stopped and looked around him. 'My, you are right Glasis. This is very odd. It looks like sorcery to me. Do you think we are being watched?' replied Iglis.

'I wouldn't be surprised with all the strange goings on. I bet she is watching us right now,' replied Glasis.

'You had better watch what you say then. If she hears you, she might cut off your trunk like she did to my brother Castian. Do you know she ate it for her tea afterwards?' added Glasis.

When they heard this, many of the elephant-like people felt uneasy and began to trumpet loudly.

'Be quiet!' said Iglis. 'We don't want to attract unwanted attention.'

'Look, what is that up there?' said one of the other elephant-like people who was standing behind Glasis.

He had been scanning the sky overhead nervously for any sign of 'she who might be watching,' but instead all he saw was Eden who was still hovering above the great army, watching and listening with great interest.

'What have you seen Rastor?' asked Glasis and he looked up to where Rastor was pointing.

'Oh, so we are being watched. I knew it!' said Glasis and he narrowed his eyes with suspicion, lifted his short trunk in the air and trumpeted defiantly.

Just as Glasis reached for his bow and arrow, Iglis shouted to him to wait.

'Don't be so quick to fire Glasis, that there is just a wee lassie,' said Iglis.

'A wee lassie you say?' growled Glasis and he narrowed his eyes again and tried to get a better look at Eden.

'Hello wee lassie. What are you doing out here in the wilds? Are you lost?' shouted Iglis.

'Hello to you too. I suppose I am a bit lost, in fact I am not entirely sure where I am,' replied Eden.

'Why, you are in the land of Westerlyn of course. You are right in the north, not too far from the town of Northdale which is where we are heading. We can take you there if you like,' said Iglis.

'Wait a minute Iglis, don't go inviting her to join us. You've not even asked her who she is, or more to the point who she is working for.

And why is she hovering in the air like that? That's what I'd like to know. It is very suspicious behaviour indeed. Have you ever known a wee lassie who can hover in the air?' growled Glasis.

'Don't mind my foul tempered cousin, he has no manners,' said Iglis.

'That's not a problem. I should have introduced myself. My name is Eden Rosencratz and I am from Ordania, Castle Draccwyne is my home,' said Eden

'Castle Draccwyne? Isn't that the home of the Ordanian Royal Family?' asked Glasis. Suddenly he stopped narrowing his eyes and opened them wide with surprise.

'Yes, it is. Queen Valda is my grandmother,' replied Eden.

'Queen who? Queen Valda you say?' asked Glasis. He began to narrow his eyes again with suspicion.

'Although we mammohofs are not from Ordania, we do know of the Ordanian Royal Family and their Queen is certainly not called Queen Valda,' growled Glasis.

'Is that right? What is she called then?' asked Eden.

'Why it's Queen Agathe of course, wife of Great King Narù. Everyone knows that,' replied Glasis.

Queen Agathe? King Narù? How can that be? It must be several hundred years at least since they were on the throne,' gasped Eden.

'Are you mad wee lassie? Of course they are the King and Queen. How can you claim to be a member of the Royal Family and not know that? I'm beginning to think that you aren't telling us the truth. Perhaps you are working for the evil one, or even worse perhaps you ARE the evil one in disguise,' roared Glasis.

The huge army of mammohofs trumpeted loudly when they heard

this.

'Who do you mean? Which evil one?' asked Eden.

'Ah, don't try and pretend you don't know that. I'm not easily fooled wee lassie. You're a sorceress and I think you are either working for the evil one or you are her in disguise,' growled Glasis.

'Well, I am a sorceress, that part is correct but I am not working for anyone and certainly no one who is evil,' replied Eden.

Glasis continued to glare at Eden, his eyes full of suspicion.

'Well, I believe her,' replied Iglis.

'Thank you,' replied Eden. 'If you don't mind, perhaps you could help me? I'm blind,' said Eden

'If you like, I can carry you on my back. It'll only take about half an hour or so until we reach Northdale,' said Iglis.

'That is very kind of you,' replied Eden. The Princess flew down and was helped onto the mammohof's back. Minutes later the huge army set off again on their journey. She released her spell and the snow began to fall heavily again.

Eden found it strange sitting on the mammohof's back as they sprinted across the frozen land. The mammohof's large feet were indeed perfectly designed for traveling in the deep snow, allowing them to move effortlessly and cover great distances in very little time.

'It's a good job I'm not afraid of heights and that I can't see,' thought Eden. She felt the icy wind blow into her face and hair for they were traveling very fast indeed. The Mammohofs of Westerlyn were very tall as a race. Iglis must have been about nine or possibly even ten feet tall.

Glasis was leading the way a few hundred yards ahead of Iglis and

Eden. He was still very sceptical and was annoyed with his cousin for offering to carry Eden. Every so often he would glance back over his shoulder and look at the Princess with great suspicion. The mammohof could be forgiven for being concerned, for an age-old witch from Ordania had been spotted in Westerlyn recently and had apparently cursed several villages close to the border. This had caused great unrest and worry amongst the mammohofs and snee menesker who were the other inhabitants of the great frozen land. Unlike Ordania, Westerlyn was not a magical land. Its people were mainly tough farmers who had to endure harsh conditions. Westerlyn also had a great army of formidable warriors made up of snee menesker and mammohofs.

During the journey Iglis began to ask Eden questions. He wanted to know how she had come to be in Westerlyn and so Eden began to tell him the story of how she and her brothers and sister and created time portals to travel between Earth, which Iglis had never heard of, and the land of Ordania.

'Are you really a princess?' asked Iglis. 'I don't mean to be rude but we have never heard of you or your family.'

'Yes, I promise you I am telling the truth but what I don't understand is that King Narù died many years ago and you are saying that he is the current king. What year is this?' asked Eden.

'This is the year 2020,' replied Iglis.

'Really? Well in that case everything makes more sense now. I think the reason you haven't heard of me is because I am from the future and more than one thousand years into the future by the sounds of it,' said Eden.

When she first heard the mammohofs mention that King Narù was still on the throne, Eden wondered if perhaps she had time travelled. The more she thought about it, the more she was convinced that this was what had happened. Her only worry now was, how she would get back to present day Westerlyn in enough time to help her friends.

6 A Trip to Auld Reekie

'Phew! What a pong,' thought Qadir and he covered his mouth and nose with his hand. When he opened his eyes he found himself standing in the corner of a small square looked onto by many windows. The surrounding buildings were high allowing very little light to reach the ground. When Qadir looked up, he could see a tiny square of light high above his head and when he looked down, he was disgusted to find his feet deep in a filthy, slimy sludge which gave off a terrible smell. He began to make his way over towards a narrow close which he thought would lead him out of the square and into the main street.

'Okay, I have twenty five minutes to find Luna and then get back,' thought Qadir as he glanced at his watch.

As he made his way through the dark close, he felt someone grab his leg.

'Hae ye a spair penny?' said a gruff voice in the dark.

Qadir freed himself from the stranger's grip and apologised for he had no money on him and certainly not any that would be of use in 1632.

'Whaur are ye fae?' said the voice again but Qadir didn't answer for he had already left the close and was now standing out in the main street. He covered his mouth and nose again for the smell was truly awful. He had hoped that the air would smell fresher outside of the small square and dark close but in many ways it was worse.

There were all sorts of people going about their business but as soon as they saw Qadir they all stopped and stared.

'Look Maw, thon laddie's fair brankie,' said a young scrawny looking lad with a dirty face. He pointed at Qadir and laughed. His mother, a heavy set woman draped in a dark shawl, looked over at Qadir. He couldn't help but notice that she was blind in one eye. She began to laugh loudly, displaying a mouth of rotten teeth.

Qadir began to make his way up the street, which he recognised as Edinburgh's Royal Mile, only it looked much different and certainly much dirtier. He was surprised at how high the houses were, stacked on top of each other and rising up as far as the eye could see. As he walked, he was careful not to slip for when he looked down he saw that the road was covered in more filth.

'Euch! I'd better be careful not to fall and land in that mess. Goodness knows what is lying on these streets. My shoes will be going in the bin as soon as I get back,' thought Qadir.

As he slowly made his way up the street, passers-by stared and pointed at him. Some of them laughed and shouted at him but he had no idea what they were saying and so he pressed on. He now had less than twenty minutes to find his sister before he returned home.

'This is not going to be easy and I don't have much time. If only I had some way of communicating with Luna,' thought Qadir. He was starting to worry that he would not find her in time and that something awful may have already happened to her. He then felt reassured when he remembered that his little sister was also a powerful sorceress.

Suddenly he heard a commotion further up the street and a group of people came running towards him, pushing their way through the crowd. Qadir watched as several people were shoved to the ground by the mob who were shouting angrily. It was then that Qadir recognised one of the men. He had seen him before when he looked into his grandmother's spyglass. The angry man was still carrying the pitchfork and waving it in the air.

'That is the same group of people I saw chasing Luna,' thought Qadir.

'She's doon that close,' shouted a small boy to the angry mob and then he pointed to the entrance to one of many dark closes that led off Edinburgh's Royal Mile.

The angry mob turned and made their way towards the close entrance, pushing more people out of the way. Seconds later, they disappeared down the dark passageway.

'I think I should follow them in case Luna is hiding in there,' thought Qadir. He remembered the image that he had seen in the spyglass of his little sister hiding in a small square. However, before Qadir reached the close entrance, he heard a girl scream and so he started to run. He forgot how slippy the ground was an almost fell. To stop himself from landing face first in the disgusting mess, he reached out to grab hold of whatever he could which happened to be the handle of a wooden cart laden with vegetables. Unfortunately his weight caused the cart to tip and the vegetables roll off onto the ground and into the slimy, sludge.

The owner of the cart roared angrily at Qadir and began to chase after him.

'I'm really sorry. It was an accident,' shouted Qadir but the man did not appear to understand and continued to pursue him.

Qadir thought about running through the close but then he remembered that it was most likely a dead end. He glanced at his watch and realised that he now had less than ten minutes left.

'Where has the time gone? I really need to hurry,' thought Qadir. He looked up and saw the angry mob re-emerge from the close and this time they brought with them two prisoners: one old lady whom Qadir did not recognise and the other was a young girl whom Qadir instantly recognised as his little sister.

'Qadir? How did you get here?' squealed Luna. She was overjoyed to see her older brother.

'I'll explain all of that later. We don't have much time. I need to get you out of here,' shouted Qadir.

'They want to kill me,' squealed Luna.

'Why would they want to kill you and why are you letting them take you hostage? Use your powers otherwise I'll use mine. We really don't have much time,' shouted Qadir.

'I'm afraid that if they see that I am a sorceress they'll punish Annie or worse, they'll kill her,' shouted Luna.

'Who is Annie,' shouted Qadir. He was following the angry mob up the street as they dragged his sister towards St. Giles and the old Tolbooth. Luna's hands were tied together with rope and so she nodded in the direction of the old lady whose hands had also been tied and who was being dragged rather roughly along the street.

'They were going to kill Annie because they think she is a witch, but I can tell if anyone has magical powers whether dark or good and Annie does not have one ounce of magic in her body. They were being very cruel and so I helped free her from a terrible, smelly prison. They were going to kill her the next day and so I used magic to open the prison door so that she could escape. We got caught and now they want to kill me as well for helping to free a witch,' shouted Luna.

'Haud yer wheesht,' roared the man with the pitchfork and he prodded Luna in the back with it.

'Luna are you seriously going to let him away with that?' shouted Qadir. He of course could have intervened but he knew that his little sister was more than capable of defending herself. However, he could not understand why she was even hesitating to use her magic. With just a few simple words she could have every member of the thuggish mob gagged and bound.

'I already told you Qadir. If I use any more magic, then they will definitely think Annie is a witch and she'll be hung or burned for sure. I can't allow that. She's just a poor old woman and they are picking on her for nothing,' shouted Luna.

'Well, what do you propose to do? We don't have much time left. I need you to do something now, otherwise I will,' shouted Qadir.

'Can we take her with us? She has nobody here, no family or friends. If I leave her here they will definitely kill her,' shouted Luna.

'Okay, whatever it takes to stop you wasting anymore time. We need to get back to Ordania remember?' shouted Qadir.

'Oh yeah, I forgot. I'll be really annoyed if I find that Asmund has made it back before me,' replied Luna.

Qadir glanced at his watch and saw that he only had four minutes left.

'Right Luna, we need to go now. *'Dèan fuasgladh,'* roared Qadir and he pointed at Luna first and then the old lady. The ropes that were tied round their wrists unravelled and fell to the ground instantly.

One of the woman who was behind Annie screamed when she saw the ropes fall off.

'Thon's a witch fur shiur an the laddie's the deil,' screamed the woman. Everyone stopped moving and turned towards Qadir.

'Are ye the deil laddie? Are these twa yer witches?' growled the man holding the pitchfork which was now being pointed towards Qadir.

'I don't know what you mean exactly. I'm here to collect my sister and if you don't mind we really need to be on our way,' said Qadir and he stepped forward to take hold of his sister's hand. However, as soon as he moved, the angry man tried to stab him with the pitch fork.

'Okay, I've had enough of you and your pitchfork. In present day Edinburgh you'd be arrested for this behaviour,' shouted Qadir and he waved his hand in the air and shouted '*bloighich*'.

The pitchfork instantly broke into tiny pieces and fell to the ground around the angry man's feet. He gasped and then covered his mouth. A look of terror spread across his face.

Qadir glanced at his watch again and saw that he had less than two minutes left and so he grabbed hold of Luna's hand and told her not to let go.

'What about Annie? I can't leave her,' said Luna and so she took hold of Auld Annie's hand.

The rest of the angry mob had now started to back off, too afraid to touch them in case they cast a spell. Quite a large crowd had gathered in the street outside St. Giles and they were watching Qadir, Luna and Auld Annie with great interest.

'Well this will certainly give them something to talk about for years,' said Luna.

'The biggest surprise is yet to come. Just wait!' said Qadir and he glanced at his watch one final time.

'Haud yersels back or they'll dae ye harm,' shouted the ring leader of the group who had taken both Luna and Auld Annie prisoner.

Ten seconds later there was a bright flash and the crowd who had gathered in the street had to cover their eyes. When they looked back they were shocked to see that the old lady, the boy and the girl had completely vanished into thin air.

One of the woman who had chased after Luna fainted on the spot and several others screamed in horror.

'We'll aw be deid by the morn. Thon laddie wis the deil, a've nae

71

doubt,' shouted one of the men.

In the meantime Qadir, Luna and Auld Annie from 15th Century Edinburgh found themselves climbing out of the enormous clock and into the hallway of Ailsa Carmichael's home.

'Ah, you are both back and in one piece I'm glad to see. Phew, I think you all need a bath,' said Nanny Carmichael as she stood in the hallway and pinched her nose.

'Who have you brought with you?' asked Nanny Carmichael upon seeing Auld Annie.

'This is Annie. I had to rescue her from some horrible people who accused her of being a witch. They were going to have her hanged,' said Luna.

'How awful, well I'm sure we can make her comfortable. Come with me Annie, I'll look out some fresh clothes that will fit you and perhaps you can freshen up in the bathroom. After that we will all go into the kitchen and have a wee *strùpag*. I'm sure you must all be hungry,' said Nanny Carmichael and then she led Annie through to the back of the house.

'Poor Auld Annie. She has absolutely no clue what is going on. I am not even sure if she understands me when I speak. I know that I can barely understand her most of the time,' said Luna.

'Okay, I need to get changed quickly and then try and find out where Eden and Asmund have gone,' said Qadir.

'What do you mean? Aren't they in Ordania?' said Luna.

'I have no idea. If only all three of you had listened and obeyed Gran, I wouldn't have to waste so much time looking for you. How did you end up in Edinburgh and in the 15th Century?' said Qadir.

'I have no idea, but I am glad things turned out the way they did otherwise I would not have been there to help poor Annie and she would have been killed for nothing. They really were barbaric in the old days,' said Luna.

'Shoes off Luna, they need to go in the bin along with mine,' said Qadir.

'Probably a good idea,' said Luna.

Chapter 7: The Snee Hex

After a quick snack, Qadir left Nanny Carmichael and Luna as they tried to help poor Auld Annie come to terms with what was happening. The old lady was indeed in shock after having been teleported four hundred years into the future. The world in which Auld Annie now found herself was indeed strange and very much different to fifteenth century Edinburgh.

'Please excuse me. I have work to do,' said Qadir and he left the kitchen and made his way through to the front room where his grandmother's spyglass was lying on a table next to the window. He picked it up and examined it closely. He noticed that the part cloudy sky inside the glass had now changed to a clear night sky with brightly twinkling stars.

'I need to check that Eden and Asmund are alright, but Nanny Carmichael says the spyglass only works in daylight. I really don't want to wait until tomorrow morning. What if they need my help?' thought Qadir.

It was then he had an idea and although it would involve using a fair amount of magic, which strictly speaking was not allowed outside of Ordania, he thought that it was his best option. His number one priority was to ensure that his brother and sister were safe.

'I need to be quick with this. It will cause a lot of confusion, but that can't be helped',' thought Qadir and then he closed his eyes, lifted his hand in the air and whispered '*solas an latha*'.

The effect was almost instant; one minute it was a dark October night on the Isle of Lewis and the next it was broad daylight. It happened as quickly as when someone flicks on a light switch. Nanny Carmichael and Luna were most surprised when they looked out of the kitchen window, Auld Annie less so as she was already dazed and confused with everything else that was happening.

'My goodness. This will create news headlines,' said Nanny Carmichael as she walked over to the window and looked outside. She knew that Qadir was behind this and quickly explained to Luna about the spyglass.

'Qadir grabbed hold of the spyglass again. He decided that he would look for Eden next and so he pictured her in his mind, said her name out loud and then held the spyglass up to the window.

Qadir watched as the clear, starry night inside the spyglass clouded over and gradually turned to more of a pale grey colour. The Prince waited patiently for the clouds inside to break and present him with an image of his sister. However, he soon realised that what he was seeing was in fact a very cloudy sky and a heavy snowstorm was making it almost impossible to see.

'It looks just like a snow globe,' thought Qadir. He stared harder for in the centre of the storm, several dark shapes began to appear.

'Where are you Eden? What I am seeing cannot be Ordania. There wouldn't be that much snow there already. It looks more like Antarctica on earth,' thought Qadir. He then began to wonder if his sister had in fact tried to go back to Westerlyn directly. This made sense to the Prince as he knew his sister was in a hurry to go there. She was terribly worried about her friends who lived in the land of Westerlyn and was desperate to go to their aid.

It was then Qadir was able to make out the large elephant-like people as they ran across the frozen landscape. There were indeed many of them and they seemed to be approaching the gates to a huge city.

'Well, at least this confirms one thing, this is definitely Westerlyn if I am seeing mammohofs,' thought Qadir.

Although he had never actually been to Westerlyn before, Qadir had a natural interest in learning about the creatures that lived in Ordania and its neighbouring lands. He had met many Ordanian olihofs before, which are distantly related to the mammohofs only more mild mannered and civilised, but he had never met a real mammohof. Fortunately however, Qadir had read a lot about the mammohofs who live out on the ice plains of Westerlyn and had seen many pictures of them. He also remembered Eden describing one when she talked about her last visit to Westerlyn several years previously.

'Okay, so I know that she is in Westerlyn, but I haven't actually seen her yet,' whispered Qadir.

As he continued to look into the spyglass, his attention was drawn to one mammohof in particular who was much taller than the rest. It was then Qadir noticed someone sitting on his back.

'Ah, so there she is. I suppose I had better check the year, just in case she too has time travelled,' thought Qadir. Although he assumed that his sister would be in present day Westerlyn, after what happened with Luna, he wasn't prepared to take any chances. Needless to say Qadir was shocked when he asked the spyglass to show him the year in which Eden had arrived, the numbers 2020 appeared in front of him.

'Oh dear, it's a good job I checked. This sure beats medieval Edinburgh. I think I had better get my winter woollies on for this one,' thought Qadir. He then left the room to prepare himself for the imminent trip to a frozen land one thousand years in the past.

It took Qadir less than five minutes to get ready. He pulled on the warmest clothes that he had with him and asked Nanny Carmichael if she had a scarf and some gloves that he could borrow. Ten minutes after looking in the spyglass, Qadir was standing in the hallway and ready to set the clock.

'You look like you are about to go on an expedition to the North Pole,' laughed Luna when she saw her older brother wrapped up and wearing a large woolly scarf, thick gloves and hat that had belonged to Nanny Carmichael's late husband.

'Well almost. I'm heading to the frozen land of Westerlyn,' said Qadir.

'I thought that there had been a bit of a melt happening in Westerlyn recently? Perhaps it might not be that cold anymore,' said Luna.

'That might be the case if I were heading to present day Westerlyn, but unfortunately it seems that Eden managed to send herself to Westerlyn one thousand years in the past,' said Qadir.

'Oh, that's not so good. You won't have very long if you are going that far back in time. I reckon you'll only have about fifteen or so minutes. Please be careful Qadir,' said Nanny Carmichael.

'Don't worry. I'll be fine. If I can survive fifteenth century Edinburgh I can survive anything,' said Qadir.

He opened the glass case of the clock and arranged the hands so that they pointed to the year 2020, then he opened the wooden door at the front and began to turn the large key.

'Have the kettle on for when I get back. I hopefully won't be long and no doubt I'll be needing a hot drink to warm me up,' said Qadir. He smiled at Luna and Nanny Carmichael and then stepped inside the clock.

'Take me to the Land of Westerlyn,' said Qadir loudly and clearly and then he carefully closed the door behind him.

'Here I go again,' whispered Qadir as he stood in the dark and listened to the clock begin to grind and groan.

A cold wind picked up as Qadir began to feel everything around him spin fast and then seconds later, he felt snowflakes against his face. When he tried to open his eyes, he discovered he was standing outside in the most terrible snow storm. The wind screamed and howled around him driving the snow into his eyes, making it impossible to see.

Qadir raised the palm of his hand towards the sky and shouted *sguir*. The snow stopped instantly and the wind disappeared allowing the Prince to find his bearings. He looked around for any sign of a building or perhaps a road that would take him to the nearest village but all he saw was a vast sea of white that seemed to go on forever. He glanced at his watch and discovered that he only had ten minutes left and so he concentrated harder and focussed his eyes on the horizon. It was then he noticed a dark shape that was moving in the distance.

'Is that a mammohof over there?' thought Qadir. As he continued to stare, he decided that whatever it was it couldn't be a mammohof as it was far too short.

'Perhaps it's a local farmer. I'll go over and ask how I get to the nearest town,' thought Qadir. To save time, he decided to use magic to help him reach the stranger quicker. He had no idea exactly how far away the person was. Without magic it might have taken him at least ten or fifteen minutes to reach the person, time which he clearly did not have. Qadir closed his eyes and whispered '*tadhail*'.

In a flash Qadir found himself standing right behind the dark figure. Although it was still quite difficult to see clearly, whoever the stranger was Qadir soon realised that they were not a farmer or even a snee menesker of Westerlyn. Although he couldn't be entirely sure for the stranger still had their back turned to him, it appeared to be an old lady who was terribly stooped and walking with a stick through the deep snow.

'This doesn't make sense, how can an old lady be walking out here in the bitter cold? She's not even wearing winter clothes,' thought Qadir.

'Excuse me, I wonder if you might help me,' said Qadir.

The old lady stopped shuffling in the snow, but she made no attempt to respond or even acknowledge Qadir's presence.

Qadir assumed that she hadn't realised he was there and that perhaps she thought his voice was just the wind and so he spoke again.

'Excuse me. I'm a bit lost and wondered if you might help me find my way?' said Qadir.

The old lady remained still with her back turned to him but still she did not speak and so Qadir moved closer. He did not want to frighten her and assuming she was most likely hard of hearing, he placed himself in front so that she could see him.

'Are you alright? Can I help you at all?' said Qadir. Once again there was no immediate response but Qadir was now able to get a better look at the mysterious old lady. No sooner had he spoken than a terrible realisation dawned on him. Now that he could see more clearly, he recognised the hat upon the old lady's head. It had a short veil to cover the eyes and a single, long black feather that pointed upwards.

'How can she possibly be here?' thought Qadir. His heart began to beat hard. The Spindle was the last person he expected to meet out in the vast frozen wilderness of Westerlyn and one thousand years in the past.

The Spindle did not move, her head remained lowered but Quentin could still see that she was grinning. The same gnarled grin that he had witnessed several years previously. The next few minutes were deadly silent as Qadir stood and watched the age-old witch, wondering what he should do next. He didn't have much time left but if he turned to walk away, he feared that she would attack him.

'This is simply too much of a coincidence to meet the Spindle out here. I feel that this is some sort of trap,' thought Qadir.

The Spindle did not move but suddenly her shrill voice filled the air around Qadir. Her scream sounded like the wind of a violent storm. Qadir tried to cover his ears in an attempt to shut out the terrible noise, but when he tried to lift his hands he found that he could not. It was as if his arms had been bound by invisible rope.

'QUENTIN BARTHOLOMEW, I KNOW YOU,' screamed the Spindle and then she began to laugh hysterically although her mouth did not move.

The terrible noise of the Spindle laughing continued to fill the air. Qadir found himself unable to do anything to block it and so he too began to scream. Suddenly there was an enormous flash that lit up the sky above Westerlyn. It was so bright that snee menesker witnessed it all over the land.

Meanwhile a short distance away in the wealthy seaport of Northdale, the mammohofs had been looking out across the frozen landscape and witnessed the bright flash in the sky. At first they thought it might be a meteor that had simply burned up as soon as it entered the atmosphere. However, many of the local people in Northdale had a different opinion as to the cause of the bright flash. They had also overheard screams around the same time as the flash and believed that some poor, unfortunate individual had fallen victim to the evil witch otherwise known as the *snee heks*.

Many people of Northdale were so terrified of the snee heks they seldom ventured beyond the toll gates. Only the mammohofs were brave enough to travel across the vast, desolate land of snow and ice.

Snee heks? That must be the evil one Glasis and Iglis were referring to. I can understand now why Glasis was so wary of me when I first met them. Well one thing is for sure, witch or no witch I can't wait around here forever. If I don't hear from my family within the next twenty four hours, I'll be venturing out onto the snow plains so I can make my way back to Ordania,' thought Eden.

Since her arrival in Northdale, Eden had been treated very well. Although she did not want a fuss and certainly did not expect any special treatment, word had spread that she was an Ordanian princess. Although they had never heard of a Princess Eden Rosencratz, there was no mistaking the fact that she was a sorceress therefore the people of Northdale felt that it was in their best interests to keep her onside, especially when an evil witch was nearby. Many of the locals believed that Eden had been sent by the gods to protect them which explains why Eden was put up in the very best accommodation they had to offer.

The day after her arrival in Northdale, Eden met with Iglis, the mammohof who had helped her reach civilisation and she discussed with him her need to get back to Ordania as soon as possible. Once she was back in Ordania, she would travel to Castle Draccwyne and speak with the current King and Queen. She would explain all that had happened and hope that they would believe her since they too were powerful sorcerers. She would then ask them to help her return to the future so that she could help the people of Westerlyn.

'But you are in Westerlyn already and the people of Northdale need your help. They have high hopes that you will protect them from the evil snee heks. In fact, apart from the old medicine man who lives in the White Tower, you are the only realy hope they have had in a very long time. Although they are tough, hardy people they are not magical like you and have no way of protecting themselves against such evil. They will be most upset if you leave them in their hour of need,' explained Iglis.

'I understand, but I wasn't supposed to be here in the first place and my friends who are in the future also need my help. The longer I am delayed here, the greater the chance of something terrible happening to them. I must get back to the future so that I can protect them. As

I speak many villages and towns across Westerlyn are being attacked and pillaged by giant eis jätte,' said Eden.

'Eis jätte? We mammohofs can easily take on a few eis jätte. Perhaps you should take Glasis and I back to the future with you, we'd happily help in the fight. Glasis and I are considered the strongest warriors in the mammohof tribe and we have killed and skinned many eis jätte over the years. If I took you to the eis grot where I live, you'd see many jätte hides suspended from the walls and ceiling,' said Iglis.

'That isn't such a bad idea Iglis, although I think we are talking about more than just a few eis jätte. We could do with all the help we can get, especially from strong warriors like you and Glasis who have so much experience. None of the mammohofs from the future will have seen eis jätte before. Until recently the eis jätte had all but disappeared and were considered extinct. However, it turns out they were merely frozen but a recent warm spell in Westerlyn has led to a thaw which in turn has revived the sleeping monsters or at least that is what we are led to believe,' replied Eden.

Suddenly the conversation between Eden and Iglis was interrupted when another, younger mammohof by the name of Thor ran into the room in a state of agitation.

'I'm sorry to interrupt but if it's not too much trouble, your assistance is required at the city gate. The people of Northdale have reported a strange, hunched figure at the toll gate. Whoever it is, claims to be relative of Princess Eden, although the people of Northdale are worried it might be the snee heks.

'A relative of mine? Old and hunched? I find that hard to believe,' said Eden. The Princess could think of no one in her family who fitted the description and therefore decided that whoever it was, they were unlikely to be telling the truth. After all, she was one thousand years in the past where no one knew her.

'I'll come down immediately and if this imposter does turn out to be the snee heks, then I'll make sure she does not enter this city. Please can you help lead me there quickly?' said Eden. Both she and Iglis jumped up from their seats and followed Thor down to the tollgates.

When she arrived at the gates, Eden could sense the fear around her. People peered out from the shadows, mothers ushered their children indoors and even some of the mammohofs were trembling with fear. As Iglis led Eden towards the gate, there was a loud knock from the other side.

'Who is there?' asked Eden, but there was no reply.

'My name is Princess Eden Rosencratz of Ordania. You say that you are a relative of mine and that you wish to see me. Can you please confirm who you are?' asked Eden again. Her voice sounded strong and confident. Suddenly a strong wind picked up and the gates to the city began to shake.

'Who are you and what do you want?' shouted Eden, but still there was no response. The wind was now howling around them and the great wooden gates had started to shake violently. Moments later the wood began to split, showering Princes Eden and the mammohofs with splinters of wood. They covered their eyes and turned their heads away momentarily but when they looked back, they were shocked to discover that the entire gate had disappeared. The mammohofs peered out onto the open plain and amidst the snow storm they could just make out a dark, motionless figure that was watching them. To help her visualise what was happening, Iglis was describing to Eden in detail, everything that he could see. As he stared harder to try get a better look at the mysterious dark shape, he noticed that it had started to increase in size. At first the change was only slight and he thought that perhaps his eyes were playing tricks. However, soon there was no mistaking the fact that whoever or whatever the dark shape was, it was steadily growing taller. The figure continued to stretch until it towered threateningly over the defence walls of Northdale.

Eden had been concentrating hard and finally succeeded in visualising everything around her. In her mind she could now see the tall, dark snee heks standing menacingly over their heads. The mammohofs and the people of Northdale watched as Eden suddenly lifted herself off the ground and flew up until she was eye level with the snee heks, then she stopped and hovered in the air. A few minutes of silence followed during which time the snee heks stared at Eden with great curiosity.

'*Cuir dorchadas air fògairt,*' shouted Eden and she pointed at the snee heks. The crowd below had to cover their ears when the snee heks began to scream loudly. The face of the evil witch changed to that of a skeletal-like creature with long, snake-like hair that flew wildly in the wind. Then, the snee heks outstretched her long, spindly arms, casting a shadow over the terrified crowd below. The noise of the snee heks screaming continued until it was so loud, the people, including the mammohofs could no longer withstand the noise and one by one they fell to the ground unconscious. When the snee heks saw the people lying on the ground, she began to laugh hysterically. Just as Eden raised her hand one more time to try and cast a spell that would hopefully banish the witch, a great silence fell over Northdale. The snee heks blew into Eden's face and turned the Princess into solid ice. The witch continued to blow on every building and every person until the entire city of Northdale and all of its inhabitants had been frozen in thick, impenetrable ice.

Meanwhile back in Ailsa Carmichael's house on the Isle of Lewis, the door of the time traveller's clock suddenly flew open and a semi-conscious, half frozen prince fell out onto the floor of the hallway.

'Qadir, whatever has happened?' shouted Luna and she ran over to where he lay on the hall carpet. When she turned her brother over, she saw the look of terror in his eyes.

'Qadir, please tell me what happened? Didn't you find Eden?' asked Luna.

'The S…Spindle. I met the Spindle,' whispered Qadir and then he passed out from exhaustion.

Chapter 8: The Forest of Lost Souls

'I must get to Castle Draccwyne and tell Gran what I saw. It changes everything,' thought Asmund. The terrible battle between Ordanians and landga wolves was ongoing in the valley below and although he wanted to run down the mountainside to help his father and grandfather, Asmund knew it was of the utmost importance that he shared with Queen Valda immediately what he had just witnessed, plus he would need to find a suit of armour before he even attempted to set foot on a battlefield amongst the jaws of so many landga wolves. He gave no thought to the fact that he had travelled back in time and would no doubt cause a lot of confusion if he turned up at the castle, he simply had to find his grandmother and share the information about Prince Espin. Within minutes Asmund had turned his back on the battle and looked towards the strange looking forest which was spread out on the hilltop behind him. He looked up towards Elfview Mountain which rose majestically above the battle scene with Castle Draccwyne sitting on top, its topmost turrets glistening in the late afternoon sun.

'The quickest way to Castle Draccwyne would be to go through the forest instead of around it,' thought Asmund as he looked up towards the thick wall of trees which separated him from the foot of Elfview Mountain. He thought that the forest looked rather strange with its thick, stumpy trees which all seemed to twist and bend in different directions. The trees were not particularly tall which made Asmund think that it must be a relatively young forest, although he could not remember seeing such a forest when he was last in Ordania.

Without a moment to lose, Asmund began to sprint amongst the gnarled, stumpy trees. He was eager to reach his grandmother as quickly as possible and inform her that Prince Espin had been carried off by an unidentified force. The sooner he reached her, the sooner she would be able to do something to help Espin, or at least that is what he hoped.

Soon the young Prince was running zigzag through the thick trees and jumping over large, overgrown roots. Although the trees were mostly short, many of them were so stooped that he had to duck to avoid smashing his head against the thick branches. He assumed that his passageway through the trees would be quick, straightforward and without hindrance however he assumed too much for the forest into which he ran was one of the most dangerous in all of Ordania; it was known to Ordanians as the Forest of Lost Souls. In most cases Asmund could be forgiven for thinking that taking a short cut through a forest wasn't necessarily dangerous but he was Ordanian born and his experience to date should have warned him that Ordanian forests are anything but straightforward, particularly when they look as ugly and odd as this one did. Most Ordanian forests are beautiful, serene places that make you feel happy whereas the Forest of Lost Souls was a sad place, filled with short, gnarled trees that seemed to weep when you walked passed them. It was a forest devoid of birdsong and where no animals chose to live. In many ways it seemed empty, nothing seemed to grow in there, even the strange-looking trees looked stunted.

There was a reason why Asmund could not remember this particular forest being at the foot of Elfview Mountain for it was not actually a forest, at least not in the truest sense. The forest gained its name when through time it became apparent that many people had simply disappeared without a trace when they tried to pass through it. It was quickly decided that the Forest of Lost Souls should be avoided at all costs. In those days there was still a lot of evil around in Ordania and it was not uncommon to stumble upon evil shape shifters from the north who had been sent as spies to gather information about the Ordanian Royal Family. Sometimes evil spells would be cast in places around Castle Draccwyne. These spells were designed to catch members of the Ordanian Royal Family by surprise, but in most cases it was ordinary folk going about their business who got entangled in the evil web.

You may be wondering who was casting such spells and sending spies to Ordania, if so the answer is a terrible warlock by the name of Lord Zadicus, who at that time resided in a place north of Ordania called Whitewitch Mountain. Asmund had already studied a fair amount of Ordanian history and he knew a lot about the evil warlock from the north, but at this moment in time he thought of nothing else other than reaching his grandmother and telling her that her youngest son was alive, that he hadn't died on the battlefield after all and so he continued to run through the Forest of Lost Souls as quickly as he could.

'Surely I must be close to the edge by now. It didn't look that big from the outside,' thought Asmund. He was beginning to tire and had to slow down when he twisted his ankle on an exceptionally large, gnarled root that protruded up from the ground. The sun was now beginning to set, casting shadows all around and although Asmund was not afraid of being in a strange forest in the dark, he knew that it would be more difficult to navigate his way and so he pressed on. After a short time he stopped to rest again for his ankle throbbed with pain. He looked around in dismay as the short, stumpy trees now seemed thicker than ever and there was no sign that he was even close to the edge.

'I've just about had enough of this strange forest. I'm beginning to feel as if I am going round in circles. I'll just have to use what little energy I have left to fly myself out of here for there isn't much time left before nightfall,' thought Asmund.

'Sgiath,' shouted Asmund and he attempted to lift off the ground however when he tried to jump, he found that he simply couldn't for his legs suddenly became very heavy, so heavy that he could barely lift them off the ground.

'I probably shouldn't have come into this strange place. I thought it would be a shortcut and now I am going to be delayed,' thought Asmund. He now realised that the forest in which he stood was no ordinary forest and he remembered his youngest sister, Luna warning him before about the dangers of some of Ordania's unknown forests. 'For once I should have actually listened to Luna, after all she is Princess of the Woods. I never thought I'd say this, but I wish she were here now. She'd be able to get me out of here,' whispered Asmund as he stood and stared around him in the middle of what now seemed like an endless forest. As he scanned the area, trying to decide a plan of action he thought he heard someone whisper. He listened again carefully for a minute or so, but since there was no repeat of the unexplained noise, he decided that it must have been the wind rustling through the trees.

'I'll send a signal into the sky to attract attention. My grandmother will hopefully see it and come to my rescue,' thought Asmund.

'I'll send up fireworks, they'll be seen by everyone. Maybe the battle will be over by now and Grandad can help,' thought Asmund. He decided to walk on a little more to where there appeared to be a gap in the trees; the perfect spot where he could send several fireworks up into the sky for all to see. As he walked forward, he suddenly realised that the trees were thinning out quite considerably and when he peered ahead into the fading light, he suddenly noticed that he was almost at the edge of the forest. Asmund couldn't believe his luck in finding the forest edge just as it was about to get dark and so he tried to run as fast as he could. When he looked ahead, he could just make out the meadow that was spread out in the valley beneath Elfview Mountain. Asmund reckoned that his exit could only have been a few hundred yards away and yet as he started to run, he got the feeling that the edge of the forest was getting further and further away. As he was running he heard more whispers, and this time there was no mistaking the voices. It was as if the strange trees were whispering in his ear.

'Run, Prince of the Mountains, run as fast as you can before nightfall,' whispered a voice in his ear. Soon Asmund's ears were filled with many unknown voices as they all shouted his name.

'Run Prince Asmund, run before it's too late,' whispered the ghostlike voices.

As he continued to sprint his way forwards, his legs began to feel heavy again. It was the same feeling he experienced when he tried to fly out of the forest. Within seconds his sprint was reduced to a jog and minutes later, he could barely walk at all. His legs were now as heavy as cement and his feet had started to stick to the forest floor. Just when he finally reached the last few trees scattered along the edge of the forest, Asmund reached forwards with his hands. He thought if he could grab hold of a branch, then perhaps he could drag himself out of the forest.

The Prince's fingertips had barely touched the branch of a lone tree which stood just outside the Forest of Lost Souls when the setting sun disappeared completely and darkness fell around him. Suddenly Asmund froze on the spot, his entire body turned to wood, his feet became gnarled roots, deeply embedded in the forest floor and his arms turned into thick, twisted branches that reached forwards. Asmund was now the latest victim to join the lost souls in the evil forest.

Chapter 9: A Helping Hand

It took Qadir several hours to fully recover from his encounter with the Spindle. When he woke up, he found himself tucked up in bed. Nanny Carmichael and Luna were sitting by his side.

'What happened?' shouted Qadir. He sat upright in bed and looked around him.

'Shhh, try to stay calm Qadir. You are back on the Isle of Lewis and in my home,' said Nanny Carmichael.

'We thought that you had been possessed. You were muttering all sorts of nonsense when you came out of the clock. I couldn't make head nor tail of most of it,' said Luna.

'Out of the clock? What do you mean? … Oh, you mean the traveller's clock. I'd forgotten about that,' said Qadir.

'I didn't find Eden, I need to go back there immediately,' said Qadir. He attempted to jump out of bed, but his sister and former nanny stopped him.

'Wait! Perhaps we should hold on until dawn. I've tried to send a message to your parents but I'm not sure how quickly they'll get it. If they have already gone to Westerlyn, it may take longer to reach them,' said Nanny Carmichael.

'I'm surprised they haven't come back for us already. It has been ages since they left,' said Luna.

'Less than two days actually,' said Nanny Carmichael.

'Yes, but in Ordania that's about three weeks. Anything could have happened in that time,' said Luna.

'Well, whatever you do, don't go trying to create any more time portals. I don't want to have to go back to Edinburgh in the fifteenth century. That really was a terrible experience. I'm surprised we didn't catch something, we should probably be quarantined now that we have been there.

Whatever happened to your friend Annie?' said Qadir, suddenly remembering the old lady whom Luna had insisted on bringing back from fifteenth century Edinburgh.

'Oh, we won't see her for a while. She's been in the bath for almost an hour. She's absolutely loving it. I've been in twice already to top up the hot water and I washed her hair. You'd think she'd died and gone to heaven,' said Nanny Carmichael.

'Qadir, can you tell us more about what happened when you went into the clock? You mentioned that you saw …' Luna paused momentarily before she said the name. 'You said that you saw the Spindle,' added Luna.

A look of terror spread across Qadir's face when the name of the terrible witch was mentioned however he soon composed himself and described everything that had happened when he arrived back in Westerlyn. Once he finished talking, a hushed silence filled the room as Nanny Carmichael and Luna contemplated Qadir's story.

'Do you think the Spindle has taken Eden?' said Luna. She was the first to speak and break the silence. What she said was exactly what the others were thinking, although no one wanted to say it.

'I have thought of that, but I'm not entirely sure. I didn't even see Eden when I was there. I didn't have long enough to look around and the conditions were terrible,' said Qadir.

'Is there anything we can do to help other than sit and wait for Mum, Dad and Gran to get back in touch?' said Luna.

'We don't know how long that will be. I need to try and do something before then and we still haven't even tried to find

Asmund,' said Qadir.

'I'm sure Asmund will be fine. At least he has his eyes to see with, but we can have a look in the spyglass for him as well just to be sure,' said Luna.

'Okay, then there is no more time to waste. I need to get up and use the spyglass again, although I think I might need to take a different approach this time,' said Qadir.

'Well, if you insist on going back so soon, I insist you eat something before you go,' said Nanny Carmichael.

After a quick bite to eat and a hot drink, Qadir was in the front room of Nanny Carmichael's home once again with the spyglass in his hand. 'I'm going to have to use some magic again. I can't afford to wait until dawn,' said Qadir.

Nanny Carmichael shrugged her shoulders. 'Do what you must. It'll give the locals something to talk about for a very long time I'm sure. It'll no doubt make front page headlines tomorrow: *Unexplained light turns night into Day across the Isle of Lewis*. We won't worry about that, your sister's safety is far more important,' said Nanny Carmichael.

'*Solas an latha,*' whispered Qadir. Within an instant, the front room of Nanny Carmichael's home was filled with bright sunshine. Without a moment to lose, Qadir held the spyglass to the window one more time and said the words '*faigh for air bana-phrionnsa Eden*'. He watched carefully as the spyglass began to cloud over. Eventually the clouds broke and the sky cleared allowing Qadir to see the location of his sister. Although he did not recognise it, he was being shown the broken gates which led into the city of Northdale. Qadir wasn't familiar with Northdale as it was an ancient, forgotten city which had been completely frozen for a very long time. No one went there anymore and over time it had been renamed the Forgotten City. The snee menesker of Westerlyn assumed that after the last big freeze, it had become virtually impossible to live there anymore. Everyone believed that the Forgotten City had been abandoned by its inhabitants who then travelled further south to the newer and prosperous city of Westercourt.

The next image that appeared in the spyglass shocked Qadir so much that he let the glass object fall from his hand. Luckily Luna was standing beside him and quickly grabbed it before it smashed on the floor.

'What did you see?' asked Nanny Carmichael upon seeing the shocked look on Qadir's face.

'I'm not entirely sure. It looked like a city that had been completely frozen and then I saw what I thought was simply a statue, an ice sculpture.' Qadir paused for a few moments before he continued. 'Then I got a closer look and it was Eden's face, but she was completely frozen in ice,' said Qadir.

Luna stifled a scream and Nanny Carmichael threw her hand over her mouth.

'I need to go now, there is no more time to lose. I need to borrow Gran's spyglass for this trip,' said Qadir. He took the spyglass from Luna, placed it carefully in his coat pocket then ran into the hallway to where his grandfather's clock stood. The hands were already pointing to the year 2020 and so he opened the door and began to turn the large key.

'But wait, you don't know where you are going?' shouted Luna.

'Yes, I do,' said Qadir and he stepped inside the clock. 'Ordania,' shouted Qadir to the clock.

'Ordania? I thought you said Eden was in Westerlyn,' said Luna.

'She is, but I need to go to Ordania first. I don't know where this frozen city is, but I know someone in Ordania who will hopefully be able to tell me,' said Qadir.

'Who do you know in Ordania from the year 2020?' shouted Luna. The clock had now started to grind and groan.

'Why, King Narù of course. He was the King in 2020 and I'm sure when I tell him what has happened, he'll be able to help. Qadir saw Luna's lips move again but he could not make out any words. A strong wind had now picked up inside the clock and the metal wheels were now groaning and creaking louder than ever. He was forced to pull the door shut and not a moment too soon as everything started to spin around him.

It didn't take long before a sweet aroma filled Qadir's nostrils, it was the smell of the last of the summer flowers to bloom in Ordania. Summer usually finished much later and autumn was a warm and colourful time of year. Even though Qadir had arrived back in Ordania more than 1000 years in the past, he still recognised the air for it was just as pure if not more so. If only he wasn't in such a hurry, Qadir wouldn't have minded exploring the beautiful Belwald forest that was situated to the west of Elfview Mountain. He had enjoyed many walks with his mother in Belwald. Qadir thought that the forest looked much the same as it did in present day Ordania, only many of the trees were understandably shorter and the forest had not yet spread out as far. Qadir looked across at the foot of Elfview Mountain and cast his eyes upwards to where Castle Draccwyne was perched, looking out over the whole of Ordania.

'My goodness, Castle Draccwyne has not changed in all these years,' thought Qadir. He began to make his way across to the footpath at the bottom of Elfview Mountain which would take him to the Castle gate. He found it a struggle at first, for the footpath was not as well used and loose rocks and gravel constantly moved beneath his feet.

'Who goes there? Identify yourself and tell me your business?' roared a gruff voice from a little further up the mountain. Qadir looked up but could not see anyone and so he did not respond and continued on his way.

'Stranger, you are now on the King's mountain. What business do you have being here and tell me your name, otherwise you may go no further,' roared the voice again.

'Please reveal yourself and I will gladly introduce myself,' said Qadir. He stopped and tried again to catch a glimpse of the mysterious speaker. Seconds later, Qadir was most surprised to see a large cat-like creature leap down from a rocky outcrop and land on the path in front of him. At first he thought it was a lion, but on closer inspection he noticed that it had wings folded neatly on its back.

'Oh, are you a tàcharan?' asked Qadir.

'Indeed I am not, but answer my questions first before you ask me any more,' growled the cat-like creature.

'My name is Qadir Rosencratz. I am here to speak with His Royal Majesty, King Narù,' said Qadir.

'What business do you have with the King? You can't possibly see him if you don't have an appointment. You'll have to come back next week,' growled the cat-like creature.

'I'm afraid that isn't possibly, you see I have just arrived from the future, more than one thousand years in the future to be precise. I am Prince Qadir Rosencratz, so strictly speaking this castle is my home, only not yet ...if you understand me,' said Qadir.

The strange cat-like creature narrowed its eyes and looked at Qadir with suspicion. It then began to circle the Prince, sniffing around his feet as if trying to uncover the truth.

'Are you a sorcerer like King Narù? You must be if you have travelled from the distant future the way you say you have. Such behaviour isn't normal and surely it can't be good for you. You certainly dress oddly and you smell strange,' said the cat-like creature.

Qadir was desperate to continue on his way for he knew he didn't have long before the clock would pull him back to the present day and so he asked the cat-like creature if he was allowed to continue on his way up the mountain.

'Jump on my back and I will take you there. It'll be much quicker than on foot. I hope you are telling me the truth. His Majesty will be the best judge. He'll know if you are lying. To answer your question from earlier, I am no tàcharan or whatever it was you said. I am originally from the land of Westerlyn. I am an örn-katt,' said the cat-like creature and then he opened his great wings and flapped them in the air.

'Thank you very much. That it is very kind of you to offer me a lift. I am in rather a hurry. Do you have a name?' said Qadir.

'Yes, my name is Iolaire,' and he purred loudly before lowering his great head. Qadir wasted no more time and quickly climbed onto the back of the örn-katt. The cat-like creature was very strong with a very wide back. Its creamy fur was incredibly thick which Qadir thought would be better suited for the cold climate of Westerlyn. As they began to fly up the mountainside, Qadir asked Iolaire why he was no longer in Westerlyn.

'I serve the King and his family now as he graciously helped the örn-katts when our mountain habitat was overtaken by evil changelings from the north. We were pushed out of the caves where we had lived and raised our cubs for generations. We had nowhere to go and many örn-katts died out on the ice plains of Westerlyn. Strong as we are, we were no match for the evil sorcery that came from the north and so kind King Narù came to our aid and attacked the evil, forcing it to retreat. I have offered to guard Elfview Mountain and make sure that no evil gets anywhere near the castle. My job is to alert the King and his son, Prince Torsten to any danger or sign of evil beings returning to Ordania,' said Iolaire. Shortly after he had finished explaining his story, the örn-katt announced that they had arrived. 'I am afraid that you must wait outside the gate whilst I seek permission for you to enter,' said Iolaire. Qadir nodded and then glanced at his watch nervously. He was worried that any minute now he would be whisked back by the time traveller's clock and find himself once again standing in Nanny Carmichael's hallway. However, just as Iolaire approached the large gate into Castle Draccwyne, there was a loud rumbling noise and the gate started to open by itself. Suddenly a loud voice boomed from inside the castle.

'Welcome stranger. I am exceptionally keen to meet with you. You may enter the castle,' boomed the voice.

'Well, it looks like His Majesty is already aware of your presence and that he is willing to let you enter. You must be telling the truth for the King cannot be fooled easily. He is one of the most powerful sorcerers ever to rule this land,' said Iolaire. The örn-katt then bowed his head in front of Qadir. 'Forgive me Your Royal Highness. I had to be sure first of all that you were not here to deceive His Majesty,' said Iolaire.

'Please do not apologise. You were only doing your job. We could do with an örn-katt like you to guard Castle Draccwyne in present day Ordania,' said Qadir. Although the Prince knew his way around, he allowed Iolaire to lead the way into the strangely familiar hallways of Castle Draccwyne. Prince Qadir was home once again and yet he felt strange to be there, one thousand years before his family had even lived. As he walked along the main hallway, he looked up at the ceiling expecting to see the huge war paintings, only to find that it was completely bare. He then realised this made sense since the painting had only been added after the Great Civil War which would not take place until 3010, nine hundred years in the future. Instead of the family portraits lining the walls with which Qadir was familiar, there were huge tapestries of wood nymphs, water kelpies and other strange creatures from Ordanian folklore.

By the time they reached the golden doors that led into the Great Hall, Qadir was growing quite agitated. He reckoned he only had minutes left before he would be made to return to present day earth. However, once he stepped inside the Great Hall, Qadir momentarily forgot about the time for when he set eyes on the King and Queen seated upon the thrones, he was truly mesmerised by their magnificence and beauty. Qadir could not believe that he was now standing in front of King Narù, the powerful sorcerer King who appeared in numerous stories and songs as well as history books. He knew that this was a special moment in his life, he only wished that he had more time to enjoy it.

'I do not know who you are young man, but I see you come with the power of a thousand stars. I can also tell that you are of royal blood. What I find strange is that you seem to be at home here in Castle Draccwne and yet you have come from far away. Please come forth and tell us your story,' said King Narù and he smiled at Qadir. He was a tall, handsome man with long, dark brown hair that fell down his back. He wore a thick beard and his blue eyes sparkled like diamonds. Qadir noticed that the King had a special glow around him, it was as if his body was full of twinkling stars.

'Forgive me Your Majesty. You are right in everything you say, however I don't have much time as I am only allowed to be here for a very short period. I do wish to tell you my story, but first of all I must ask for your assistance in helping me stay here a little longer,' said Qadir. He was trying not to sound too impatient, but his wrist watch now told him that he had less than two minutes left before being transported back.

'Certainly, if a little more time is what you need, then I can easily grant you that. However, it takes a lot of power to be able to stop time and only the most powerful of sorcerers can do it. I can tell that you are very powerful, just like me and if you take my hand we can use our powers combined to make it work,' said King Narù. Qadir did not take one second to consider it, he had no time left and so he stepped forward and took the King's hand. As soon as their hands touched, both King Narù and Qadir began to shine brightly. Suddenly two of the most powerful sorcerers ever to have lived in Ordania, but who lived more than one thousand years apart, were brought together and their magic combined created a force like no other.

'By the power of the stars, I ask that the sands of time stand still,' shouted King Narù.

'Sguir cliongraich a'ghleoca,' shouted Qadir.

There was a short pause before anyone spoke again, and then an eerie silence filled the Great Hall. 'Our wish has been granted, now please be seated and tell me your tale. I did not recognise the words that came from your mouth. What were they pray tell?' said King Narù.

'The words you heard come from a language called Scottish Gaelic, an old language spoken in parts of a small country called Scotland.

'Scotland? I've never heard of it. Is that where you are from?' asked King Narù.

'No, not quite. I am Ordanian born, although I have been living in Scotland for a while,' said Qadir. He then sat down and told King Narù and his beautiful Queen Agathe his story from when he was born, then sent to earth for his protection and finally how he and his siblings had returned to Ordania. Meanwhile outside the castle walls, there was not one other heart in the entire Kingdom that was beating, no insect buzzed and no birds flapped their wings for life had been temporarily paused.

Once Qadir had finished telling his tale, including his reason for traveling back to the year 2020, King Narù stood up from his throne where he had been seated and listening intently to everything Qadir had to say. The King walked over and shook Qadir firmly by the hand. 'Prince Qadir Rosencratz, it is an honour to meet you and although I would very much like to sit with you for a few more hours and find out more about the future, I know you are eager to reach your sister. Tell me more about this frozen city that you spoke of and I will do what I can to help,' said King Narù.

Instead of trying to describe the vague picture that he'd seen, Qadir had a better idea. He withdrew his grandmother's spyglass from his pocket and held it to the light.

'Faigh for air bana-phrionnsa Eden,' said Qadir and then he waited patiently until the cloudy sky inside the spyglass began to clear. It wasn't long before the same snowy image appeared in the glass and an outline of Eden became clearly visible, frozen and suspended in mid-air. Qadir asked King Narù to look into the spyglass to see if he recognised the mysterious frozen city behind Eden.

'Indeed I do recognise this city and it would appear that the main gate has been completely removed from its hinges, usually it is never open for long. I can tell you that this is the city of Northdale which lies at the most northerly point of Westerlyn,' explained King Narù.

'Northdale? I've never heard of it. Although I have never really been to Westerlyn, I have studied many maps and the only place in the north that I can remember was called the Forgotten City. I just assumed that it was the ruins of some old city, abandoned long ago,' said Qadir.

'Well, all I can say is that there is evil at play here. No city can freeze instantly like that, even if it is located in the far north of Westerlyn. My son and I were there only a few months ago and it was a happy, vibrant city. However, I do remember there was a growing fear among the people that a form of evil was present outside the city gates. Many of the inhabitants were afraid to venture outside. I didn't see or hear anything when I was there and assumed it was simply rumours, however I am wondering now if perhaps there was some truth in it,' said King Narù.

'I think I know the answer to that. I visited Westerlyn very briefly a very short time ago. I could not tell you exactly where I was; I found myself out in the open under a terrible snow storm. I can't say for sure if I was close to the city of Northdale or any city for that matter, for I was prevented from travelling any further,' said Qadir.

'Whatever it was must indeed me strong to impede your journey Prince of the Stars,' said King Narù.

'Well, some would think that it is a miracle I survived at all for not many do. I had the misfortune to encounter a terrible witch who is unimaginably evil. She is known in present day Ordania as the Spindle and I was most surprised to find her back in the year 2020. Perhaps this is the same evil that the people in Northdale spoke of,' said Qadir.

'The Spindle? That is a strange name and not one I've heard before. There is an evil witch who walks these lands currently, but she has many names and many different faces. She can appear in the form of dark, strange-looking animals or a frail old lady, bent over and walking with a stick....'

'That's her,' shouted Qadir, interrupting the King. 'I'm sorry Your Majesty, it's just that your description of an old lady is exactly how the Spindle has appeared when I met her on two occasions,' said Qadir.

'Well, all I can say is that it is of great concern to me to know that an evil witch can be around these lands for more than one thousand years. She must indeed be powerful and I have a responsibility to the people of Westerlyn as well as to the people of Ordania to remove such evil,' said King Narù.

'If you don't mind me saying so Your Majesty, if she has been around for as long as we think, at least we know that she hasn't managed to take over the entire land. In most cases the Spindle stays hidden, out of sight and it is only when some poor, unfortunate individual stumbles across her that something terrible happens,' said Qadir.

'If that is the case, how do we explain the entire city of Northdale being frozen in ice, along with your sister? They certainly did not stumble upon the witch by accident. If she is indeed the same witch who the people of Northdale claimed was lurking around outside the city walls, it would appear that she found them. We should head there immediately, hopefully the spell can be reversed but I think that it will take our power combined to undo the work of such evil,' said King Narù.

It took less than an hour for the King to arrange their departure. Both Qadir and King Narù flew from Ordania to Westerlyn on the backs of örn-katt: King Narù sat on the back of Iolaire and Qadir on the back of another örn-katt by the name of Eliolah. First they travelled northwest over the western slopes of the Esterway mountains and then across the great lakes. Finally the green land spread out below them began to change colour until they could see the start of the great snow plains of Westerlyn. Most of the journey was a blur to Qadir and he paid little attention to the landscape for he was desperate to reach the city of Northdale; all he could think of was rescuing his sister. In the back of his mind he knew that once he had rescued Eden, then he would need to return home immediately and began the next search for his brother Asmund. Fortunately time continued to stand still and throughout their entire journey, not one living creature stirred on the ground below them.

They flew for ages over what seemed like an endless world of ice and snow until eventually King Narù pointed ahead to the skyline of Westerlyn's most northerly town. By the time they landed it had started to snow again and Qadir was glad of the warm furs which King Narù had given him to wear before they set off on their journey for the air was bitterly cold. They landed just outside the open gate which led into the city of Northdale. There were frozen bodies lying all around the entrance, but Qadir was only interested in reaching his sister who he could see almost as soon as he arrived, poised in mid-air and frozen solid. Why she was in mid-air, he did not know. He only hoped that the spell could be reversed.

'There is my sister, Princess Eden Rosencratz. Do you think we can break the Spindle's spell?' asked Qadir and he pointed up to the frozen Princess, suspended fifteen feet in the air.

'We won't know until we try, but I fear it will drain our energy for a while. We might struggle to free the entire city from its frozen slumber,' said King Narù.

'In that case I will return with Eden and my entire family and we will make sure that the spell is reversed,' said Qadir.

'That does mean these poor people will have to wait an awfully long time to be rescued, over one thousand years according to your calculations,' said King Narù.

'Yes, I hadn't thought of it like that as it only takes me several minutes to travel one thousand years into the future. What should we do?' said Qadir.

'Well, do remember that we have already used a lot of our energy to freeze time, which by the way can only be stopped for so long. I don't think that spell will last much longer. Let's do what we came here to do and rescue your sister. Once we have done that, we can decide what the best course of action will be for the others. However, I think your idea might be the only option. This evil creature whom you call the Spindle is very powerful indeed,' said King Narù.

'Do you think that she is still around?' said Qadir as he scanned the area nervously.

'Who knows, but I suppose we will find out when you try to break her spell. Now, you must hurry young Prince for time is now against us. As I said, the spell to freeze time will not last much longer and if I have understood correctly, when the spell does break, you will be instantly transported back to the future,' said King Narù.

Without a moment's hesitation, Qadir flew up to where his sister was suspended in mid-air and placed his hand on her frozen shoulder. He looked at her pale, expressionless face and whispered gently in her ear 'Awaken Princess Eden of the Seas and Lakes. I have come to take you home.' King Narù joined Qadir in the air and he held Qadir's hand. He placed his other hand on Eden's head and then he too spoke to her; 'Awaken Princess from the future, shake off the dark spell that holds you in a frozen sleep,' said King Narù. The King then leant forward and kissed Eden on the forehead. Within seconds what had been a dark, heavy sky cleared and a galaxy of twinkling stars appeared. Just as Qadir and King Narù lifted their heads to look up, a beam of starlight shot down from the sky and bathed Eden's frozen body.

'Hold on to her now, otherwise she will fall,' said King Narù.

Qadir wrapped his arms around his sister and within seconds her complexion began to change from pale, frosty white to pale pink. Suddenly Eden fell heavily into her brother's arms and then ever so gently he lowered her to the ground. The Princess began to stir, although at first she said nothing and did not seem to have any recollection of what had happened.

'Qadir, is that you? What happened? I'm so cold,' whispered Eden. Her voice was weak and she shivered.

'Yes, Eden it's me. I've come to take you home,' said Qadir.

'To Castle Draccwyne?' whispered Eden, her voice was very weak.

'No, not straight away. I have to take you back to Lewis, to Nanny

Carmichael's house then once you are better, we will take you back to Castle Draccwyne,' said Qadir.

'Young Prince, the spell to freeze time is beginning to weaken. I'm afraid we don't have much time,' said King Narù.

'Your Majesty. I need to thank you for everything you have done. I wish I could stay longer, but I must go back with my sister and then try to find my brother. After that I promise that I will return to Northdale and free its people from the Spindle's spell,' said Qadir.

'It has been an honour to meet you Prince of the Stars and to know that in the future, Ordania and its people will be in very safe hands. The people of Ordania will wait for your arrival in many years to come, they will speak of the prophecy of the Starry Prince and his siblings. I bid you and your sister farewell,' said King Narù and he blew Qadir and Eden a kiss goodbye.

'Who was that?' whispered Eden as she cuddled into her brother's fur coat for warmth.

'That was the King of Stars, he really was just as magnificent as the history books said he was,' said Qadir. Moments later both Qadir and Eden began to feel disorientated. When everything finally stopped spinning, they found themselves in complete darkness. The air around them suddenly became a lot warmer and it smelled old and musty. At first Qadir sat still, unsure where he was or what had happened and then he heard a rustling noise to his right, followed by a loud creak. A bright beam of yellow light suddenly streamed into the darkness and the familiar voice of Luna filled their ears.

'Qadir, is that you in there? Have you got Eden this time? You took ages. What kept you?' said Luna.

'Hi Luna, yes it's me and yes I've got Eden this time,' said Qadir. He smiled, shook his head and then asked Luna to help him lift Eden out from their grandfather's clock. Although she was now fully awake, she needed to go to bed for a while in order to recuperate fully. Qadir understood better than anyone what if feels like after an encounter with the Spindle and what better place to be than under the watchful, caring eye of Nanny Carmichael.

Chapter 10: The Reawakening

'It's time to find out where Asmund is,' said Qadir. He had his fingers crossed behind his back when he said it. Secretly he hoped that when he looked inside the spyglass one final time, he would see his brother safe and well back in Castle Draccwyne. He took the spyglass out of his coat pocket and started the entire process all over again.

'Don't you want to get some sleep first and leave it until tomorrow morning before you look for Asmund?' asked Luna.

'I could wait, but what if he is in difficulty like you were or Eden. Don't you think I should at least find out where he is? He might be absolutely fine, living in Castle Draccwyne and enjoying Bellamina's wonderful cooking, in which case we don't need to do anything,' said Qadir.

Moments later a huge look of relief began to spread across Qadir's face when the familiar outline of Castle Draccwyne appeared in the spyglass.

'This is the best news I've had all day. I just need to get a sighting of Asmund and then I think I will go to bed and catch up on some sleep,' said Qadir.

However, Qadir could not see his brother anywhere near the castle, all he could see was Elfview Mountain and a strange looking forest which spread out in the valley below.

'Those trees at the foot of Elfview Mountain look very odd. I don't recall there being a forest there at all, just an open meadow which takes you down into Brookden Valley,' thought Qadir.

Qadir was now becoming increasingly concerned that the spyglass had not yet been able to present him with an image of his brother and he began to wonder if the strange forest had something to do with it.

'Luna, I need to ask you a favour. Since you are Princess of all Ordanian forests, could you please take a look at this and tell me what you think?' said Qadir.

Luna was intrigued and carefully took the spyglass from her brother and looked inside.

'Oh, it's Castle Draccwyne. So Asmund made it home after all. I'm so annoyed that he beat me. You mustn't tell him what happened to me or I'll never hear the end of it. He'll tease me for years,' said Luna.

'Luna, look carefully. Can you see Asmund anywhere?' said Qadir.

'No, I can't. Wait, why are there so many people standing still at the foot of Elfview Mountain and staring into space? It looks like they are playing a huge version of musical statues, except they seem to be standing still for an exceptionally long time,' said Luna.

'People? I didn't see any people,' said Qadir and he took the spyglass off his sister to have another look.

'I don't see any people at all, just a whole load of short, ugly trees. Most of them don't even have any leaves,' said Qadir.

'Well, I didn't see any trees, just lots of people, so what does that mean?' said Luna.

'I'm not really sure, but it looks as if an early night is out of the question. As for you Princess of the Woods, you are coming with me this time,' said Qadir. He then looked at the spyglass one final time and asked for the year to be revealed.

'3010? So he didn't make it to present day Ordania after all. Why does that year sound familiar?' said Qadir.

'3010? Why, that was the year of The Civil War. Don't you ever pay attention in history class?' said Luna.

'The Civil War involved landga wolves didn't it?' asked Qadir.

'Yes, it did. It also involved grotta ghoul and evil shape shifters, just like the war we were involved in. Grandad Andris and Dad both fought in the civil war,' said Luna.

'I suppose that means I could bump into Abnocta Mirus again. That's so annoying considering I already killed him,' said Qadir.

'Perhaps you could just kill him sooner and then Grandad Andris would not be bitten and he'd still be alive today. Qadir, why didn't we think of this before? The time traveller's clock is a brilliant way of going back in time to stop terrible things from happening,' said Luna.

'If only it were that easy. I'm afraid that it is strictly forbidden to go back in time and try to change history. Nanny Carmichael warned me of that before I went to fetch you,' said Qadir.

'But I managed to stop Annie from being killed and brought her back here with me. Surely if that wasn't allowed something would have happened by now?' said Luna.

'Yes, I've been wondering about that. I'm sure if Gran found out, she wouldn't be happy that you brought someone back with you from the earth year of 1632. However, we don't actually know for sure what would have been the outcome for Annie, perhaps she would have been executed, perhaps not. You will have to tell Gran about Annie at some point and don't be surprised if she says that she must be returned to fifteenth century Edinburgh,' said Qadir.

'Well, whatever Gran says. I won't let them kill Annie,' said Luna.

'We can worry about that later. In the meantime we must to go and bring Asmund back. This is the last time that I can use the time traveller's clock therefore I cannot afford to mess this up. If I don't find Asmund before I am brought back to earth, someone else will have to go and fetch him,' said Qadir.

Before they set off, they said goodbye to Nanny Carmichael who was in the bedroom taking care of Eden.

'This should hopefully be our last trip into the past. It won't be too long before we are back. I'm taking Luna with me. We aren't going quite as far back as last time, the year 3010. We might even see you there Nanny Carmichael,' said Qadir. Luna said goodbye to Annie who was sitting in the front room staring at the TV. Ever since she had been shown how to change the channels, Annie sat constantly flicking through every single one and laughing at whatever appeared on screen.

'Qadir, please tell me that you're not going to wear that old moth eaten fur coat again? Where on earth did you find it anyway? I'm sure it has fleas,' said Luna as she watched her brother get ready for their trip to Ordania.

'No, I don't think I'll need that on this trip. I'll have you know that the fur coat is an antique, over a thousand years old. King Narù gave it to me before we travelled to Westerlyn. I bet you I could sell it at a good price,' said Qadir.

'I think it should be buried in the back garden,' said Luna with a disgusted look on her face.

'Okay, let's do this,' said Qadir as he opened the door of their grandfather's clock once again, arranged the hands so that they pointed to 3010 and then gave the large key one single turn.

'I was going to say hopefully this will be straight forward, but I don't want to tempt fate. Right Luna, in you come,' said Qadir and he climbed inside the clock, Luna followed.

'Elfview Mountain, Ordania,' shouted Qadir and Luna together.

As soon as everything started to spin, Luna closed her eyes and giggled. 'This reminds me of when I travelled from Aunt Eva's house to Lewis using her magic tea set. How long will it take us and when will we know that we have arrived?' shouted Luna.

'We already have. Open your eyes,' said Qadir. Luna did as Qadir said and found that they were already standing at the foot of Elfview Mountain between the ugly forest and the pathway that would lead them up to Castle Draccwyne.

'Oh, that was quick. Isn't it great to be home?' said Luna.

'Yes, but we don't have time to get too comfortable. We haven't been born yet, remember? Now, turn right around and look at the strange forest behind us. Can you still see the people you were talking about?' said Qadir.

Luna turned around, but could see no forest. Instead she saw hundreds of people standing perfectly still. Some had their hands held high above their heads, others reached forwards. The only thing they had in common was that they did not move.

'Oh my. Are all those people dead?' gasped Luna.

'So you can still see them? That is strange, to me they look like ugly, leafless trees but you see people. I really don't understand any of this,' said Qadir.

'Wait, I can see one tree, but the rest are just people who seem to be pretending to be trees. I wonder how long they have been like that. It all looks rather creepy,' said Luna.

'Why don't you ask the tree what's going on?' said Qadir.

'Oh yes, of course. Why didn't I think of that?' said Luna. As Princess of the Forests, she was the only one who could see through the spell. Luna could communicate with all of the trees in Ordania therefore it made perfect sense that she should try to get some information as to why all of these people were standing at the foot of

Elfview Mountain pretending to be trees.

As Luna passed among the motionless people, she noticed that many of them were Ordanian soldiers. However, there were also other people and creatures from Ordania such as; varken mensen, tàcharan as well as men, woman and children from the towns and villages that lay in the valleys below Castle Draccwyne. She noticed how each and every one of them had an expression on their face which suggested they had been caught by surprise.

The only real tree amongst the enormous gathering of people stood right in the centre. It was an oak tree which Luna remembered from present day Ordania, although it now looked much younger and shorter than she remembered. Luna could speak to every tree spirit in the land and she had spoken with this tree on many occasions in present day Ordania. When she first approached the tree and placed her hand against its trunk, the tree made no response. Luna waited several minutes before she tried to speak. She could sense almost immediately that the young tree was afraid.

'Dear gentle spirit. You need not fear me for I am Luna Rosencratz, Princess of all trees. I am from the future therefore you do not yet know me,' whispered Luna. After several minutes the tree still did not respond, although the Princess did detect the slightest vibration pass up through the trunk and along its branches. The young oak tree could in fact hear every word Luna said and it was thinking hard about the name *Luna Rosencratz*, for there was a story that had been whispered over generations from tree to tree about a princess who would one day arrive and ensure the safety and protection of all Ordanian forests. The young oak tree was wondering if this could indeed be her. Never before had it met a human being who could speak to it in the way Luna had. The Princess did not even need to move her lips to speak, she used only her mind. As soon as Luna's hand had touched the trunk, the tree felt safe and reassured. For years it had remained silent and sad, growing ever so slowly amongst the crowd of poor unfortunate souls who had the misfortune to walk across an area of land where an evil spell had been cast. Those who did not make it through the forest before sunset, soon found themselves unable to move. Their legs and arms would grow heavy and eventually their feet would be rooted to the ground. They would reach forwards in a desperate attempt to escape the terrible forest that was now consuming them. Soon afterwards they would appear as leafless, gnarled and twisted trees.

It was therefore difficult for the young oak tree to respond at first for it had now been so long since it last communicated with another living being. Of course there was still the possibility that Luna was not in fact who she said she was and the young tree was afraid that she might be the evil one who had cast the spell, come back to count how many victims she had managed to catch in her web of deceit.

'Tell me of this evil being whom you fear so much? Did it do all of this?' asked Luna again.

She listened carefully and eventually, from deep within the heart of the tree came the softest whisper.

'The Dark Spirit of Shadows did this many years ago and I am trapped. No flowers grow around my roots, no woodland animals use me for refuge and no birds sing on my branches for I am doomed to grow amidst this sea of lost souls. The magic that cast the evil spell is so powerful that even Queen Valda and King Andris cannot see through it,' whispered the oak tree.

'I can see through the spell and I was able to see that you were the only real tree among them all. That is why I am here, to ask you what happened,' said Luna as she gently caressed the trunk of the tree.

The young oak tree then went on to explain to Luna in detail about the evil being which it referred to as the Dark Spirit of Shadows and how it had come in the hope of trapping members of the Ordanian

Royal Family. The tree also warned the Princess that she had to be careful and leave the forest before sunset otherwise she too would be trapped, exactly what the Dark Spirit of Shadows had been waiting patiently for.

'Don't worry about me. I won't be trapped. My brother and I will try and break this evil spell around you so that you can breathe again. I know you from the future and you are now a large, strong tree so you will survive this evil, trust me,' said Luna.

For the first time in years, the oak tree felt much calmer. It felt soothed by the Princess' soft touch and the gentle words which she spoke through her mind. Never before had the tree known a human being who could understand it and therefore it thought that what Luna had said, must in fact be true. This being must indeed be the Sorceress Princess whose arrival had been talked about for almost one thousand years, an exciting story that had been whispered on the wind from tree to tree across the whole of Ordania.

'My brother and I will help you be free from this suffocating evil before we return to the future,' said Luna and she kissed the tree trunk gently.

Qadir had been waiting patiently on the edge of the forest for his sister to return and was worried that she was taking too long. On the other side of the hill he could hear the noise of the ongoing battle, although he had not yet realised that the noise was indeed the very battle that his father and grandfather had told him all about. Had he known, Qadir would probably have found it difficult not to take part. However, he was very pushed for time and as much as he wanted to, he could not go and explore the area. Deep down he desperately wanted to try and see his grandfather again, alive and strong the way he remembered. However he kept reminding himself that he could not waste the opportunity to rescue his brother and that as soon as they found him, they had to return to the future immediately and then hopefully make their way to Westerlyn to help their grandmother and parents in the fight against the terrible eis jätte.

'So much to do and so little time. Where has Luna got to?' thought Qadir.

Just as Qadir was about to call on his youngest sister, she suddenly reappeared out of the forest.

'Ah, there you are. I thought something had happened and I was just about to come and look for you,' said Qadir.

'Qadir, you must help me to break the evil spell that has caused this. I know we are here to rescue Asmund, but we cannot leave until we have helped to free all of these people,' said Luna.

'By people, you mean all of these short, strange looking trees?' asked Qadir.

'Yes, they are not trees but people who have been trapped by an evil spell cast by someone whom the tree referred to as the Dark Spirit of Shadows,' explained Luna.

'Oh, hopefully it's not her again! She certainly gets everywhere if it is her. She has made her presence known in every century that I have visited, in fact every millennium. Was there ever a time when she didn't exist?' said Qadir.

'I don't understand. Who do you mean?' said Luna, sounding confused.

'Why the Spindle of course. She has had many different names and many different faces over the centuries, but I have no doubt that this Dark Spirit of Shadows that you speak of is in fact her,' said Qadir.

Suddenly Luna looked over Qadir's shoulder and let out a short scream.

Qadir froze on the spot, fearing the worst. 'I shouldn't have said her name out loud,' thought Qadir.

'Is she behind me Luna? Can you see her? What does she look like?' said Qadir.

'Sorry, it isn't the Spindle. I didn't mean to scream. It just came out. Look behind you!' said Luna and she pointed to one of the strange looking trees that stood right on the edge of the forest. Its twisted branches seemed to reach out towards them as if begging for help.

Qadir turned and looked, but of course all he could see was a short, gnarled, leafless tree.

'What exactly am I supposed to be looking at?' asked Qadir.

'Oh, I am sorry. I keep forgetting that you can only see trees whereas I see real people. Asmund is standing right over there,' said Luna and she pointed again.

Without a moment to lose, Qadir ran over to the tree which Luna had pointed to. He placed his hand against the tough bark, closed his eyes and whispered.

'Great Spirits from the stars above, help free my brother with your love,' said Qadir.

Suddenly the tree was illuminated and as soon as Qadir opened his eyes again, he watched the transformation take place. Gradually the spindly branches of the tree changed to fingers and then to arms. Within seconds, his brother's face appeared out of the bark and the gnarled, twisted roots on the forest floor, changed into feet; Asmund collapsed onto the ground.

Qadir knelt down and turned his brother over. Fortunately he was breathing and shortly after Qadir whispered his name, Asmund opened his eyes and looked up at his older brother.

'Hey, how did you get here?' said a rather bewildered looking

Asmund.

'Oh, that's a long story which we will have to save for later. I just need to get you out of here and back to the future. Can you stand?' said Qadir.

'Yes, of course I can stand. I'm not really sure what happened. Did I pass out?' said Asmund.

'You fell under an evil spell,' said Luna.

'Oh, you're here too. I hope you realise that I made it back before you, so I win,' smiled Asmund.

'You haven't won Asmund. In fact you messed up! You are almost thirty years too early and we had to come and rescue you,' smirked Luna.

Suddenly Asmund's memory came flooding back, the soldier and the landga wolf in the wood and how he had witnessed the battle field where his own father and grandfather were fighting a bloody battle.

'We must get to Castle Draccwyne and try to find Gran. I've just remembered I have urgent news that I must tell her immediately,' shouted Asmund.

'We don't really have much time Asmund. I'm afraid that any minute now we will be whisked back to earth. Can't you just speak to Gran once we get back?' said Qadir.

'No, you don't understand. We need to do something now. I can't wait thirty years to tell her. That will be too late. If I tell her now, she can do something about it,' said Asmund.

'Do something about what?' asked Qadir.

'Whatever it is it will have to wait, I promised the oak tree that I would not leave here until we had broken this evil spell and freed the people,' said Luna.

'What people?' asked Asmund.

'I'll explain later, just trust me. These trees that you see around you are not trees, but real people who have fallen under a spell. Now let's hold hands and combine our powers to free them,' said Luna.

Before Asmund had the opportunity to ask any more questions, his sister had taken hold of one of his hands and then Qadir took his other hand. Soon they were joined in a circle and as soon as he heard Qadir and Luna begin to chant, Asmund joined in.

'Great Spirits of the Stars above, release these people with your love,' chanted Qadir.

'Great Spirits of the Woodland trees, help these people to be free,' chanted Luna.

'Great Spirits of Mountains deep and old, break this spell, let the truth be told,' added Asmund.

There was a blinding flash which spread throughout the Forest of Lost Souls and when Qadir and Asmund opened their eyes again, they watched as one by one each of the short, gnarled, leafless trees changed into human beings who as soon as they were released from the spell, fell to the ground. In total it took only a few minutes before what had been the Forest of Lost Souls, became a sea of people who sat upright on the ground, rubbed their eyes and looked around them, somewhat confused and bewildered. In the middle of the sea of people, stood a beautiful young oak tree. It waved its branches gently in the wind as if to thank the children for their help.

'You were all under an evil spell, but we have broken it and you are now free to go on with your lives. Your friends and families will have been searching for you for quite some time therefore they will be overjoyed to see you again and I am sure there will be much rejoicing,' said Qadir.

It was then that Qadir began to feel the now familiar sensation of the time travelling clock calling him back, a tingling that started in his toes and then made its way through his body until his head felt light and dizzy. Being the most experienced time traveller out of all of them, he quickly grabbed hold of his brother's hand and then his sister's and not a moment too soon for seconds later Qadir, Asmund and Luna vanished into thin air, leaving the already confused and bewildered crowd of people scratching their heads and wondering what in all of Ordania was going on.

'What's happening?' shouted Asmund.

'Where are we?' shouted Luna.

'We are on our way back to the future,' said Qadir.

Shortly after he spoke, the wind died down, the strange feeling of giddiness stopped and the children found themselves standing silently in the dark. Qadir fumbled around and moments later succeeded in opening the door of his grandfather's clock from the inside, letting the warm light from the hallway of Nanny Carmichael's home flood inside.

'Welcome home you three. You are just in time for supper,' said Nanny Carmichael. She was over the moon to see all three children home safe and well.

'I think I'm going to go straight to bed if that's alright with you. The past twenty four hours have been the most exhausting ever,' said Qadir. 'How is Eden?'

'Eden is doing brilliantly, in fact after you left I had a hard job trying to make her stay in bed. She was determined to climb into your grandfather's clock and join you,' said Nanny Carmichael.

'Okay, goodnight everyone. Now, please stay out of trouble and whatever you do, do not use any more magic,' said Qadir. He turned to his brother and sisters who were sitting in the front room of Nanny Carmichael's house, chatting to Annie. The old lady from Edinburgh was admiring her new hairdo which Nanny Carmichael had given her. Luna handed Annie a mirror and as soon as the old lady saw her own reflection, once she had recovered from the initial shock, she laughed hysterically. '*She looks jist like ma ain mither,*' laughed Annie.

Chapter 11: Making Headlines

The following morning Qadir slept until midday. He even missed breakfast, which was most unlike him and Nanny Carmichael was concerned enough that she went into the room three times to make sure that he was alright. Each time she was reassured when she heard gentle snores coming from the bed. She then left the room, gently closing the door behind her.

Shortly after the clock struck one o'clock, the front door of the house swung open and a familiar figure appeared in the doorway.

'Good afternoon. Is anyone home?' shouted the voice of Granny Bartholomew.

'Gran, you're back?' squealed Luna with delight.

'Yes, I'm back, but not for long. I've come to collect all of you and then we must return to Westerlyn immediately,' said Granny Bartholomew. She entered the hallway and quickly removed her coat.

Shortly after she was joined in the hallway by the twins and her old friend Ailsa Carmichael.

'Would you care for a cup of tea Vronnie? You should at least have a quick rest to recover from your journey,' said Nanny Carmichael.

'Yes, okay that would be lovely. I could do with a cuppa for I have been fighting eis jätte for days on end and I'm exhausted. I'm getting far too old for fighting monsters,' said Granny Bartholomew. She kicked off her shoes, threw herself down in one of the arm chairs and placed both feet on the footstool.

'Oh, I am sorry. I see you have a visitor. Forgive me for muttering gibberish, I didn't see you there,' said Granny Bartholomew when she noticed Auld Annie sitting in the corner of the front room, staring in awe at the magnificent Queen who had arrived straight from the battlefield.

Luna didn't know what to say and so she looked over at Nanny Carmichael nervously. Nanny Carmichael smiled back and then introduced Granny Bartholomew to her *old friend* Annie who she said was visiting from Edinburgh.

A look of relief spread over Luna's face and then she, along with Eden and Asmund settled down on the settee in the front room to listen to Granny Bartholomew tell them about the situation in Westerlyn. However, she was now reluctant to talk any more about monsters, magic and battles since an earthling was present in the room. Instead she changed the topic to her eldest grandson who she noticed was missing.

'Where is Quentin?' said Granny Bartholomew, remembering to use her grandson's earth name.

'I'm here,' replied her eldest grandson. He appeared in the doorway looking rather sleepy with unkempt hair.

'Goodness me, have you just woken up? You certainly are in holiday mode. Well, I'm afraid holidays are over for now as I need you all to come home and help me attend to some urgent …. Ahem, *business*,' said Granny Bartholomew.

'You will no doubt be bored and fed up sitting around. I hope you haven't been in any trouble and getting up to mischief? Especially you my dear Luna,' said Granny Bartholomew and she cast her youngest granddaughter a glance.

Luna's face reddened. She knew that her grandmother was referring to the incident from the previous summer when she had accidently cast a spell on her neighbour, sending him to Ordania and then after that she ran away with him. Her grandmother had to come looking for her and Luna got herself into all sorts of bother.

'They have all behaved impeccably,' smiled Nanny Carmichael.

'I'm glad to hear it. Now, I am afraid I need everyone to gather their things and then we'll be off. By the look of things, Quentin badly needs some fresh air and exercise. Isn't that right Quentin?' said Granny Bartholomew. She emptied her tea cup and glanced over at her eldest grandson who had been yawning constantly from the moment he entered the room.

'Right, I need to collect a few of my belongings that I forgot the last time I was here and then we'll be off,' said Granny Bartholomew. She stood up from the armchair and began to make her way through to the bedroom.

'Well, it was very nice to meet you Annie. I hope you enjoy your stay on Lewis,' said Granny Bartholomew. She smiled at the old lady who had sat perfectly still and silent in the corner of Ailsa Carmichael's front room.

Just as Granny Bartholomew began to make her way across the hallway to the spare room where she had left her belongings, the daily newspaper fell through the letterbox.

She bent down and scooped it up from the floor. Just before she placed it on the hallway table, Granny Bartholomew happened to glance at the headline on the front page.

Local Ladies disappear following unexplained light Phenomena

'Goodness me, whatever has been going on here?' said Granny Bartholomew as she began to read the front page article.

Ailsa joined her in the hallway and listened as Granny Bartholomew began to read aloud.

Two local elderly ladies have gone missing under mysterious circumstances on the same evening unexplained light anomalies appeared above the skies of Lewis, turning night into day. It has been suggested that both ladies in their eighties may have been abducted by aliens. Brighid Macleod aged 83 and Ealasaid Mackenzie

82 failed to return home yesterday after a routine bus trip. Families have described the behaviour as out of character and have asked the public to contact police if they have any information about their whereabouts. According to police reports, both ladies stepped off the bus one stop earlier than normal at Timsgarry, along with a group of four school children who are thought to be on holiday on the island. Police have asked the children to come forward and assist them with their enquiries. The disappearance of both ladies comes at the same time many local people reported an unexplained light that was so bright, it temporarily turned night into day. Although the strange light phenomena remains unexplained by scientists, many believe there is a connection between the mysterious lights and the disappearance of Ms Macleod and Ms MacKenzie.

Granny Bartholomew paused from reading and looked up from the newspaper.

'Perhaps things haven't really been that quiet here after all. Okay children, I think you have some explaining to do,' said Granny Bartholomew.

The walk from Ailsa Carmichael's home down to the beach was a long one as Granny Bartholomew asked the children to explain to her in detail everything that had happened since she had left them two days previously. Once the children had finished explaining, Granny Bartholomew stopped walking and turned towards them. There was a blank expression on her face and the children could not tell whether or not she was cross with them.

'Okay, so let me just recap to see if I have understood correctly. Despite being told that under no circumstances must you use magic whilst on earth, three of you managed to create time portals that sent you back in time and your brother had to go looking for you. Luna went back to Edinburgh in the year 1632 and almost got burned at the stake for witchcraft, Eden went one thousand years back in time to Westerlyn where she, along with an entire town were frozen by an evil spell and Asmund went back in time almost thirty years to when the Great Civil War was ongoing in Ordania and got trapped by an evil spell that turned him into a tree? Did I miss anything?' said Granny Bartholomew and she looked at all four of her grandchildren with raised eyebrows.

'Not really Gran, I think that just about covers it,' said Asmund.

'Well, you have forgotten one thing,' said Granny Bartholomew.

'Have we? What have we forgotten?' said Luna.

'You have forgotten the part where three of you meet the extremely angry sorceress who strips you of your magical powers and sends you to a very strict boarding school for the next five years with no holidays and study classes at weekends,' said Granny Bartholomew.

'But that didn't happen to any of us Gran,' said Luna.

'It's just about to,' roared Granny Bartholomew and she glared at her grandchildren.

The penny suddenly dropped and all four children stood in silence, unsure what to say next. They felt ashamed for having caused so much trouble. After a short pause, Granny Bartholomew spoke again and this time her voice was much quieter and calmer.

'Of course I am not annoyed with Qadir, quite the opposite in fact. If it wasn't for him, goodness knows what might have become of you. It seems like he is the only one with any sense at all,' said Granny Bartholomew. She turned to her older grandson and smiled.

'I really am very proud of you Qadir and I don't think it will be too long before you return to Ordania on a permanent basis and leave the name Quentin and your life on earth behind you. Your immense bravery and commitment to helping others who are in trouble tell me that you are almost ready,' said Granny Bartholomew.

'On another more positive note, you have also managed to answer a few questions for me that have left me scratching my head for years.

I do remember the strange forest at the foot of Elfview Mountain. It never seemed to have any life about it, there was never any spring blossom or autumn colour. Your grandfather and I stayed clear of it and then one day, the very same day the Great Battle was ongoing, the strange forest simply vanished leaving behind one single oak tree which is still there to this day.

Anyway, we have to get going for there is a battle to be fought. We can't hang around chatting any more, but once the battle is over we will need to talk about this again. I need to be able to trust that in future you will be responsible with the great gifts that have been bestowed upon you. First of all, let us focus on helping the people of Westerlyn,' said Granny Bartholomew.

By this point they had reached the beach which had been chosen as a new spot by Granny Bartholomew to create a portal that would transport her and the children from earth straight to Westerlyn. It was the same beach where another portal linking earth to Ordania had remained hidden for many years and it was also on this very beach that Granny Bartholomew first arrived on earth as a small child many years ago.

'Before we travel, I must warn you that you won't have any time to stop and think as soon as we set foot back in Westerlyn. You will need to be prepared to defend yourself and have your wits about you. One strike from the claws of an eis jätte will take your head clean off. They stand thirty or sometimes forty feet tall and their roar is loud enough to blow your eardrums. The eis jätte will stop at nothing when they want to feed, which is constantly. They hunt relentlessly in huge packs and there are now thousands of them all over Westerlyn.

'Where did they come from Gran and why are they attacking all of a sudden?' asked Qadir.

'That is a very good question and one that I have been trying to answer. A recent warm spell in Westerlyn has brought about a melt.

There have been terrible avalanches in the mountains that lie between the land of Westerlyn and the Wolfhaven. The snee menesker believe that the ice melt has something to do with the rise of the eis jätte,' said Granny Bartholomew.

'I don't understand. How can ice melting cause these monsters to attack?' asked Eden.

'I thought eis jätte were extinct,' said Asmund.

'Many believed the eis jätte to be extinct for they haven't been seen for thousands of years. The local people believe that the avalanches have unveiled deep, hidden caves in the mountains where eis jätte have been living for centuries. However, I am not so convinced that these occurrences have anything to do with the current mild spell of weather. I sense foul play and I have the feeling that something or someone powerful is behind it,' said Granny Bartholomew.

'What do you mean Gran? Who do you think is behind it?' asked Qadir.

'I am really not sure, but I can sense their power and it is strong and very dark. Evil still lurks in the cold shadows of the Wolfhaven. I always felt that there was a power much stronger than the landga wolves and their evil leader, Abnocta Mirus. Although we managed to ban evil from entering Ordania, we did not destroy it. I think that whatever or whoever it is, they might be planning to enter Westerlyn and then try to enter Ordania. There is no protection spell between our land and the land of Westerlyn,' explained Granny Bartholomew.

'Do you mean that Abnocta Mirus was working for someone else? I can't imagine anyone or anything being strong enough to control Abnocta Mirus,' said Qadir.

'Oh, I can tell you that there is greater evil out there and much stronger than you could ever possibly imagine. Now, are we all ready to go?' said Granny Bartholomew.

'Yes Gran, we are,' said Luna.

'Let's chase those eis jätte back into their caves,' said Eden.

'I can't wait to get some action,' said Qadir.

'What about you Asmund, are you ready to face the eis jätte?' asked Granny Bartholomew. She had noticed that her youngest grandson had not said anything.

'Yes, I am ready Gran. I was just thinking about what you said,' answered Asmund.

Since the moment she arrived back on earth, Asmund had been desperate to share with his grandmother the news that he brought from his recent trip to Ordania whereby he witnessed his grandmother's youngest son being carried away from the battlefield by an evil shapeshifter. However, he had to find the right moment, it wouldn't be easy to tell his grandmother that her youngest son did not die on the battlefield after all. Could he still be alive and living in the cold, desolate lands that lie to the north of Ordania? Asmund wondered if perhaps the evil being who had once kidnapped his sister, was not lying after all. Whoever he was, he told Eden that he was her Uncle. So many questions were now racing through Asmund's mind, but he decided that he would wait for now did not seem like the right moment.

Little did he know, his grandmother had been asking herself the same question for several years. Although she had never said anything to her family, the Queen had often wondered if there was indeed any truth in the story that her granddaughter shared with her following her kidnap. However, the Queen found it difficult to believe that the evil stranger who lived in Whitewitch Mountain could possibly be her beloved Espin.

Chapter 12: Fighting Eis Jätte

One by one the children followed their grandmother into the portal which suddenly appeared between several rocks on the beach. They glanced around the area cautiously for they did not want to be seen by any of the locals. The events of the past forty eight hours had already caused quite a stir in the community and there were now several police officers in the area, trying to find the missing pieces of the jigsaw that might explain the disappearance of two local ladies. What they were looking for exactly, the police did not know but they did want to speak to a group of teenagers who were last seen getting off the bus in front of the old ladies. They knew for a fact that one of the teenagers was blind, therefore it wouldn't take them long to trace the children to the home of Ailsa Carmichael.

'It sounds very windy,' said Luna as they entered the portal and the world around them temporarily became very dark.

'That isn't the wind you hear howling, that is the sound of eis jätte. Now, get ready to fight,' shouted their grandmother.

'Three, two, one..,' counted Qadir and then he found himself standing in broad daylight. The sky was overcast and snow lay on the ground. He looked around and saw his grandmother, brother and sisters standing behind him; each one scanning the area cautiously.

'Well, it all seems pretty quiet here at the moment,' said Asmund. However, no sooner had he spoken than a terrible roar as strong as a gale force wind sounded from behind almost knocking everyone off their feet.

'Here we go,' shouted their grandmother. The children watched as their grandmother spun around in the air. She no longer looked like an old lady but the powerful, sorceress Queen that she was. The creature that now towered above them was indeed terrifying. It many ways it resembled an exceptionally large bear that stood forty feet tall on legs as large as tree trunks. It was covered in thick, white fur with long, muscular arms weighed down by enormous forepaws. Huge, curled horns protruded from each side of its head and its mouth hung open, displaying a set of razor sharp teeth. The eis jätte took a swipe at the Queen, but luckily she leapt into the air just in time. The children were amazed at how fast and nimble their grandmother was.

'*Thalla!*' shouted Queen Valda and she threw a ball of green fire into the face of the terrifying monster.

'*Reòth!*' shouted the Queen again. This time she pointed at the eis jätte with her forefinger, sending out a beam of blue light which struck her assailant full force in the chest. The giant snow monster instantly stopped moving for it had been turned into solid ice.

The Queen's grandchildren clapped and cheered, they were clearly impressed by their grandmother's performance.

'Well done Gran. You made that look so easy,' shouted Asmund.

'Look behind you, now let's see if you can do the same,' shouted their grandmother. The children quickly turned around and saw several enormous eis jätte sprinting towards them over the ice. Their large feet thumped against the frozen ground causing minor earth tremors. The children were surprised at how fast the creatures could move and it didn't take long before they found themselves surrounded by several hungry mouths. The children and their grandmother stood in a circle and faced outwards.

'When I give the word, we will attack but don't move until then,' said Queen Valda.

The eis jätte lowered their enormous heads and stared at the children hungrily. They began to close in, a deep growling noise could be heard coming from their throats.

'Hold back, wait for my signal,' whispered the Queen. She sensed her grandchildren's discomfort and was worried that they would not be able to resist attacking the terrifying beasts who were now so close they could feel their breath against their skin. To have any chance of beating so many of them at once, they would have to combine their powers and strike at the same time.

'On the count of three I want you to help me create the largest fireballs,' whispered Queen Valda.

'Ullaìch? Trì, a dhà, aon,' whispered Queen Valda.

'Teine!' shouted all four children and their grandmother at once. They lifted their hands at the same time and released enormous balls of fire which struck several of the eis jätte causing them to roar angrily. Everyone covered their ears, except Eden who suddenly roared back so loudly the eis jätte took a few steps backwards.

'Slàraig,' roared Queen Valda and they all ran towards the eis jätte who were still stunned by the roar which had come from Eden.

'Stay behind me Eden. I'll protect you,' shouted Asmund.

'I don't need protecting. My senses are sharper than ever now that I have my lost my eyesight. Watch this!' shouted Eden. The blind Princess held her arm outright with her palm facing one of the eis jätte.

'Tha seo thugad,' shouted Eden. A wave of powerful energy shot out from the palm of her hand and struck one of the eis jätte, sending the beast flying backwards and crashing into the hard snow and ice.

Asmund hardly had any time to congratulate his twin sister for seconds later he almost jumped out his skin when another ferocious roar sounded from behind him. The eis jätte responsible was so close to Asmund that he could feel its breath on his neck. Fortunately Asmund noticed just in time and he had to leap into the air to avoid the terrible claws that suddenly took a swipe at him.

'*Bodach-sneachda,*' shouted Asmund. As he leapt through the air, he pointed at the enormous eis jätte which continued to take swipes at the Prince with claws as sharp as daggers. Suddenly the enormous arms stopped moving and the eis jätte froze on the spot.

'Hey, you turned him into a snowman. That was clever Asmund,' shouted Qadir upon seeing his younger brother's work.

'Ha, ha. This is great fun. Watch your back Qadir. There are two more behind you,' shouted Asmund.

Qadir spun around and came to face to face with two more eis jätte who charged at him, roaring so loudly Qadir thought his head might explode.

'Ist!,' said Qadir and he snapped his fingers. The deafening noise coming from the eis jätte stopped instantly for his simple spell had silenced the beasts.

'Great, now I can at least think clearly,' said Qadir. Both eis jätte were confused when their terrible roars suddenly vanished. No matter how hard they tried, they could no longer make even the slightest noise.

'*Stoirm-shneachda,*' shouted Qadir. As he said the words, he raised both hands and wiggled his fingers in the air as if imitating rainfall. Suddenly both eis jätte vanished and in their place a thick shower of snowflakes fell through the air and landed on Qadir's shoulders and at his feet.

'You are starting to show off now,' said Queen Valda and she smiled at her eldest grandson.

The battle against the terrible eis jätte raged on for what felt like hours. Just as they had beaten one group of terrible monsters, more appeared over the horizon.

Soon it started to grow dark and the children began to feel weary, although interestingly enough their grandmother, despite her age did not show any signs that she was in the slightest bit tired.

Just as sunset approached, the number of eis jätte began to decrease until they stopped coming altogether.

'Is that it? Have we won?' shouted Asmund.

'No, not quite. I think it's over as far as tonight is concerned. Eis jätte prefer to move in daylight for they have quite poor eyesight,' said Queen Valda.

'We might as well have a rest. Shall I use some magic to make us a tent? We can't sleep out here in the cold,' said Luna.

'Rest? Who said anything about resting? We need to travel to the City of Westercourt and there is no better time to travel than during the wee small hours, when the eis jätte are asleep,' said Queen Valda.

Although they said nothing, all four children looked rather miserable when they heard that they would spend the night travelling, rather than huddling around a camp fire before snuggling up in a tent.

'We don't even have any transport and my limbs ache so much, I don't think I could walk,' whispered Luna to her brothers and sister.

'I think Gran is right. Tired and sore as I am, it makes sense to reach to the City of Westercourt by nightfall and it would certainly be better than staying out here in the middle of nowhere,' said Eden. She was actually quite looking forward to going to the city for she had been there before had been made to feel very welcome. Furthermore, her grandmother had told her that her friends Henrik and Megriit had been rescued from their farm and were now safe and well behind the city walls. Eden was now very much looking forward to being in their company again.

'You needn't all look so glum. You'd think I was asking you to walk all the way to Westercourt,' said Queen Valda.

'Aren't we going to walk? How else will we get there? I'm too tired to fly,' said Asmund.

'Young people these days simply don't have the stamina that your grandfather and I had when we were young. I'll have you know when I was your age I travelled everywhere on foot and I fought all sorts of monsters along the way. However, you needn't worry for I have arranged transport to take us to our destination. In fact it should be here shortly,' said Queen Valda.

'Oh really? What kind of transport? Snowmobile?' asked Luna.

'No, but it is the best way to travel in the frozen lands of Westerlyn,' replied the Queen.

'Eis cougar?' said Eden.

'Eis cougar indeed. I had forgotten that you'd already travelled by eis cougar the last time you were here,' said the Queen.

'What are eis cougar?' asked Luna.

'You'll soon see for yourself for they will be here shortly ....in fact here they come,' said Queen Valda.

The children could hear the distinct sound of tiny bells ringing and when they looked in the direction of the sound, they saw two enormous sleighs bearing lanterns which appeared quite bright in the fading light. Each sleigh was being pulled by eight large cat-like creatures with enormous padded paws which moved effortlessly across the frozen ice and snow. They also had thick, creamy furs to protect them from the cold and large ears and eyes to help them hear and see in the dark.

'Greetings Your Majesty, Your Royal Highnesses. Please step aboard and we will take you somewhere much warmer and certainly more comfortable where you can eat and rest before dawn,' said a rather large, burly man who was driving one of the sleighs. He stood up, removed his hat and bowed several times.

'My name is Piotr and this is my good friend, Falke,' said the man and he pointed to the driver of the second sleigh. The man called Falke then stood up, removed his hat and bowed several times. Both men were the personal sleigh drivers of Lord Finhildur, the Leader of Westerlyn who resided in the city of Westercourt.

It didn't take long for the Queen and all four children to climb onto the sleighs and once on board they discovered warm blankets and flasks of spicy, cinnamon tea had been provided to keep them warm during the journey. Several minutes later the sleighs turned around and headed back out across the open plain in a north westerly direction.
The way ahead was dark and the children saw nothing as they sped almost silently across the snow and ice with just the sound of tiny bells in their ears. The only light came from several small lanterns which were suspended from each of the sleighs and it was just bright enough to allow the children to see each other's faces; red glowing cheeks and sparkling eyes full of excitement. They knew that more adventure was just around the corner; no doubt the dawn would bring more surprises their way.

Chapter 13: The Halls of Erifort

Queen Valda and her four grandchildren arrived outside the gates of Westercourt shortly before dawn. When the sleighs pulled up outside, they discovered a huge army of soldiers standing guard outside the city walls. There was nervous tension in the air and it took much longer than usual for the city gates to be opened and allow both sleighs to enter. The inhabitants of Westerlyn's largest and main city had lived peacefully for many years but reports of eis jätte attacks in the east had filled them with terror. The once vibrant city was now trembling in a hushed silence. The eis jätte had not yet reached the fair city, although many feared that it was only a matter of time before they did. The army of snee menesker had been standing guard for days on end, holding enormous spears that pointed east, waiting for the first eis jätte to appear on the horizon.

Although Eden could no longer look upon the streets of Westercourt the way she did the last time she was here, she could sense their emptiness and she could feel the fear amongst the hidden people.

'This is not the way I remember things. This was a happy, lively city the last time I was here,' said Eden.

'Who can blame them with hundreds of hungry eis jätte wreaking havoc in the east of their country,' said Qadir.

The journey from the city gates to the Halls of Erifort was a short one and before they knew it, the sleighs had pulled up in front of the steps that would lead them inside the official residence of Westerlyn's great leader, Lord Finhildur. The children knew Lord Finhildur for he and his great army had helped in the fight against the landga wolves several years previously. As soon as they stepped off the sleighs and looked up the steps towards the main doorway, they recognised the familiar face of Lord Finhildur waiting for them at the top. Although he smiled at them, they could tell that he was troubled. His face was full of concern and he looked as if he hadn't slept in days.

'Welcome, Your Majesty and Your Royal Highnesses to the City of Westercourt. Please come inside and make yourselves at home. Once you have had refreshments and the chance to rest, we can meet,' said Lord Finhildur.

'Thank you Lord Finhildur. I only wish the circumstances that brought us here were different and we could enjoy your wonderful city but never fear. We will do our very best to make sure that life in Westerlyn returns to normal as soon as possible,' said the Queen.

'I hope so, Your Majesty. We are forever indebted to you and your family for you have always shown us great kindness. My army is weak from fatigue and from the cold, they have not dropped their guard in days. We cannot take our eyes of the east for one minute, lest the terrible eis jätte appear and attack our city. It is most exhausting and worrying for Westercourt and all its people,' said Lord Finhildur.

'I can tell you that the numbers of eis jätte in the east are indeed great, but they seem to be moving south east, rather than west. Although I cannot give a guarantee, there is a chance that the eis jätte may not travel this far west. An army of Ordanian warriors is standing guard on the south east corner between Westerlyn and Ordania and another army has already been sent to the border between Westerlyn and the Wolfhaven. My son, Prince Adair and his wife, Princess Isabella are with them,' said Queen Valda.

'Your Majesty, I hope you are right. Although, this isn't good news for the snee menesker who live in the south east of the country. I should send more soldiers but it is a long way and if they travel by day, they would only be attacked by eis jätte. Why do you think the eis jätte are moving south east?' said Lord Finhildur.

'I cannot be sure, but my gut feeling is telling me that the purpose of these beasts is simply to clear a pathway that leads from the Wolfhaven to Ordania via Westerlyn. Something or someone has discovered that there is no protection spell between our land and yours and they have resurrected these prehistoric creatures to help remove any possible obstruction before they make their move,' said Queen Valda.

'The gut feeling of a powerful sorceress Queen such as yourself is seldom wrong. This is very interesting, yet equally alarming news Your Majesty,' said Lord Finhildur.

'Hopefully my son will have more news for me when I see him next. In the meantime, we really should try to manoeuvre some of the soldiers towards the south east for the area is vast and there are still many villages that are unprotected. The Ordanian army is already spread too thinly. I think we underestimated just how many eis jätte there would be. If travelling by daylight is a problem, then let me travel with your men. I will make sure that they arrive unharmed. My granddaughter, Eden wishes to remain here to help protect the city. However, the children must all rest for a while for they are exhausted,' said Queen Valda.

'Indeed, you must all rest. I will have you shown to your rooms immediately,' said Lord Finhildur.

It was late morning before the children were woken by their grandmother. She allowed them enough time to rest and recharge, then they discussed the plan that she and Lord Finhildur had come up with.

'Have you even been asleep Gran?' asked a sleepy looking Qadir as they all sat around the breakfast table in the grand dining room of Erifort.

'Oh, I had forty winks. You don't need as much sleep when you are an old timer like me. I'm sorry I couldn't let you sleep longer but there is so much to do,' said Queen Valda.

After breakfast Queen Valda and Lord Finhildur sat and talked the children through the plan of action. Eden would remain in

Westercourt for the time being and protect the city from possible invasion. Although Queen Valda was quite certain that the eis jätte would not come this far west, she didn't want to take any chances. It would indeed be awful if they dropped their defences and then were attacked. With the Princess of the Seas and Lakes on guard, eis jätte were unlikely to gain access to the walled city. Queen Valda then went on to explain how further south, the army was weary from battle and that they needed reinforcements therefore some of the men from Westercourt would travel south to provide much needed support. They would travel along with Queen Valda, Qadir and Asmund. The Queen gave Luna the choice of either staying with her sister or joining them.

'Gran, if the army needs more reinforcement then I have an idea which will make a huge difference. I know where we can find a formidable army, one which is quite used to dealing with eis jätte. However, for this to work, one of us will need to head north,' said Eden.

'What is this army that you speak of and where would we find them? I know all armies in Westerlyn and I think we have exhausted almost all of them,' said Lord Finhildur.

'They can be found in Northdale and they are a huge army of mammohofs,' replied Eden.

Qadir suddenly sat upright and began to listen more carefully as soon as he heard his sister mention the city of Northdale. He had of course made a promise to King Narù that he would return and help to free the people. He wondered if perhaps it was now too late to do anything.

'Northdale? There is no such place. If you head north from here you will come to no more than a few villages and farms along the coastline and if you head inland you will eventually come to the ruins of an ancient city, long since abandoned. After that you will come to a place called Deamhan's Drop and believe me, you wouldn't want to go there,' said Lord Finhildur.

'An ancient abandoned city? That must be Northdale,' said Eden. The Princess then proceeded to tell the story in full of how she accidently time travelled to Westerlyn one thousand years in the past. She described how she met the huge army of mammohofs, led by Iglis and Glasis and how they took her to the City of Northdale. Finally she explained how she had tried to confront an age old witch called the Spindle, only to be frozen in ice along with every other inhabitant of Northdale. Qadir took over at this point and described how he went to her rescue along with King Narù of Ordania.

Lord Finhildur could hardly believe a word he was hearing and when Eden mentioned the names Iglis and Glasis, he gasped loudly.

'Iglis and Glasis are legendary here in Westerlyn. They were two of the bravest warriors who led a formidable army of mammohofs around the year 2020. Every child in Westerlyn has studied them in school and heard about them in adventure stories passed down by their parents and their parents before them. I can't believe that you've actually met Iglis and Glasis. Now, correct me if I'm wrong, but you are also suggesting that you'll bring them back, to join in the fight against the eis jätte?' said Lord Finhildur. For the first time in weeks, concern vanished from his face and he looked alive again. His eyes sparkled with excitement.

'She is telling the truth. The city is called Northdale, King Narù knew it well and he took me there to rescue Eden. We used up so much of our energy freezing time to stop the traveller's clock from pulling me back that we could not free everyone. I promised the King that I would return to help the people of Northdale,' said Qadir.

'My goodness, this is fascinating and indeed fantastic news. Why didn't you tell me all of this before?' said Queen Valda.

'Well, to be honest Gran, there has been so much happening. I really haven't had the chance and I actually kind of forgot about it,' said Qadir. He looked embarrassed when he said it for he had fully intended to keep his promise, but he had been so preoccupied with trying to find his sisters and brother that it had slipped his mind.

'Well, it does look as if you have a responsibility to yourself, King Narù and the people of Westerlyn. One thousand years later or not, you must keep your promise. After all, better late than never. Indeed you should travel to this town you call Northdale, although I do not know what you will find when you get there. If the spell was indeed cast by the one whom nowadays we refer to as the Spindle, it will be strong and will hold forever unless someone can break it. If anyone can, it will be the Prince of a Thousand Stars. I doubt if anyone has beat you to it, it sounds as if the people of Westerlyn were unaware of this place called Northdale and the fact that its inhabitants were trapped under and evil spell,' said Queen Valda. When she spoke she looked over to Lord Finhildur.

'Everything that I have heard today is new to me. This town you call Northdale, must be what we now refer to as the Frozen City. It has always been assumed that the city was abandoned following the big freeze of 2030 which made it impossible to farm, therefore impossible to live. As for Iglis and Glasis, no one ever knew what became of them and their army but they have remained heroes for young snee menesker ever since. If you can indeed wake them from their frozen slumber, it would be remarkable. However, I am not quite sure how they would be after all this time. The fact that they could be alive at all simply makes my mind boggle. I am afraid I don't really understand sorcery and spells but it fascinates me,' said Lord Finhildur.

'Well, the difference is they are under a powerful spell which will preserve them and if Qadir succeeds in breaking the spell, they will simply wake up and it will feel as if only a few minutes have passed by,' explained Queen Valda.

'Won't they be in for a surprise,' said Asmund.

'Wait, I thought it was forbidden to time travel and change the past?' said Luna.

'We aren't talking about changing the past, we are talking about changing the future,' said Qadir.

'Okay, enough talking. I think it is time we lifted our bottoms off these rather fine chairs and set about doing some work. There is a one thousand year old army badly in need of an alarm call and then a county to be saved, so chop chop,' said Queen Valda and she stood up from the table.

'I don't think you should travel alone Qadir. Why don't you and Asmund travel together and I will take Luna with me instead?' suggested Queen Valda.

'That sounds like a good idea. You could probably do with some help. From what you have told us it is quite a job trying to break a spell cast by a witch as powerful as the Spindle,' said Asmund.

'Okay, it's settled then. Qadir and Asmund will head north, Luna and I will head south to meet with your parents and Eden will remain here in the City of Westercourt. I don't suppose you could spare a few more eis cougar to transport my grandsons?' said the Queen to Lord Finhildur.

'Of course, I will provide the very best and I will insist that Piotr and Falke accompany them too,' said Lord Finhildur.

That evening Queen Valda and Luna set off with several hundred soldiers from the city of Westercourt and began to make the long journey south. Qadir and Asmund set off on their journey aboard a large sleigh, pulled by eight eis cougar and driven by Piotr and Falke, two snee menesker who were very experienced in travelling across the frozen wilderness of Westerlyn.

Eden remained in the Halls of Erifort where she met up with her old friends; Henrik and Megritt who had once looked after her when she was lost. Eden's face lit up when she was shown into the small library on the first floor of Erifort and heard the familiar voices of Henrik and Megritt who were waiting to see her. Although they grinned from ear to ear when she entered the room, they were of course shocked to discover that Eden was now blind.

'Princess Eden, it is wonderful to see you again. Megriit and I have often wondered about you. We are both terribly sorry to hear about the accident,' said Henrik.

'It is wonderful to be with you again Henrik and Megriit, I almost said it is wonderful to *see* you again,' said Eden and she laughed. 'To be honest, I'm actually getting quite used to being blind. My other senses feel so much sharper than before and so I can hear and smell so much better. If I try really hard, I can sometimes see images in my mind and anyway, I haven't forgotten what you both look like.'

'We want to thank you and your family for coming to rescue us. Our home has been destroyed but thanks to your grandmother, we were brought here to safety. We are so honoured and humbled and cannot believe that the Queen of Ordania herself went out of her way to rescue us. We had all but given up hope and were hiding beneath the ruins of our home, struggling to stay warm against the cold. We were too scared to move or make a noise in case the eis jätte heard us. Several of them tore our house apart, but luckily part of the roof collapsed and half buried us otherwise we would have been eaten alive. We lay still for days and I cuddled Megriit to keep her warm. We had to eat snow in order to drink. We could hear the eis jätte prowling around the ruins of our home, trying to find us. They have very poor eyesight, but a very sharp sense of smell,' said Henrik.

'Just like me,' said Eden.

'Yes, indeed. It was terrifying, especially for my poor Megritt. She hasn't said a word since, she got such a scare. We had been lying there for days and then we heard a commotion outside. The eis jätte began to roar loudly and then we could hear someone digging around us. Megritt started to weep for she thought it was one of the eis jätte searching for its meal. You do not know what a relief it was when suddenly our hiding place was discovered and your grandmother's face appeared. She helped us out and said that you had sent her. When we crawled out of our hiding place we were shocked to see several dead eis jätte lying around. We could not believe that your grandmother had managed to bring down these monsters all by herself. Although Megriit still has not spoken, she is smiling again which is a very good sign. Thank you Princess Eden, thank you so much,' said Henrik and he knelt on the floor before Eden, took her hand and kissed it.

'I'm sorry you had such a terrible ordeal and I only wish that one of us could have come sooner. It must have been terrifying for both of you. You have nothing to thank us for, you and Megriit would have done the same for you are good people with true hearts. If only the world was full of more Henrik's and Megriits, then there would be so much more happiness around,' said Eden.

'I spoke with Gran and we would very much like it if you and Megriit came to live with us in Castle Draccwyne once everything has been resolved here in Westerlyn,' continued Eden.

'Oh, my. That would be an honour indeed. However, I do not think a grand castle is the right place for simple farmers like us. It wouldn't seem right,' said Henrik.

'Why Henrik, that is nonsense. Just a short while ago I was a normal schoolgirl whose only experience of being in a castle had been when I visited Edinburgh Castle with my Dad during the holidays,' said Eden. She then realised that Henrik had no idea where Edinburgh Castle was or indeed what it was.

'What I am trying to say is that until recently I also could never have imagined living in castles and being called *Princess* and *Your Highness* and if someone had told me what was going to happen, I would have laughed my head off. However, I have taken to it like a duck to water and so will both of you. You would never have to work again,' said Eden.

'Never work again? I don't think that sounds right. We snee menesker are raised to believe that we must work for a long as we are physically able. My own father worked until he was ninety three, in fact he was at work out on the ice plains when he passed away. He stopped for a quick break, sat down with a hot mug of my mother's homemade hot punch and he died,' said Henrik.

'Oh, I'm sorry to hear that Henrik. I think it's terrible that your father never got to enjoy any retirement after working so hard,' said Eden.

'No, you have got it all wrong Your Highness. The snee menesker believe that it is much more honourable to work until you die and if we are given the chance to remain strong enough, right up until we take our last breath so that we can continue working, then that really is the best way to die,' said Henrik.

'Hmm, I hadn't thought of it like that. Would you consider coming if we offered you some work?' said Eden. She felt uncomfortable saying it, but it sounded as if it might be the only way she could get Henrik to agree.

'Yes, we would need to feel that we were contributing in some way. We would not be happy living in a grand castle and doing nothing in return for your kind hospitality,' replied Henrik.

'Okay, I am sure we can sort something. I will speak with my grandmother. Perhaps you could take care of the Castle Gardens, with some help of course. Megriit could maybe help Bellamina in the kitchen. Bellamina isn't getting any younger and she could do with some support,' said Eden.

'It would be an honour for both of us to assist in any way we can but work we must!' said Henrik.

Chapter 14: The Frozen City

It was dawn once more by the time the sleigh carrying Qadir and Asmund finally reached its destination, although the sky remained grey and overcast.

'If you look straight ahead you will see what remains of the Frozen City. I'm afraid that most of it is buried under thick ice, some of which is six feet thick. I am not sure what you expect to find here,' said Piotr.

They pulled up outside what was once the gateway into Northdale, although it was now impossible to pass through. The entire city was barely recognisable to Qadir who had already been here briefly to rescue his sister.

'Are you sure about this Qadir? It doesn't even look like a city. In fact it looks more like rocks covered in ice,' said Asmund as he stepped down off the sleigh and walked over to have a better look.

'Don't forget that this city has been frozen for at least one thousand years. Since then more ice and snow has appeared on top of it, so it's not surprising that it is barely recognisable as a city,' said Qadir.

'It's also hard to imagine that there are any people under there at all, especially an entire army whom we expect to fight a war for us in a day or two. I'm not trying to be funny, but don't you think they'll look a bit worse for wear after having been buried under ice for such a long time?' said Asmund.

'Didn't you hear what Gran said? Once the spell wears off, they'll look much the same as they did on the day the spell was cast,' replied Qadir.

'Well, good luck with trying to explain to them what has happened. I think it will be a huge shock for them to discover that they are now one thousand years into the future. I wonder what it would be like for us if we travelled one thousand years into the future. I wouldn't mind a shot of Grandad's travelling clock at some point. I would use it to travel forwards to see what will happen,' said Asmund.

'I think that sometimes we are better not knowing what might or might not happen. We are not allowed to change anything, so why take the risk of finding out something you'd rather not know and can't do anything about? I say that you should only time travel if you absolutely have to. If it hadn't been for you messing around with magic, I would never have thought of time travelling,' said Qadir.

'Well, I think it's exciting. Now, where do we begin?' said Asmund.

Both princes looked around the area carefully but saw no signs of any clear entrance into what remained of Northdale. Meanwhile Piotr and Falke watched on from the sleigh, wondering what in all of Westerlyn the Princes hoped to achieve so far north and in an area which most snee menesker considered to be the world's end.

After several hours of trying out simple spells, they still had no luck. Tired and frustrated, both princes gave up and sat down on the ground.

'I'm exhausted,' puffed Asmund.

'I think we are trying too hard. Perhaps we should just take a rest for a while and stop thinking about it. Mum always says that when something doesn't work, rather than get frustrated and tired, it's better to walk away for a while and come back later with a clear mind,' said Qadir.

'Let's have some lunch. I'm starving,' said Asmund and he opened his backpack and removed his packed lunch which had been given to him when he left Erifort.

'There is only so much pickled fish you can eat. What do you have in yours?' asked Asmund.

'Pickled fish of course,' smiled Qadir. 'You can have some of my kornbrot if you want.'

Both princes sat munching away and chatting merrily for the next half hour. It helped them to take their mind off the difficult task in hand, although both Piotr and Falke were concerned that they were taking far too long. It got dark early this far north and both drivers were hoping to be back home with their families before nightfall. Qadir had decided not to share with them the real reason they were here in case his plan did not work.

'I have an idea!' said Qadir as he swallowed his last mouthful of pickled fish mixed with kornbrot.

'I don't think we can do this alone. We need to ask the Great Spirits to help us,' said Qadir.

'Maybe we should have brought Eden and Luna with us. Will we be able to call upon the spirits of the seas and forests without them here? I'm not even sure if we can call on any of the Great Spirits when we are outside of Ordania,' said Asmund.

'Well, we won't know until we try I suppose. Come on, let's get to work,' said Qadir and he stood up.

Soon both Qadir and Asmund were standing side by side, facing what remained of the ancient seaport called Northdale. They had their eyes closed with their hands raised and they were concentrating hard.

Great Spirit bright of the Stars above, bring us light, bring us love,

Great Spirit blue of lake and sea, help us set these people free,

Great Spirit born of rock and stone, change this ice to flesh and bone,

Great Spirit of woodlands old and wise, release these prisoners, open their eyes.

Both princes repeated the chant several times and each time they finished the last sentence, the wind around them grew stronger and clouds began to swirl in the darkened sky above their heads. Piotr and Falke watched on from where they remained seated on the sleigh. Never before had they seen real sorcerers using magic and they were most intrigued. Just as the Princes finished chanting their spell for the fourth time, there was a loud rumble of thunder overhead. When they all looked up, they saw the biggest of storms swirling furiously in the sky above the remains of Northdale.

'If it gets any darker, we won't be able to see anything,' shouted Asmund. He was struggling to be heard above the noise of the wind which was now screaming past their ears.

'How do we know that it is working? All it seems to be doing is creating a storm, just what we don't need,' continued Asmund.

'I'm not really sure what's happening, but we can't give up now,' roared Qadir. Both princes began to chant again, only this time they had to scream from the top of their lungs for the wind was now so loud.

Great Spirit bright of the Stars above, bring us light, bring us love,

Great Spirit blue of lake and sea …..

The Princes were interrupted when a huge bolt of lightning shot down out of the sky, striking the ground in front of them and causing the greatest of cracks to appear in the ice.

'Wow, hang on. We were asking you to help us Great Spirits, not fry us,' shouted Asmund.

Suddenly the noise of the wind stopped and was replaced by a shrill laughter. Neither of the princes knew where it was coming from and they scanned the area to see who or what was making the noise. It was then that a loud voice boomed out from nowhere.

'Hello Prince of the Stars, we meet again. I'm afraid that if you have come to break my spell, then you are wasting your time. No one will ever defeat me. I have walked these lands for centuries and have yet to meet anyone who can match my power. You had better run along, otherwise I will be forced to kill you,' came the voice of the Spindle and she began to laugh again.

Both princes looked up to the sky once more, for it seemed as if her blood curdling laugh was coming from the storm clouds above their heads. When they looked up they noticed that a hole had appeared in the centre of the storm and peering down through it was an enormous eye.

'Yikes, that's freaky,' shouted Asmund.

'Don't say or do anything,' whispered Qadir.

'She says that she's going to kill you, but I'd like to see her try. She'll have to get past me first,' said Asmund.

Qadir stared back up at the enormous eye that continued to peer down through the storm clouds.

'Why have you done this to the people of Northdale? What harm did they ever do to you? Surely after all this time they deserve to be free from your spell?' shouted Qadir.

At first there was no response and then after a few moments of silence the Spindle started to laugh again. The storm clouds began to swirl once more and the howling wind returned with more strength than ever.

'Young boy, you have too many questions and I have no desire to answer them,' screamed the Spindle. Suddenly more bolts of lightning shot out from the sky and struck the ground in front of the Princes. One of them almost hit Asmund and he had to jump to avoid it.

'We have come to free the people of Northdale and there is nothing you can do to stop us. We won't leave here until we have broken your spell,' shouted Qadir.

'Is that so? Well, you will be here for a very long time. How does one thousand years sound?' said the Spindle and she began to laugh hysterically again. Soon her terrible laugh turned into a scream, so loud that Qadir and Asmund had to cover their ears. It was then that a long, spindly cone-like shape began to descend from the swirling storm clouds above. It continued to descend until it touched the ground and formed an enormous tornado.

As the Spindle's tornado moved across the landscape, it consumed everything in its path.

The terrible screaming continued overhead making it impossible for Qadir and Asmund to think clearly. Qadir kept his hands over his ears and struggled to keep his feet against the strengthening winds. It was then he heard his brother shout and when Qadir turned to look, he witnessed Asmund, along with the sleigh carrying Piotr and Falke being lifted up into the air by the raging tornado. He watched on helplessly as one by one they disappeared through the hole in the storms clouds where the eye of the Spindle had appeared.

Chapter 15: The Road to Iara

Queen Valda and Luna travelled through the night by eis-cougar alongside several hundred soldiers from the City of Westercourt. They barely slept during the journey for they were on the constant look out for more eis jätte. As soon as it began to grow light the roar of the snow monsters could be heard once again. It wasn't long before vibrations could be felt on the frozen ground as the forty foot giants began their daily hunt.

'Well, no rest for the wicked,' said a rather tired looking Queen Valda. The Queen and her granddaughter began to cast various spells on the pack of eis jätte that suddenly appeared out of the freezing fog and tried to attack the soldiers.

The great army was naturally unnerved by the attack and although the Queen and the Princess successfully finished off each and every one of the large, hairy beasts, nevertheless the soldiers remained nervous for the rest of the journey. They scanned the horizon constantly, expecting more eis jätte to appear at any minute. Fortunately, there were no more attacks and they arrived safely at the first army camp where Princess Isabella was staying.

As soon as the army of snee menesker appeared along with Queen Valda and Princess Luna, there was a loud cheer from the camp.

'Her Royal Majesty Queen Valda and Her Royal Highness Princess Luna of Ordania have arrived. All rise!' shouted the army captain. As the sleigh pulled into the centre of the camp, the soldiers stopped whatever they were doing and stood up. As the Queen passed by, the soldiers bowed and saluted.

'Greetings Your Majesty. It is an honour to welcome you. Princess Isabella is waiting in the main tent. Would you like me to fetch her?' said the Captain.

'Thank you. If you don't mind, I'd rather go inside and out of the cold for a while. Can you please take me to her?' said Queen Valda.

'Of course your Majesty. Please follow me,' said the Captain.

Queen Valda and Luna followed the Captain to the main tent which was only a short distance away. Once inside, they found Princess Isabella seated and in deep conversation with the army General.

'Good Morning Isabella. How are things?' said Queen Valda. Isabella had her back turned and did not see her mother-in-law and daughter walk in.

'Oh, Good Morning. It's great to see you. Are there just two of you?' said Isabella. She got up from her seat and hugged them.

'Yes, only two of us at the moment I'm afraid, but not for long. This is just a short visit for me, I came for an update and to bring Luna to you. Later today I plan to travel further east to where Adair is stationed. If all goes well, we should be joined by Qadir and Asmund in a few days. Let's just say that I think everyone will be in for a surprise when they do arrive for they should bring with them much needed support,' said Queen Valda.

'Really? I'm intrigued to know more. Why don't you join me for a quick cuppa and we can fill each other in on what has been happening,' said Isabella.

'That sounds like an excellent idea. Hopefully we can finish before any more eis jätte appear,' said Queen Valda.

The camp had several watchmen who took turns to scan the horizon for any signs of the snow monsters and as soon as they caught sight of their looming shape, they would ring the camp bell. Fortunately, no bell rang for the next thirty minutes or so, just enough time for Queen Valda to bring Isabella up to speed on everything that had happened since they last met. Isabella was of course very excited to hear that both of her sons might return with the support of an ancient army and one that was very experienced in slaying eis jätte. Queen Valda was also eager to know how things were progressing in the south east and soon their conversation focussed on the current situation at the border between Westerlyn and the Wolfhaven.

'Adair has moved closer to the border along with several hundred soldiers. They are staying in a small town called Iara which lies at the foot of the Back Mountains. This is the spot where most of the eis jätte are arriving into Westerlyn. It seems you were correct when you said that they are coming over the mountains, rather than from inside. Adair and his men are going to try and block their path. It won't be an easy job but they have to try. Our soldiers are close to exhaustion but hopefully the arrival of the army from Westercourt will boost their morale and if what you have told me is true, if Qadir does arrive in a few days with a great army of mammohofs, then we might be in with a chance of winning this fight,' said Isabella.

'I knew that the eis jätte hadn't simply woken up. These creatures have not been around for a very long time and the only thing to explain their sudden reappearance is dark magic,' said Queen Valda.

'Hmm, I was afraid you might say that. Who do you think is behind it and why have they chosen to resurrect a prehistoric creature? If this is dark magic, then whoever it is must be powerful so why don't they just show themselves instead of hiding behind an army of monsters?' said Isabella.

'I think that it is a cunning plan, designed to throw us off scent. Whoever or whatever it is, they want us to believe that these creatures have simply woken up after having been dormant in the mountains for centuries. This army of eis jätte are not intended for Westerlyn, the plan is to send them to Ordania via Westerlyn and as soon as they arrive, they will cause enough distraction to allow someone to sneak unnoticed over the border into Ordania, at least that is my theory anyway. As to who this person or being is, I have absolutely no idea but I do intend to find out,' said Queen Valda.

'In that case we should probably head in the direction of Iara. We can follow the route that the eis jätte are taking and block any who cross our path. So far not one beast has made it over the border into Ordania and we appear to have pushed a lot of them back towards the Black Mountains,' said Isabella.

'That is probably the best idea. The closer we get to the source of the problem, the more chance we will have of finding out who or what is behind it. I want to see what is happening on the other side of the mountains,' said Queen Valda.

'Do you mean cross over into the Wolfhaven?' said Isabella.

'Yes, absolutely. I fully intend to challenge whoever or whatever it is and put an end to their evil spells,' said Queen Valda.

'But Valda, we haven't set foot in the Wolfhaven for a very long time. We have absolutely no idea what we will find on the other side,' said Isabella.

'I can tell you what we will find, we will find the perpetrator behind all of these eis jätte attacks and when I get hold of whoever it is, they will be sorry for all the trouble they have caused,' said Queen Valda.

Queen Valda and Luna needed to rest for a while and so they took refuge inside Isabella's tent however no sooner had the Queen nodded off than the alarm bell sounded, indicating they had company.

Within minutes Queen Valda, Isabella and Luna were outside the tent and attacking more eis jätte. This time the fight lasted over an hour and by the time the last beast came crashing down onto the ground, the Queen and her granddaughter were running out of steam.

'I don't think I can keep this up for much longer,' mumbled Luna as she staggered back towards the camp.

'You can rest now. Please go back to the main tent and take my bed,' said Isabella and she kissed her daughter on the forehead.

'Perhaps one of us should remain at the camp. They will need protecting if any more eis jätte appear. Strong and brave as they are, it takes several soldiers to try and bring down one single eis jätte,' said Isabella.

'Why don't you and Luna stay here? I can manage by myself and I will have Adair to support me once I do get there,' said Queen Valda.

'Are you sure? I don't think you should travel alone. Perhaps we can spare a few soldiers to go with you at least,' said Isabella.

'Do you think I will need a few soldiers to protect me? It's more likely that I will have to protect them if we come into contact with any eis jätte. If anyone does come along, it will only be to keep me company on the road,' said Queen Valda.

'I want to go with you Gran. Please let me come,' pleaded Luna.

'That is for your mother to decide, not me,' said Queen Valda. 'What do you think Isabella?'

'Hmm, I'm not sure that's such a good idea. It will be very dangerous so close to the border. We don't know what or who might be there,' said Isabella.

'Dangerous? I'm not a baby any more. I have spent the past two days fighting eis jätte and I have finished off every last one. Qadir and Asmund got to go off on their own and no one seems concerned that their quest might be dangerous and anyway, I'll be with Gran. Dad will be there too,' said Luna.

Later that day and once they had rested, it was agreed that Luna, along with six of the best foot soldiers would accompany Queen Valda on the next stage of her journey. This time, instead of travelling by sleigh the Queen and Luna sat on the back of snee yaks, which is Westerlyn's answer to a camel; strong, heavy set creatures, perfectly adapted for living in extreme, harsh conditions. Queen Valda's only concern was that the snee yak might appear as a tasty snack to any eis jätte that they encountered.

'Fingers crossed our transport will still be in one piece by the time we reach Iara. *Tioraidh*!' said Queen Valda and she waved goodbye to her daughter-in-law.

'I will join you in a few days, once Qadir and Asmund arrive. Let's hope they bring good news with them,' said Isabella.

Isabella watched on until the snee yak carrying the Queen and Luna were mere specks in the distance. Although she hadn't said anything, she was worried about all of her children and would not settle until she knew that both of her sons were safe and well and the entire family were back together again.

Chapter 16: Dangerous Curiosity

'I'm becoming a dab hand at fighting eis jätte,' said Luna. She had just polished off her eighth monster since leaving the camp and was starting to find it all too easy.

'There should be fewer eis jätte the closer we get to Iara. Your father will be stopping any more from getting through into Westerlyn,' said Queen Valda.

'Gran, what exactly will be doing when we do get to Iara? I'm getting a bit bored fighting eis jätte all the time, it's not even a challenge any more,' said Luna.

'Well, I'm not entirely sure what we will do. First of all I will need to speak with your father who will bring me up to speed with everything that has been happening. Once I have spoken with him, I will decide what to do next. It won't be long now until we arrive,' replied Queen Valda.

In the distance they could just make out the dark outline of the Black Mountains which marked the boundary between the Land of Westerlyn and the Wolfhaven. The small town of Iara lay at the bottom of the mountains.

'I've always wanted to visit the Wolfhaven. I wonder what it's like?' said Luna.

'You've always wanted to visit the Wolfhaven? You make it sound as if it is a holiday hotspot. I'll have you know that the Wolfhaven is a place where nobody wants to be. It's cold, desolate and packed full of evil creatures,' said Queen Valda.

'Even so, I'd still like to go with you. Eden has already been,' said Luna.

'Yes, but that was not through choice. She was kidnapped and taken there against her will. I'm afraid that if I do end up crossing over into the Wolfhaven, I will do so alone and there is nothing that will change my mind. The Wolfhaven is far too dangerous for you, so please put that idea out of your mind. You will stay in Iara under the watchful eye of your father,' said Queen Valda.

Luna wanted to protest but she knew that it was no use arguing with her grandmother and so she remained silent for the remainder of the journey. Over the past few days she had begun to feel as if her family did not take her seriously enough and that they did not consider her capable of looking after herself. Soon she was lost in her own thoughts and as the Black Mountains drew closer, she began to imagine what it would be like over on the other side.

'I wish my family would stop treating me like a baby. It's not fair that Qadir and Asmund get to off on their own adventure without any adults to supervise them. Eden got asked to stay behind to protect an entire city by herself whereas I get dragged around everywhere like a small child who can't be left alone. It's as if no-one trusts me to do anything on my own and all because I messed up just one time. I'm going to prove to my family once and for all that I am a powerful sorceress who doesn't need looking after,' thought Luna as she looked out over the frozen landscape.

It wasn't long before the road along which they were travelling began to narrow and a signpost written in the language of the snee menesker, informed them that they had finally arrived in the town of Iara.

"Veelkome an gri stette ven Iara"

The area surrounding the village was heavily guarded by soldiers and they saluted the Queen as soon as the small caravan of snee yak appeared on the road. The gates that led into the small town were opened immediately, allowing Queen Valda and Luna to pass through without stopping. Once inside, they looked around cautiously but saw nothing untoward. Iara was a quaint market town where tradesmen travelling between Ordania and Westercourt often stopped for the night. The village square was surrounded by several inns, a few small bars and a couple of restaurants. They did however notice that there was no-one out on the streets, except for the soldiers who constantly walked up and down. Every shop they passed had a sign in the window or door saying 'Closed until further notice' and almost all of the tiny cottages had their wooden shutters tightly fastened, even though it was now mid-afternoon.

'The local people are obviously too afraid to venture outdoors and who could blame them?' said Queen Valda as they stopped outside the town hall. A soldier who was standing guard in the town square told them that they would find Prince Adair inside.

'Mum, Luna, what a surprise,' came the voice of Adair. He had heard them approach and had come outside to investigate.

'Hello Adair. We've just come from Isabella's camp and Westercourt before that. How are things?' said Queen Valda as she stepped down off the snee yak.

'Please come inside and I'll bring you up to date. Where is everyone else?' said Adair. He walked over and hugged his mother and his youngest daughter.

'By everyone else you mean Qadir, Asmund and Eden? I'll fill you in once we get inside but it's all good news so far,' said Queen Valda.

Both Queen Valda and Luna followed Adair inside the entrance to the town hall. Adair and his army had been allowed to use it as their base and they had been in the middle of a meeting with an army general and captain. He invited them to sit around the table and they spent the next hour or so catching up on everything that had been happening.

Adair could not help but notice that his youngest daughter had barely spoken since her arrival. In an attempt to engage her in conversation he reached over and tousled her hair.

'Are you alright darling? You seem very quiet. Aren't you pleased to see your old Dad?' said Adair.

'I'm fine Dad, just a bit tired. We've been travelling for days and I haven't had a proper rest,' replied Luna.

'Well, you can rest here tonight. We are staying in the local inn. It's very cosy and comfortable.' said Adair.

'I'm surprised you are able to sleep at all being so close to the border with the Wolfhaven. Although, it's a lot quieter here than I was expecting,' said Luna.

'First of all eis jätte normally sleep when it's dark so it is the ideal opportunity for us to rest too, although sometimes we sneak up on them in the night and attack when they least expect it. Anyway, I'll probably stay awake and keep vigil. You and your grandmother can catch up on sleep, it sounds as if you need it more than I,' said Adair.

Once they were seated inside the town hall, Adair began to explain to Queen Valda in detail everything that had been happening.

'When we first arrived there were hundreds of eis jätte spilling over the mountainside into Westerlyn. We fought them for several days until their numbers seemed to decrease. Although there are fewer than before, they are still coming over the mountains. As soon as we drop guard, there is usually another attack,' said Adair.

'We need to get to the root of the problem, otherwise this may go on for a long time and your soldiers will tire,' said Queen Valda.

'Many of them are already exhausted. When you say that we must get to the root of the problem, do you mean we should travel over the mountains and into the Wolfhaven?' said Adair.

'Indeed, that is what I intend to do,' replied Queen Valda.

'It will be difficult to convince the soldiers to travel with us. I know that they are tough but their physical strength is no match for evil sorcery,' said Adair.

'You have misunderstood me. I intend to cross over into the Wolfhaven but I will do so alone. I will not expect anyone else to risk their life by coming with me. You must stay here and look after Luna,' said the Queen.

'Mum, forgive me for saying so but that is madness. I cannot possibly let you go there alone,' said Adair.

'Son, I must go. You needn't worry about me for I have faced more evil over the years than you could ever possibly imagine and I am still here to tell the tale,' said Queen Valda.

There was silence for the next few minutes as Adair contemplated his mother's plans. He was trying to come up with another reason why she should reconsider however he knew how difficult it would be to try and talk her out of it.

'When do you plan on carrying out this ludicrous plan?' said Adair quietly.

'As soon as possible, probably after nightfall and once the eis jätte are resting. I will go once everyone else has gone to bed. There should be full moons tonight which will make it easy to navigate over the mountain,' said Queen Valda.

'Mum, a lady of your age should not be climbing mountains that lead into unknown evil and certainly not on your own. What is your exact age these days anyway? You won't ever tell us. I reckon that you must be at least ....'

'Stop! That's enough discussion about my age. A Queen's age is a Queen's business. I'll have you know I could outrun you and this entire army, so no more talk about *a lady of my age*', said Queen Valda.

That evening Queen Valda, Adair and Luna retired to the local inn where they ate merrily and were entertained. The people of Iara felt safer that night than they had felt in weeks for they now had three powerful sorcerers to protect them. They were able to relax and wanted to show their special guests warm and kind hospitality. The innkeeper was beside himself, never before had royalty visited his humble inn and he intended to pull out all stops to ensure their stay was the most comfortable. After dinner Queen Valda, Adair and Luna were invited to sit by the fireside where they enjoyed mugs of hot punch and listened to songs and tales about long gone days in the Land of Westerlyn. Many of the tales and songs made reference to Glasis and Iglis, two of the bravest mammohofs ever to have lived in the land.

Many of the songs that they heard were often sung by the snee menesker at times when they needed courage, especially by soldiers before they went to war. Several of the soldiers who had been enjoying the inn's best ale, began to sing one to their royal guests.

Oh, we're off to fight the jätte, we're off to face our foe,

We're off to crush our enemy, over the ice we go,

We won't stop till it's over, not until we've won,

We will fight into the night until the rising sun,

Our hearts are made for winning,

Our hearts are pure and bold,

We won't stop until they drop,

Then we'll take their gold.

Oh, we're off to fight the jätte, we're off to face our foe,

We're off to crush our enemy, over the ice we go.

The fun and frivolity continued until late in the evening. Everyone was having a fabulous time and they were able to forget briefly about the threat on the other side of the Black Mountains.

'I can't wait to see the looks on their faces when Qadir and Asmund return with Glasis and Iglis as well a one thousand year old army. They won't believe it,' said Queen Valda.

'Explain to me again how this all came about? It sounds as if an awful lot happened in the short time we left the children,' said Adair.

Queen Valda spent the next twenty minutes explaining in more detail everything that had happened on Lewis. Luna, who had been seated beside her father and grandmother decided that this was the perfect opportunity for her to leave the room. Apart from the fact that she was bored with adult company, she also didn't want to hang around and see her father's reaction when he found out that she had misused magic again. Adair and Queen Valda were soon engrossed in conversation and did not notice Luna slip out of the room.

The night sky was crisp and clear when Luna stepped outside. As soon as she felt the icy cold air against her cheeks, she was glad that she had pulled on her heavy coat. The courtyard in front of the inn was bathed in bright moonlight making it easy for Luna to look around. When she glanced across to the far side, she spotted several soldiers standing guard. Luna did not want to be caught and so she ducked under the shadow of the building. When she looked back across at the soldiers, they appeared not to have noticed her and so she sneaked round to the back of the inn to avoid being seen.

Behind the inn, she discovered a garden which sloped down to the embankment of a frozen river. The river bordered a pine forest which marked the boundary between Iara and the Black Mountains.

'This is the perfect opportunity to explore. I only wish I had a tàcharan and then I could fly over those mountains,' thought Luna as she looked up at the mountain range. She walked to the bottom of the garden and opened a small gate which led into the dark pine forest.

'Solas!' whispered Luna and a bright ball of light appeared in the air, lighting up the path in front of her. Now that she was able to see the way ahead, she began to make her way along the small footpath that meandered through the trees. As soon as she passed beneath the first few pines, she heard the hoot of an owl overhead. It seemed to come from the tree directly above her. Luna loved owls and she looked up in the hope that she might see it, but it was too dark and so she shone her light through the branches. It didn't take long before she caught sight of two huge saucer-like eyes staring down at her through the branches.

'Hello there, you are a beauty aren't you? My name is Luna. What's yours?'

The owl continued to stare at her in silence through the branches.

'Aren't you going to speak?' said Luna again. As Princess of the Ordanian woods, she was able to converse with every living creature that made the wood its home. However, Luna wasn't in Ordania and she began to wonder if this was why the owl was not responding.

'Are you able to understand me at all? At least give me a hoot,' said Luna. Just as she was about to give up and continue on her way, the owl blinked its large eyes, opened its beak and hooted twice.

'Ah, so you can understand me?' said Luna. 'Are you going to tell me your name?'

'Hoo, Hoo Harailt,' hooted the owl.

'Harailt? I'm very pleased to meet you,' said Luna.

'Whooere are yooou from?' hooted Harailt again.

'I'm from Ordania. I am Princess Luna Rosencratz and I live in Castle Draccwyne,' replied Luna.

'Tu whoo, tu whoo, pleased to me yooou,' hooted Harailt.

'Do you live in this forest Harailt?' asked Luna.

'Tu whoo, no, I am from another forest that lies on the slopes of the Black Mountains but I have had to leave and find a new place to live, tu whoo,' said Harailt.

'Why have you had to leave your home Harailt?' asked Luna.

'Tu whoo, the dark shadow from the east has risen and has made its presence felt on the mountains. It is too dangerous now to stay there. You too must be careful. This forest won't be safe for much longer as the shadow continues to spread west,' said Harailt.

'Who are speaking about Harailt? I am not afraid of whoever it is. I am a sorceress and I am here with my family to help Westerlyn. In fact, I am on my way now to try and find some answers. No-one has the right to scare you out of your home. Perhaps you can help me find some answers,' said Luna.

'Tu whoo, tu whoo. How can I help yooou?' hooted Harailt.

'I need you to fly me up and over the mountains, so that I can see what is happening on the other side. You needn't be afraid for I can protect you,' said Luna.

'Tuwhoo, but how can I carry you? I am tooo small,' replied Harailt.

'That is easily remedied. If you fly down from the tree I can make you bigger,' said Luna.

At first Harailt was unsure what to do and he continued to sit on his branch and stare down at the Princess. However, he quite liked the idea of being made bigger. He thought that it might help him defend himself as he moved from forest to forest, trying to find a new home. It wasn't easy trying to re-establish yourself in a new area and quite often he would come across hostility. The more Harailt thought about it, the more he liked the idea of being large enough to carry a child on his back and so he opened his wings and glided down from the branches. He landed in front of Luna's feet and stared up at her with his large, blinking eyes.

'Tuwhoo, will you let me remain bigger or will I return to my normal size afterwards?' asked Harailt.

'It's entirely up to you. If you like being bigger, then you can stay like that otherwise I can reverse the spell. Why don't you try it first and see if you like it?' said Luna.

'Tuwhoo, tuwhoo, okay Princess Luna. I will carry you over the mountains,' said Harailt.

'That's great Harailt. As I said you have nothing to fear for I will protect you,' said Luna. She lifted her hand in the air and held it above the owl's head.

'*Fàs,*' whispered Luna.

Within thirty seconds, Harailt the owl was five or six times his normal size. He stood proud on the forest floor, puffed out his chest and opened his large wings to admire them, flapping them gently in the night air. 'Tuwhoo, tuwhoo, thank yooou Princess Luna,' said Harailt.

'You are very welcome Harailt. Now, if you don't mind let's head over the mountains while the moons are still bright,' said Luna.

Moments later, Luna had climbed onto the soft feathered back of the owl and before she knew it, they had left the forest behind them, passed through a gap in the pine trees and were flying through the night sky. The owl's large wings beat silently against the cold wind.

Chapter 17: Keeping a Promise

By the time the screaming stopped and Qadir was able to think clearly, the storm clouds had completely vanished.

'If only I had acted quicker, I could have prevented her from taking my brother, Piotr and Falke,' thought Qadir. He looked up to the sky and wondered what had become of them. Everything had happened so quickly.

'What have you done with my brother?' shouted Qadir angrily. He continued to look up at the sky, but there was no sign of the witch or his brother. The only sound to be heard was the echo of his own voice.

Without a moment's hesitation, Qadir began to invoke the Great Spirits once more. He secretly hoped that it might make the Spindle return and when she did, he would make sure that she did not leave again until she told him where his brother was.

'Great Spirits of the Starry Sky,

Great Spirits of the Mountain High,

Great Spirits of the Woodland Trees,

Great Spirits of the Lakes and Seas,

Join me now, bind our power,

Let this be our finest Hour.'

Within seconds the wind began to howl once more, storm clouds gathered overheard and the high pitched laughter of the Spindle returned.

'I can see that you have still not learned your lesson, boy. I told you, you will never break my spell,' came the chilling voice of the age-old witch.

'What have you done with my brother? I demand you return him and the others,' shouted Qadir angrily. The Spindle continued to laugh loudly and although he still could not see her, soon he could feel her evil presence surround him.

'Aren't you afraid of me boy? I could crush you into pulp right now. I'd drink your blood and chew your bones. Oh and your flesh would taste so sweet, just like your brother. Hmm, yes indeed he was tasty. I plan to eat you and then I'll find that blind girl again and I'll eat her as well … ha, ha. I'll eat all of you,' shrieked the Spindle. She screamed with delight at the prospect of eating all four children and then began to laugh hysterically once more.

'You are a liar. I don't believe that you have eaten my brother and I dare you to try and eat me. Come on, I dare you …..I'm waiting,' shouted Qadir as he continued to look up at storm clouds overhead.

Suddenly a giant hand on the end of a long, spindly arm shot out from the clouds, grabbed hold of Qadir and lifted him off the ground. It squeezed Qadir so tightly, he could barely breathe. Desperate to free himself, he punched and kicked as hard as he could but the witch only tightened her grip.

Qadir gasped for air, he found it difficult to shout or even scream and he threw his head back and looked up at the storm. It was then that a face appeared in the sky, but it was not the Spindle's, it was the face of King Narù.

'We meet again Prince of Light,' came the voice of King Narù. 'I have waited one thousand years for your return; I knew that you would keep your word. Now, together we will use the light of the stars to banish this evil and free the people of Northdale once and for all. They deserve to live the rest of their lives the way nature intended.'

'*Sorchar nan Reul*,' whispered Qadir. His voice was barely audible against the wind and he was close to passing out. The enormous hand continued to lift him higher and just as he reached the hole in the clouds, he looked through and caught sight of a lone star, shining high above the land.

'*Sorchar nan Reul*,' whispered Qadir again. This time, a bright beam of light shot out from the lone star and struck the Prince. It seemed to revive him and soon he was able to fight back. Within moments, Qadir's entire body was aglow with starlight. When he looked back up at the storm clouds, there were more beams of light, only this time they shone from his eyes. The Prince looked directly into the eye of the storm with his starry gaze. The howling wind stopped almost instantly, only to be replaced with the sound of the Spindle screaming. The storm clouds vanished as did the giant hand which had been squeezing Qadir. He gasped, taking in huge gulps of air; it was such a relief to be able to breathe freely again. It was then that he caught sight of the Spindle for the first time; she no longer had any storm clouds to hide behind. The ancient witch was momentarily stunned by what had just happened; never before had she encountered such power.

For the first time ever, Qadir found himself looking directly at the Spindle's cruel face. Suddenly her empty eye sockets began to burn with fire. He could not stare for long, for soon he felt a searing pain in his body. Unknown to Qadir, he was feeling the pain of all of the many victims who had suffered the wrath of the witch over the centuries. Qadir would never forget the terrible pain that he felt that day and had he not been the powerful sorcerer that he was, he would surely have died. Instead, he lifted his hand in the air and pointed at the witch as she began to scream, wriggle and writhe in front of him. This time it was the Spindle who was trying to escape but she couldn't for Qadir had trapped her.

'*Dèan fuasgladh*,' roared Qadir. More beams of starlight shot out from his fingers and made their way towards the frozen city. Suddenly the Spindle stopped screaming, she took one last look at Qadir and then vanished, leaving a thick, black cloud of smouldering ash in the air. Qadir watched as the ash fell down onto the frozen city below, covering it like a blanket of black snow.

By the time Qadir touched down onto the ground, the ancient seaport hidden beneath thick ice had begun to glow bright blue. He watched in amazement as Northdale slowly became visible and took its first breath of fresh air for over a thousand years. It didn't take long for the ice to recede and soon Qadir was able to look upon Northdale's majestic skyline, see the city in its entirety and marvel at its size. As he made his way over to the main entrance, he noticed movement on the ground.

'Ouf! What in all of Westerlyn happened? Have we been on the grog again? Wake up you meat head,' shouted Iglis and he shook his cousin by the shoulder. He was lying on the ground, just inside the city gate.

'Wh…What happened? Did I get knocked out?' replied Glasis.

'Look, the wee lassie has gone. Do you think the snee hex took her?' shouted Iglis. As he spoke he scanned the sky for any sign of Eden or the witch.

'I don't know, but there is definitely something fishy going on here. Look, it's as if everyone has been asleep on the ground,' said Glasis. Both mammohofs looked around the streets that led into Northdale and watched as their entire army of fellow mammohofs picked themselves up, rubbed their sleepy eyes, shook their elephant-like ears and wiggled their short trunks.

'Hmm, I smell witchcraft and evil witchcraft at that,' said Iglis.

Suddenly the entire army of mammohofs trumpeted nervously. Although they were very brave warriors, they were afraid of the snee hex and the sudden reminder that she might still be in the area unnerved them.

'Look, there's a laddie over there. I haven't seen him before,' said Glasis. He trumpeted loudly and pointed towards Qadir, who was watching them from just outside the city gate.

'Hello. My name is Qadir and I came here to rescue you. Are you Glasis and Iglis by any chance?' said Qadir.

Glasis as well as some of the other mammohofs who were standing nearby began to laugh.

'You came to rescue us? Don't make me laugh. Do we look like we need rescuing by a young laddie?' roared Glasis.

'I'm only telling you the truth. I have just freed you all from an evil spell that has kept you frozen in thick ice for over a thousand years. I think the *wee lassie* that you referred to is my younger sister Eden. She is safe and well in the City of Westercourt.

'Frozen in ice for a thousand years? What utter nonsense. I suppose that means the current year is ……..' Glasis stopped talking momentarily and tried to do the basic maths, however arithmetic was never his strongest subject and the fact that his brain had been frozen for the past millennium made it even more difficult for him.

'It is the year 3020,' said Qadir. He could sense the great mammohof's frustration and thought he should save him the trouble of having to work it out.

'I knew that,' growled Glasis. 'It still doesn't prove that you are telling us the truth,' he added.

'Well, what will it take to prove to you that I am telling the truth? We really don't have time to waste for there is a war going on in Westerlyn at the moment and we are all needed,' said Qadir.

'A war? If there was a war then we'd know about it. Do you know that we are the strongest army in these lands? No war should ever be fought without us,' continued Glasis.

'Yes, I am fully aware of how strong you are and that is why I came to break the spell which has kept you frozen for so long. Your help is very much needed in the south east of Westerlyn. The country is being ravaged by an army of eis jätte as I speak,' said Qadir.

'Eis jätte you say? That'll be an easy war to win. I'll have you know I've skinned more eis jätte in my time than I've had hot dinners,' said Glasis and he puffed out his chest with pride.

'That's brilliant news, in that case you won't mind helping us then? An army has already been sent from my home country of Ordania and from Westercourt, but we will need more help,' said Qadir.

'What did you say your name was again?' said Glasis.

'My name is Qadir Rosencratz of Ordania,' said Qadir.

'Rosencratz? Yes, I do believe that was the name of the wee lassie. She mentioned a Queen Valda too, do you know her?' continued Glasis.

'Yes, of course I know her; she is my grandmother,' said Qadir.

'And I suppose you'll be one of those magical folk, just like the wee lassie?' added Glasis.

'If you're asking whether or not I am a sorcerer, then yes I am. Now, are you prepared to help your country?' said Qadir.

Before any of the mammohofs had a chance to answer, another strange light appeared in the sky above the city. Qadir instantly went on the defence, worried that the Spindle was making a return. However, he sighed a huge relief when the face of King Narù reappeared between the clouds and smiled down at them.

The mammohofs looked up and gasped, they recognised King Narù of Ordania instantly.

'Greetings brave warriors; Glasis and Iglis. I have come to tell you that everything you've heard is true. The young man before you now, is indeed Prince Qadir Rosencrtaz of Ordania and he returned today to free you, just as he said. I have waited one thousand years for this day to happen. The witch's spell was very powerful and it took our power combined to break it. Now you and all the people of Northdale can carry on with your lives as before, except that now you live in the future. As for me, at last I can now rest. However, before I go I wish to protect this town so that the witch can never attack again,' said King Narù.

'Well, now do you believe me? Will you help to save your country?' said Qadir.

'Oh aye young Prince, we believe you and of course we will fight but first we must eat; I'm starving,' said Glasis.

'We mammohofs travel fast. It won't take us long to get to wherever we have to be, but Glasis is right, we must eat first,' said Iglis and then he trumpeted loudly which signalled to the other mammohofs that it was time to eat. As you can imagine, they were all ravenous after having not eaten for such an incredibly long time. One by one they marched off further into the city to find food, but told Qadir that they would be back before sunset and that they would travel all night long until they reached the town of Iara. After one thousand years of being idle, the great mammohofs of Westerlyn were itching for a fight.

'As long as the stars, sun and moons continue to shine above the city of Northdale, its inhabitants will be safe from the witch,' said King Narù. His voice was kind and gentle and once he had finished speaking, he blew the city a kiss.

Qadir watched as sprinkles of stardust rained down on the city. Shortly afterwards, hundreds of rowan trees began to push up through the snowy ground outside the city walls. They continued to grow until they were tall and heavy with berries.

'These enchanted rowan trees will also stop the witch from coming anywhere near Northdale. They will remain forever green and the red berries will never fall off. Goodbye and good luck to you Prince Qadir. This is your time to shine. Until we meet again,' said King Narù and he waved goodbye to Qadir.

'King Narù, before you go, can you please help me find my brother? The witch took him earlier,' said Qadir.

There was a short silence before King Narù spoke again.

'My dear Prince, I have asked the Great Spirits and all they can tell me is that your brother has already gone to the stars. They say he is with your grandfather now. I am very sorry that I can't tell you more,' said King Narù. The image of the great king faded leaving Qadir standing alone, outside the city gates of Northdale. A terrible numbness passed through his body and then a feeling of dread rose from the pit of his stomach when the realisation dawned on him of what King Narù had said.

'Asmund has gone to the stars? It can't be true. I don't believe it. Asmund can't be … dead,' whispered Qadir. As soon as he said the word, his head began to spin and he thought he might be sick. He then staggered backwards before collapsing onto the ground. Qadir buried his face in his hands in an attempt to muffle his scream.

Soon the sky overheard was clear again. The colours of orange and pink in the western sky suggested that it would soon be dark, however Qadir barely noticed anything. He seemed unaffected by the cold air that surrounded him and he paid no attention to the stars as one by one they began to appear high above his head. Had he been looking, he would have noticed that his own star as well as that of his brother, were now shining brighter than ever.

Chapter 18: Walking With the Enemy

As Luna flew silently through the night sky upon the soft feathered back of Harailt, she cast her eye down the mountainside in the hope she might catch sight of the mysterious enemy whom her grandmother had mentioned. The problem was Luna had absolutely no idea what she was looking for, she hadn't even considered if the enemy would be in the form of a human, monster or other. All she knew was that she had to be the one responsible for catching the perpetrator behind the eis jätte attacks and when she did, she would use her magic to bring an end to his evil plan. What excited Luna more than anything was the fact that she would be the one who saved the day. She imagined the looks on the faces of her brothers and sister when she returned home triumphant and everyone knew that she had conquered the enemy all by herself.

'They'll never leave me out of their plans ever again and force me stay home while they go on adventures. I should think they'll come to me for advice in future,' thought Luna.

Luna hadn't realised just how big the black Mountains were and soon they reached such a high altitude, she began to shiver and her teeth chattered. She realised that the clothes she was wearing were not nearly warm enough and so she used magic to conjure up a thick cloak. When she pictured the cloak in her mind, which is what sorcerers do just before they make something appear, she thought of her grandmother who regularly wore long cloaks when she took to the sky.

'If I am to be taken seriously, I need to start dressing like a proper sorceress princess. I think I'll choose a black cloak too, so that I can travel undetected at night,' thought Luna as she soared through the cold mountain air on the back of the owl.

It wasn't long before Luna caught her first glimpse of the land on the other side of the Black Mountains, known as the Wolfhaven. Harailt seemed uneasy as soon as the ground began to level out and the great desolate plains became visible under the moonlight. Luna had half expected the land below to remain empty and desolate for miles, expect for the odd mangy landga wolf scavenging around for food here and there. However, both Luna and Harailt were in for a shock for shortly after they left the Black Mountains behind them, they could see enormous torches of fire dotted all over the ground below and they seemed to be moving. Luna continued to peer down, trying to see who or what was holding the burning torches but they were too high to see anything clearly. Luna asked Harailt to fly a little lower so that she could get a better view but the owl was so nervous, he started to tremble.

'Oh, please, Your Highness. I don't think that is such a good idea. What if they see me? They will be suspicious if they see such a large owl. They'll know it isn't natural. Tuweet Tuwhoo,' hooted Harailt.

'Don't worry Harailt. I have everything under control. It is they who will be scared when they see me. If it makes you feel better, I'll make us invisible, they won't see a thing,' said Luna and then she shouted *Do-fhaicsinneach*'. The Princess and the large tawny owl became invisible instantly.

'Now we can get a bit closer, in fact you can get really close for they will never see us,' said Luna.

The owl trusted her and began to swoop downwards and continued until they could see the burning torches up close. It was then that they had the shock of their lives for they discovered that the vast plains of the Wolfhaven were not quite so desolate after all; a terrifying army as wide and as long as the eye could see filled the landscape. Luna spotted thousands of eis jätte first for all, for even though they were slouched and asleep on the ground, their bulky shapes still towered above everything else. However, not all of the army was asleep and it wasn't long before Luna spotted the shapes of landga wolves moving in and around the sleeping eis jätte.

The War of the Wolves which took place several Ordanian years ago, had seen the destruction of the Landga Wolf leader and it was believed that since then, what was once the formidable Landga Tribe, was now very close to extinction. The few Ordanians who were brave enough to venture over the border into the Wolfhaven since the Great War, had reported seeing only a few very thin and undernourished landga wolves. However, the landga wolves on the ground below Luna were certainly not thin and undernourished, instead they were enormous beasts with strong, muscular backs and even more surprising, they were all dressed in full battle armour.

'Gran always said that landga wolves would not survive without a powerful leader. They must now have a new leader. I wonder who that might be?' thought Luna. Suddenly several of the landga wolves looked up at the night sky and howled. Harailt began to tremble with fear, his instinct was to climb higher into the night sky, away from the evil on the ground below. Sensing his fear, Luna told him once more to be calm and then much to the owl's dismay, she asked him to fly even closer to the ground.

Soon the noise around Luna's ears became almost deafening. Amidst the howls and growls of landga wolves, came the familiar hissing sound of the ancient, evil cave dwellers, known to Ordanians as the grotta ghoul. Indeed, Luna could now see many tall, skeletal-like creatures running around on the ground, their large, bat-like wings flapping furiously in the night breeze. There were also other evil creatures which Luna did not recognise; among the great army were unfamiliar heavyset soldiers who were dressed in armour. They held long spears in one hand and great axes in the other. Luna thought that their heads resembled those of a rhinoceros for each one had two enormous horns protruding from their noses. The rhinoceros-like soldiers snorted and grunted impatiently, they were eager to begin fighting. Great puffs of steam from their nostrils were visible against the cold, night air.

'Hmm, by the look of things someone has been building themselves an army and I intend to find out who and why before anyone else does. If Gran and the others saw this, they would certainly be worried. I'm not even the slightest bit afraid. I know that I can do this by myself. I will find the leader and creator of this army and then I will defeat him. However, I'll need to do it quickly before Gran gets here, otherwise she will take over and everyone will say that it was her who saved the day and that she had to rescue me. I am not going to let that happen, not this time. This is my challenge,' thought Luna to herself. She then asked the tawny owl to let her down onto the ground.

'Are you sure that's wise Your Highness? There are terrifying monsters everywhere,' hooted Harailt.

'Yes, but we are invisible. They won't see us,' shouted Luna.

'But they will hear us if we continue to talk so loudly,' hooted Harailt.

'I really don't think so, not above all this noise and raucous,' shouted Luna. Sure enough, the air around them was filled with the howls, growls, snorts, grunts and hisses of the huge army. It was in fact so noisy that it was highly unlikely the voice of Luna or the hoots of Harailt would be heard at all.

'I tell you what Harailt. Once I am on the ground, you can fly back towards the mountains. I won't need you anymore. I'll make sure you remain invisible until you reach Westerlyn,' said Luna.

It soon became obvious to Harailt that he would not be able to convince Luna to return with him and seek the help of the Westerlyn and Ordanian armies. Although Harailt felt guilty about leaving the Princess behind, he knew that he would be of little use to her on the ground.

'I will come back for you in the morning and take you home if you like?' suggested Harailt.

'That won't be necessary Harailt, but thank you for offering. I have a lot of work to do here and I don't imagine that I'll be ready to go home as soon as that,' replied Luna.

'It doesn't feel right leaving you here by yourself amongst all these monsters, tuweet tuwoo,' hooted Harailt.

'I will be absolutely fine. I'm a dab hand at fighting eis jätte and landga wolves. You really don't have anything to worry about but if it makes you feel better, I will call you if I do need your help,' said Luna.

'But how will you call me? Tuweet Tuwoo,' hooted Harailt.

'I am a sorceress aren't I? That means I can do absolutely anything. My Gran once used a form of mental telepathy to talk to me. I'll try the same with you, just stop worrying. I'll be fine,' replied Luna.

Shortly after that, Harailt found a small clearing to the left of the huge army, beside a few dead looking trees. He landed softly and silently on the ground and waited patiently as Luna climbed off his back.

'Thank you Harailt. You've been very kind to me and I hope that we will remain friends. When the tawny owl turned his large head to look at the Princess, he realised that he could not see her, for she was invisible. He was eager to get going, especially when he heard the roar of the terrible army to his right. A fight had broken out between two of the large, rhinoceros-like soldiers. The burly beasts pushed and punched each other to the ground and began rolling around. The crowd nearby began to shout and cheer as they watched the fight unfold. Soon the burly soldiers had rolled over to the spot where Harailt and Luna were standing. To avoid being crushed by the heavy horned soldiers, each one weighed more than a ton, Harailt opened his wings and prepared to take off into the sky whereas Luna reached for the branches of the dead tree, ready to pull herself up to safety, however the fight was suddenly interrupted when an enormous landga wolf jumped through the air and landed between them.

'Right, that's enough! Break it up you two. Any more of this and I'll take you to his Lordship and you know what'll happen then,' snarled the landga wolf. Luna noticed that his armour was different to the armour worn by other landga wolves. He appeared to have an air of authority about him and Luna thought that he might be of a higher rank.

'Sorry Officer Morticus. We got a bit carried away. Please don't take us to his Lordship,' pleaded one of the rhinoceros-like soldiers. This strange looking species was native to the Wolfhaven and went by the name of raganosi. Unlike rhinoceros, which in many ways they resembled, they moved around on two legs and they were meat eaters. They also had a thick, tough skin which most arrows or spears could not penetrate. They were notoriously muscular and strong. If you ever offend a raganos, it would most likely charge at you and if being struck by one ton of solid muscle didn't kill you, then its two foot long nose horns would most definitely do the trick.

'Morticus the Crusher? Surely that can't be him?' thought Luna. She had read about the formidable landga wolf who was second in command after Abnocta Mirus and it had been assumed that he had died during the War of the Wolves, just like his evil leader.

The ragonosi warriors stopped fighting, picked themselves up off the ground and returned to their posts. Officer Morticus gave them one last look, growled and turned to move away. However, as he turned, he paused momentarily for his nostrils had picked up the scent of something unusual. He turned back to the raganosi and eyed them with suspicion. 'Have either of you been eating children again? I can smell a human and it must be coming from one of you. Next time you shouldn't be so greedy and keep them all to yourself. Where did you manage to find a child anyway? Have you been wandering close to the border? I've a good mind to report you for leaving your posts without permission,' growled Officer Morticus.

One of the raganos warriors whose name was Baltrus started to look panicked.

'Officer Morticus, I promise I've not been eating any children, chance would be a fine thing. In fact I don't know the last time I even ate a human. It must be at least a year ago. I did see two old ladies wandering close to the edge of the forest the other day, but I chose not to eat them because old ladies tend to be really tough and chewy and not that tasty. I'd much rather wait until we get into Westerlyn and eventually Ordania and then there'll be plenty of children for us all to eat. Oh, my mouth is watering at the thought,' said Baltrus and he licked his lips.

'Well, someone has been close to a human because I can smell one right now. I'm going to keep my eyes on all of you,' growled Officer Morticus and then he turned and disappeared amongst the huge army of soldiers.

'Phew! That was close,' whispered Luna.

'Are you sure you won't change your mind and fly back with me?' hooted Harailt.

'No Harailt. I must stay here, but you should probably go now. The invisibility spell won't last forever. You should travel now to avoid being seen,' said Luna.

'Okay Your Highness, if you insist. Please remember to send me a signal if you want me to come back for you. I will do so immediately,' whispered Harailt. Shortly after that the great owl lifted quietly and swiftly into the night sky, leaving Luna standing on the ground beside the dead trees and the terrifying army of eis jätte, raganosi, landga wolves, grotta ghoul as well as numerous other evil creatures.

'I'm leaving now. Please be careful, tuweet tuwoo,' hooted Harailt.

'Goodbye Harailt and thank you,' said Luna. Neither the owl nor Luna thought to wave for they still could not see each other. Soon Harailt was high in the night sky and winging his way back towards the Black Mountains.

'Now it's time to find out more about this mysterious leader whom Morticus referred to as his Lordship. I wonder if he's another landga wolf?' thought Luna.

She began to make her way through the army of monsters. As she walked past, she pinched her nose and screwed up her face for the smell was truly awful, particularly when she passed by several raganosi warriors. 'Phew! I think some of them could do with a bath. What a nasty smell,' thought Luna.

Most people would have been terrified if they had been as close as Luna now was to the various monsters and ghouls that made up the evil army, however Luna did not seem in the slightest bit phased. She was determined to use this opportunity to prove to her family once and for all just how powerful and fearless she was. As she passed through the crowds of monsters, several heads turned when they suddenly picked up the scent of the invisible princess.

'Grrr, I smell human flesh and it's fresh. Which one of you is hiding the meat? Come on, share it with me. I ain't eaten in days,' growled an exceptionally large, overweight raganos warrior by the name of Hergius.

'Well, it ain't me that's for sure. I can smell it too. Maybe it's him,' growled another warrior called Saulius. It wasn't long before several raganosi warriors were accusing one another of hiding fresh meat and as Luna continued to make her way through the crowd, several fights broke out among the very hungry soldiers.

By the time Luna had reached the centre of the huge army, almost half of the raganosi warriors were fighting. The noise was truly deafening as the burly beasts punched and kicked one another. Luna was glad when she finally reached a wide open space where the air was much fresher and she could escape the smell of the monsters. However, she was surprised to discover a campsite with a large marquee tent standing in the centre. Luna stopped and stared, wondering who might be inside. Two landga wolves stood guard outside the entrance suggesting that the occupier must be someone of importance.

'Hmm, curiouser and curiouser. I wonder who might be inside?' thought Luna. She approached the tent cautiously for although she was still invisible, she was now aware that the enemy could pick up her scent, depending on which way the wind was blowing. Luna was also beginning to tire, she had forgotten just how much energy she would need to remain invisible for such a long time. She would have to find a hiding place soon, otherwise she'd run the risk of being caught when the invisibility spell wore off, which inevitably it would.

'I'll just have a quick look inside and then I'll go and find a hiding place where I can rest and recharge my batteries,' thought Luna. She approached the two landga wolves who stood guard outside the marquee. As she tiptoed past, one of them growled and swung its great head in the direction of the Princess. For a split second Luna was worried that perhaps her invisibility spell had already begun to wear off and that maybe the great wolf had had glimpse of her, however it appeared that once again he had simply picked up on her scent.

'Did you smell that Keshnar? I could swear there's a human near here,' said the landga wolf who stood guard on the left hand side of the entrance.

'Yes, Lucias, indeed I did. It was very strong and fresh too. How could a human be in our camp and still be alive? Do you think we should mention it to his Lordship?' replied Keshnar.

'It'll keep until Officer Morticus comes back out. I think they are in the middle of a very important meeting,' replied Keshnar.

Luna was quite relieved once she had gotten past the landga wolves standing guard outside. Moments later she found herself inside the large marquee tent which was much warmer and quieter than outside. It was quite dark, expect for a strange, orange glow that seemed to flicker in the centre. Inside the tent she found herself in some sort of makeshift entrance hall. When she looked straight ahead she saw another doorway which seemed to lead into the centre where the strange light flickered. There were two chairs sitting right outside the entrance, on either side. As she drew close to the entrance, she heard voices, although at times they sounded more like deep growls.

'So Morticus the Crusher is in here. I wonder who he is talking to,' thought Luna. She stepped a little closer to the door and tried to listen to the voices inside.

'Your Lordship, our soldiers are ready to attack any day now. In fact I'd say that they are desperate to get going. The raganosi are fighting amongst themselves all the time at the moment because they are fully charged and ready for battle. Once they have prepared themselves for war, they can only wait and hold back for so long before they literally go mad and eat and punch everything around them. I once saw a raganos snap an entire tree in half with his teeth he was so frustrated,' said the voice of Officer Morticus.

Soon Luna was right outside the door and she began to peer inside, hoping to catch a glimpse of the mysterious lord. Once she stuck her head further inside the tent, Luna was able to see the cause of the strange, flickering light. Although it looked like a real fire, Luna knew that real flames inside a tent made of canvas was highly unlikely and so she came to the conclusion that they were made by magic. It was quite difficult to see at first because it was so dark, although she could just make out the shapes of two individuals; the flickering light had cast their long, dark shadows against the inside wall of the tent.

Suddenly there was movement to the left and Luna recognised Officer Morticus, the flames that burned in the enchanted fire had reflected against his shiny armour.

'Yes, I think it is now time to release the raganosi along with the eis jätte. We need to double our efforts and make sure that we have more soldiers than they could ever possibly cope with. How many of them have been seen near the border?' said a voice from the dark shadow, hidden in the far corner of the tent.

'If you mean the family, then yes I believe some of them are already present. The children's father is still there and apparently his mother, the Queen has also arrived and she brought with her one of the girls,' said Officer Morticus.

'Yes, but what about the boy? Is the boy there? He is the only one who is dangerous to me. If we can kill him, the rest will be easy,' growled the voice from the dark shadow.

'There has been no sighting of the boy for some time, although I'm sure it is only a matter of time before he does arrive. Perhaps now is the time to attack, while he is away and their defences are weaker,' said Officer Morticus.

'You might be right. The eis jätte that I sent over the border first were really only to test the water. I think that their soldiers will be almost exhausted by now and will probably think that the worst is over, at least that is what I want them to believe. That is why I have sent fewer eis jätte over the mountains these past few days. They will be in for a surprise when the *real* army arrives over the Black Mountains in a day or two,' said the voice from the dark shadow.

There was a silent pause for a few minutes before anyone spoke again. It was Officer Morticus who eventually broke the silence.

'If you don't mind me saying so, you seem preoccupied my Lord. Is anything the matter?' asked Officer Morticus.

'There is something that troubles me, although I don't know what it is. I have had this feeling before in the past. It's almost as if …' the voice in the dark stopped talking and slowly began to turn round until it was facing the flickering flames of the strange enchanted fire.

Luna's heart was now thumping hard against the inside of her chest and she tried to hold her breath for fear she might be heard. She stared intently at the dark, looming figure as slowly but surely it moved forwards into the light. It was dressed in a long, dark robe, very similar in fact to the robe that Luna herself was wearing. Luna strained to catch a glimpse of the face hidden within the dark hood, but she saw nothing. Suddenly the figure stopped moving and seemed to lower its head as if it were deep in thought.

'Morticus, do you sense anything peculiar?' said the dark, robed figure.

'Indeed my Lord. For the past ten minutes or so I have picked up the scent of a human. I also picked up the same scent when I was out walking amongst the soldiers earlier,' said Officer Morticus.

'Yes, the scent of a human and no ordinary human either. I think we have a visitor,' growled the dark, robed figure. Suddenly it lifted one of its arms and pointed a long, bony finger in the direction of the entrance, exactly where Luna was standing. Realising that they were now aware of her presence, she wanted to turn and leave the tent. She had stayed longer than intended and she could feel her invisibility spell beginning to weaken. As she attempted to step backwards and retreat from the tent, she found that she couldn't. It was as if her feet had been glued to the spot.

Do-fhaicsinneach, do-fhaicsinneach … do-fhaicsinneach,' said Luna in a desperate attempt to make herself invisible again. She was in such a panic that she forgot herself and shouted out the words loudly on the final attempt to make herself invisible.

'My Lord, did you hear that? I heard a voice inside the tent,' growled Officer Morticus.

'Yes, I heard it alright and I can see who is responsible,' said the dark, robed figure. He continued to point at Luna and then suddenly a bright green light shot out from the tip of its finger. It struck Luna full force and caused her to body to violently convulse. She tried to escape but it was no use, she felt trapped like a fly in the web of a giant spider. Slowly she began to feel herself be drawn further into the tent towards the flickering flames and the dark, robed figure.

'Now, who do we have here I wonder?' said the Dark Lord of the Wolfhaven.

Chapter 19: The Medicine Man and the Witch's Lair

Qadir pulled himself up off the ground and lifted his tear stained face to the sky. The stars were now shining brightly and he looked to them for reassurance. When he looked up he could see the stars from all of the sorcerers past and present but there were two stars in particular that he wanted to see more than any other; his grandfather's as well as that of his younger brother Asmund. It didn't take him long to find what he was looking for, in fact it was almost as if the stars had found him.

'So the stars above Starrydell can be seen from Westerlyn as well as from Ordania,' thought Qadir as he stared in wonder at the thousands of twinkling stars and wondered who they all belonged to. He knew that each star would have its own story to tell and no doubt held secrets and stories of adventures from the past.

'It's almost as if the sky is full of secret adventure stories. If only I could listen to all the stories that they had to tell. Now they have all fallen silent, to shine for eternity above these lands,' thought Qadir. He was then filled with an even deeper sadness when he thought of his brother and the fact that he never had the chance to take part in all of the adventures that he was planning.

'How can you be gone Asmund? Your star still shines brightly. I cannot believe it,' murmured Qadir to himself and he wiped more tears from his eyes.

'I have failed Great Spirits of Sorcerers past and present. I have failed my brother and I have failed all of my family. Please forgive me. I should have done more to protect my brother,' said Qadir out loud as he looked up at the twinkling stars.

In the back of his mind he knew that there was still a job to be done and a battle to be won. He hadn't forgotten that the people of Westerlyn were counting on him, yet still he could not find the strength to carry on. After all, how could he return to face his family only to tell them that Asmund had died? At first they would be overjoyed to see the army of mammohofs arrive, they would want to celebrate even before the war was over but then everything would change as soon as someone asked Qadir where Asmund was.

'It will destroy the family,' thought Qadir. 'I can't go back now. I will just have to send the mammohofs to travel back by themselves. I won't tell anyone what has happened until the war has ended, there is nothing to be gained by telling them before,' thought Qadir.

It was then that Qadir thought about the wives and families of Piotr and Falke and he knew that he had to let them know immediately what had happened to them. As he stood wondering what to do, he suddenly felt something touch his shoulder. When Qadir turned his head, he was startled to find a beautiful white bird perched on his left shoulder.

'Where did you come from?' whispered Qadir and he began to stroke the peaceful creature. Although no sound left its beak, the bird continued to stare at Qadir and in his mind it seemed to speak to him.

'I have come from the stars to bring a message from your grandfather. He asks that you enter the City of Northdale immediately and seek the help and counsel of an old and wise medicine man, known as the Ollamhan. He will be able to help you for he is experienced in dealing with the witch who took your brother. If you can hurry, there is still time to save him. This should not be his time but if you don't hurry, then you will be too late. The Ollamhan is the only one who can help you find the witch's secret lair,' said the bird.

'Of course, I will go and find this Ollamhan. I thought it was already too late, King Narù said so,' said Qadir.

'Your brother had gone to the stars but your grandfather has sent him back. He has breathed life back into your brother but he is stll trapped and unless you find him soon he will die and there won't be anything your grandfather or anyone can do,' said the white bird and then it took off into the sky. Qadir watched as it rose higher and higher until it disappeared completely.

Although Qadir was still far from convinced that the so called Ollamhan or medicine man whom the white bird referred to would be of help, he decided that he had nothing to lose and so he made his way inside the city gates. He passed through the bustling streets in a daze, staring at the people as they went about their business. It was hard to imagine that only a short time ago, this entire city had been frozen and silenced for over one thousand years. One of the first giveaways that the people of Northdale were from the distant past, was of courses their old fashioned clothes. However, it was Qadir who appeared the odd one out and as he staggered along the main streets, many passers-by stared at him.

When he reached the top of the main street, he saw a very familiar figure standing on the street corner and conversing with one of the locals; it was Iglis, the mammohof. When he saw Qadir he waved him over.

'Hello young laddie. You look troubled. We were just about to head back to the city gates. The soldiers are just stocking up on a few provisions for the journey and then we'll be on our way,' said Iglis.

'Hi Iglis. That's fine, but before I can go, I need to speak to someone urgently. Perhaps you can help me. I'm looking for a person known as the Ollamhan. Do you know who that is and where I might find him?' said Qadir.

'The Ollamhan you say? Yes, I've heard that name mentioned before. It's an odd name and outlandish, not one you're likely to forget. I've never met him myself, apparently he never ventures outside but I do know that he lives at the top of the White Tower. He turned and pointed towards a single white tower that looked down over the city. 'I believe he's one of your kind,' added Iglis.

'What do you mean he's one of my kind?' asked Qadir.

'I mean that he's magical. He's not from these lands originally,' replied Iglis.

'Who is he and what exactly does he do?' asked Qadir.

'I really couldn't tell you but I do know that he has lived for a very long time. In fact they say he's possibly the oldest man that ever lived. They say he's completely insane but if anyone ever survives and encounter with the snee hex, they are taken straight to him because apparently he makes the most amazing medicine. Excuse me for asking but why are you going to see him if you don't know anything about him?' said Iglis.

'I'm not entirely sure but I think he might be able to help me find my brother,' said Qadir.

'We will gather the army and wait for you at the city gates. We will not leave without you,' said Iglis.

'That won't be necessary. If I'm not back within a couple of hours, please make a head start. I can always catch up,' said Qadir. He thought that the chances of the wise old medicine man having any good news for him were extremely slim. However, there still was the tinniest hope that his brother could be alive therefore it was definitely worth a chance.

Qadir left Iglis and began to make his way towards the white tower which dominated the skyline of Northdale. As he made his way through the cobblestoned streets, he soon realised that it was further away than he thought. It took him almost half an hour before he finally arrived at the foot of the white tower. Qadir stopped and looked up, he could only see one window at the very top that looked southwards over the whole of Westerlyn.

Qadir walked right around the tower but could not find any sign of a doorway. Concerned that time was being wasted, he decided that the only way to try and speak to the Ollamhan was to fly up to the top of the tower and knock on the window.

Qadir flew up to the tiny window and rattled his knuckles against the glass and waited for a response. After several minutes no one appeared and so he tried again. Eventually, he heard a muffled voice from inside but could not make out what it said. Qadir knew it wasn't right to stare in through a person's window but he was growing impatient and was now prepared to take the risk of upsetting someone.

After the third knock, he heard the muffled voice again and so he leaned forward and tried to peer inside. The window was quite dirty making it difficult to see. Suddenly, an angry face appeared at the window, shaking a fist. If this was indeed the Ollamhan, he was much smaller than Qadir had imagined. He had an exceptionally long beard and although Qadir could not see everything, he was sure that it must have reached the floor. His tiny head was bald, except for some curly, wispy hair around the sides. He wore spectacles on the end of his pointed nose and his eyebrows were long and white.

Qadir watched as the angry little man jumped up and down frantically and gestured with his hand for Qadir to move away from the window. As Qadir still had no idea what the little man was saying, he shrugged his shoulders and pointed to the window latch. Eventually, the little man realised that Qadir was not going to leave and so he thrust open the tiny window, almost hitting the Prince in the face. Luckily Qadir ducked just in time.

'How many times do I have to tell you, I don't want any today,' shouted the angry little man.

'You don't want any what?' replied Qadir.

'Why, fiskbrot or whatever it is that you are selling. I don't want any and that's that,' shouted the little man.

'I'm not selling fiskbrot or anything for that matter. I'm here to speak with the Ollamhan. Is that you?' said Qadir.

'Who? The Ollamhan? I've never heard of him,' said the angry little man.

'Oh, really? I was told that he lived here in this tower. Do you know where he does live?' said Qadir.

'Do I know where who lives?' said the angry little man.

'The Ollamhan,' replied Qadir and he sighed deeply.

'Who? The Ollamhan? I've never heard of him,' said the angry little man for the second time.

'I'm sorry to have troubled you. I was clearly given the wrong address,' said Qadir and he turned away from the window and began to fly back down towards the ground.

'Wait young man! Where did you learn to fly through the air like that?' shouted the little man.

'I am a sorcerer from Ordania and I am here to help the people of Westerlyn. I am using magic to fly. I am afraid that I am in a hurry and can't really stop to chat. I need to try and find someone as quickly as possible,' said Qadir.

'Perhaps I can help you. I'm not from here originally but I have been here for so long I know every inch of this city,' replied the little old man.

'I already asked you, but you said you had never heard of him,' said Qadir.

'Never heard of who?' said the old man.

Qadir could feel himself growing irritated and he paused momentarily before he responded.

'I'm looking for someone known as the Ollamhan,' said Qadir.

'Well, why didn't you say so? I know where you can find him,' replied the little old man.

'You do? I thought you said …, actually it doesn't matter. If you could please tell me where I might find the Ollamhan, I would be most obliged,' said Qadir.

'The proper way of course would be to knock on the door but you have to do so correctly otherwise he may not answer,' said the little old man.

'Which door? Can you tell me where I might find this door? I really am in a hurry,' said Qadir. It was now obvious from the Prince's voice that he was losing patience.

'Why the door into this tower of course,' replied the little old man.

'There aren't any doors, that's why I flew up to the window and knocked on the glass,' said Qadir. He hadn't intended to sound as angry as he did but he was now so exasperated that he couldn't help it.

'Why of course there's a door. Where there is a window there is usually a door,' replied the little old man and he pointed towards the ground, directly below where Qadir was hovering.

'It's a yellow door, hard to miss … no, wait it'll be green today. It depends what day of the week it is,' continued the little old man.

Qadir rolled his eyes and flew back down to the ground. Once his feet had touched back down on the cobblestones he looked at the wall of the white tower but there was still no sign of a doorway.

'You must knock properly if you want to speak with him,' shouted the little old man from the window above.

'There is no door and so I can't knock. I really must go, thanks for your ... help,' said Qadir and he began to walk away from the white tower.

'Of course you can't see the door, you haven't even knocked yet. The door never appears until you knock,' shouted the little old man.

'This had better be worth all the hassle,' murmured Qadir and he quickly turned round, walked back towards the white tower and rattled his knuckles against the whitewashed bricks.

'That wasn't a proper knock. If you don't knock properly, it won't work,' shouted the little old man.

'How am I supposed to know what the proper way is?' shouted Qadir, sounding irritated again.

'My, don't they teach young people anything these days? The proper, civilised way to knock on someone's door is this,' said the old man.

'Two single knocks, followed by three quick knocks in succession and then finish with another two single knocks ... *'tap, tap .. tap, tap, tap .. tap, tap,'* shouted the little old man.

'This is absurd! Iglis was right, he is insane. He has probably been incarcerated inside this tower for a good reason. There's no door, so he can't get out. Here I am entertaining this madness when I really should be trying to find my brother, never mind lead an army to war,' thought Qadir.

He raised his knuckles one final time and knocked against the whitewashed bricks; *knock, knock ... knock, knock, knock ... knock, knock.'* Much to Qadir's surprise, within seconds a bright green door with polished brass knockers appeared in front of Qadir. There was no number on the door but there was a brass plate with the name *Osvaldur Gunnvald* etched on it.

The door flew open and the little man who had been at the window was standing in the doorway and looking up at Qadir. His head reached no higher than Qadir's waist and his beard was so long it trailed on the ground.

'My goodness, how did you manage to get down from the top of the tower so quickly?' said Qadir.

'That really isn't the proper way to greet someone at their front door,' said the man.

'Oh, I am sorry. My name is Qadir Rosencratz and if at all possible, I would like to speak with the Ollamhan,' said Qadir. He was trying hard to disguise any sarcasm in his voice. He then thought that he'd play along in case the strange, little man closed the door in his face and he'd have to start all over again.

'You seem to be very angry and mistrustful. A sorcerer prince should really be more in control of his emotions, especially if he is to try and rescue his younger brother from the witch's cave,' said the man.

'So you are the Ollamhan? Please, tell me what you know of my brother? Is he alive?' said Qadir. He made sure that his voice sounded much calmer this time.

'I have many names, I believe that the Ollamhan is one of them although I haven't heard in a long time. I much prefer the name my mother gave me which is Osvaldur but you can call me Osvald. In response to your other question, the answer is yes, your brother is still alive but only just,' said Osvald.

'Thank you Osvald. Please tell me what you know about my brother? How do you know that he is alive?' said Qadir.

'If you come upstairs I'll show you what I have seen. Please, come inside, it shan't take long. However, I must warn you that it isn't all good news,' said Osvald.

'But he is alive, isn't he?' asked Qadir.

'Yes, but he is very weak and he is trapped in the most awful place,' said Osvald. 'Quick, follow me.'

Qadir followed Osvald inside the green door. Once inside, the door vanished completely.

'I hope it isn't as difficult to get out of here as it was to get in,' thought Qadir.

He looked around inside the hallway and marvelled at the giant sweeping staircase. When he looked up, the stairs seemed to go on forever. As he began to climb, he noticed that the walls inside the circular building were covered from top to bottom with paintings of places in Ordania.

Qadir recognised the Esterway Mountain range on one painting with Elfview Mountain clearly visible in the foreground, Castle Draccwynne sitting majestically on top. He saw paintings of Brookden town as well as the Fair Forrest and the seaside resort of Janlee. There was even a painting of Crystalhaven, the wealthy seaport that lay on the southern coast of Ordania.

'Osvald, I know all of these places. Do you come from Ordania?' said Qadir.

'Well, almost. I am originally from a tiny island that lies off the south east coast of Ordania, called the Isle of Hope. Have you heard of it?' said Oswald.

'Yes, I think I have, although I do not think it is called that any more,' said Qadir.

'That is correct. It is now called the Isle of Tears and from what I've heard, that is probably a more appropriate name for it now. I certainly have no desire to ever go back, although the reason why escapes me at the moment. This is the problem when you have a brain as old as mine, full of too many memories and information. The locals think I am a bit mad and they might be right but they also come to me for advice. I can see things that they can't. Like yourself, I was born with a special gift. However, the island where I spent my childhood was very small and I was the only one born with special powers. Many of the locals were afraid of me and quite often I was blamed when bad things happened. Some believed that I was a bad omen and they tried to chase me away from the island.

When a terrible plague arrived from overseas killing almost everyone, I was blamed and so my mother sent me away on a boat. I think she intended for the boat to take me to the east coast of Ordania. She knew that the people on the mainland were more accepting of magical folk and she thought that I would have a better life there. Perhaps she thought that I would settle in Janleee and that she would come over and visit me, however she fell ill and died shortly after she sent me away. There was a terrible storm that night out at sea and the wind blew me off course. My boat began to drift north and eventually I sailed right around the land through some of the most dangerous waters ever. Eventfully I arrived here in Northdale where I have lived ever since. Although the folk here are non-magical and are sometimes a little wary of me, they are never unkind and they have accepted me,' said Osvald.

By the time they had reached the top of the staircase, Qadir found himself standing in a circular room. There was a large fireplace with two armchairs at either side. An old, black kettle sitting on the hearth began to whistle emitting thick puffs of steam as soon as they stepped forward into the room. 'Perfect timing,' shouted Osvald. 'Do you have time for some tea?'

'Normally I would say yes, but I really am pushed for time,' said Qadir.

'Well, if you don't mind I need to drink a cup. It helps my old brain work better and I can think more clearly,' said Oswald and he began to prepare himself a hot drink. In the meantime he invited Qadir to sit down on one of the armchairs. Although eager for more information about his brother, Qadir sat down and looked around the room. On the opposite side, closest to the small window was a tiny bed. Next to it sat a small bedside table upon which sat a lamp as well as an enormous pile of books that looked as if they were about to topple over. There were books piled everywhere; on every shelf, chair and table and they covered most of the floor.

Once they were seated by the fire, Osvald walked over to a small writing bureau. He opened a sealed compartment and carefully lifted out a small, dark jar which he then placed on a small table in front of Qadir.

'You must take just one single drop of the liquid in this jar and then you will be taken to where your brother is but I must warn you that what you will discover there will be terrifying,' said Osvald.

My brother and I have already had to face a fair amount of evil, including the evil witch who took him. I have managed to defeat her on many occasions so I am not afraid. I just want confirmation that he is alive and then I will find him. After that we must head south and help in the war,' said Qadir.

'Well, let me tell you, even if you are successful in rescuing your brother, he will be in no fit state to fight in a war. I can tell you that he is alive but only just. If you don't act fast, I fear it will be too late. The witch will be much stronger than normal for she will be in her own territory,' said Osvald.

Osvald unscrewed the lid of the strange, dark bottle and then he picked up a spoon that lay on the table. Qadir watched as the old man carefully poured some of the thick, black liquid onto the spoon. He then held it up in the air and asked the Prince to take it.

'How can I be sure that you aren't poisoning me?' said Qadir as he eyed the strange liquid suspiciously.

'I suppose you can't be sure but what do your instincts tell you?' said Osvald.

'Qadir paused for a few seconds and then he carefully took the spoon from Osvald's hand and quickly swallowed the liquid.

At first nothing happened and he started to wonder if perhaps Osvald was mad and had given him nothing more than a spoonful of old cough medicine. However, just as Qadir was about to tell Osvald that nothing was happening, he began to feel light headed and a warm, tingling sensation fill his toes and fingertips.

Osvald stared at the Prince with wide eyes.

'Well? Is it working yet?' shouted Osvald sounding rather excited.

'What is it supposed to feel like? I just feel light headed and I have pins and needles. I hope this isn't some sort of game Osvald. I'll be really annoyed if it is,' said Qadir.

'I can assure you that this is no game young Prince. Now, move over towards the fireplace and look into the flames. Ask the fire to show you where your brother can be found. It's an enchanted fire and now that you have drunk my special potion, you can use the fire to transport you to wherever he is. Please, you must hurry young Prince. Your brother can't hold on forever and the potion that I made for you will only work for so long,' shouted Osvald.

Qadir cast his eyes towards the fireplace to see if there was any truth in what Osvald was saying. He soon felt quite hypnotised by the bright, flickering flames.

'Please show me where I can find my brother, Asmund Rosencratz, Prince of the Mountain High,' shouted Qadir. As he continued to stare into the flames, a dark shape began to appear.

'What can you see? What can you see?' shouted Oswald excitedly.

'I'm not really sure what I am looking at … I think it's the entrance to a cave,' said Qadir.

'Yes, yes it will be. Now, you must go inside the cave but be warned what you will see is not for the faint hearted,' shouted Oslvald. His voice was now so high he sqeaked like a mouse.

'How can I go inside?' muttered Qadir as he continued to stare through the flames. However, he didn't need to wait for Osvald to answer. Shortly after he spoke, he began to feel as if he were floating. Before long, Qadir found himself floating over the flames which were surprisingly cool and into the mouth of the mysterious cave. Although it was dark inside the cave, he soon noticed the glow from another fire burning deeper inside. Qadir began to move towards it.

As he made his way down the long, dark passageway towards the orange glow, Qadir heard the sound of someone running towards him, followed by a scream and then the familiar sound of the Spindle laughing.

Whoever was running towards Qadir, they sounded very close and so Qadir stepped to one side, leant his back against the wall and held his breath.

'Solas,' whispered Qadir. Almost instantly the dark cave was brightly lit allowing him to see more clearly.

'Hello, who's there? Is that you Asmund? This is Qadir,' shouted the Prince. Seconds later, exhausted and half terrified, the familiar face of Asmud appeared in the cave.

'Qadir, you'd better get out of the way. Quick, RUN!' gasped a rather exhausted looking Asmund.

'Asmund, you're alive? I thought you were dead,' shouted Qadir. He was overjoyed to see his younger brother again.

'I might not be for much longer if we don't get out of here. She really isn't happy that I escaped,' puffed Asmund. He appeared pale and shaken, quite different from the young, confident brother that Qadir was used to.

'Do you mean the Spindle? Where is she?' said Qadir. He grabbed hold of his brother and tried to support him. Asmund could barely stand he was so exhausted.

'Qadir, we need to get out of here ... NOW!' screamed Asmund.

Suddenly the cave was filled once more with the Spindle's spooky laugher. Both Asmund and Qadir turned and looked back down the dark passageway. Qadir was not prepared for what he saw, the age-old banshee was floating along the passageway towards them. Her long, spindly arms and fingers were outstretched and reached forwards as if trying to grab hold of her prize meal which had escaped the cooking pot. She appeared illuminated, casting an eerie light against the wall of the cave as she drew closer.

'I'm not afraid of her Asmund. Trust me, I can deal with this,' said Qadir. He asked his younger brother to stand behind him and then he turned to face the Spindle.

'Are you afraid of me now boy?' screeched the Spindle.

'No, I'm not afraid of you. I have come to take my brother home. I knew you were lying when you said that you had eaten him,' replied Qadir.

'Teine,' shouted Qadir and he pointed at the Spindle. Flames shot out from his fingertips and struck the banshee. The empty eye sockets in her skeleton-like face suddenly lit up before she opened her mouth and proceeded to spit. Qadir had to move quickly to avoid being sprayed by her venom.

Her ghost-like voice filled the air around them as she screamed '*You cannot escape*'.

The Spindle raised her bony finger one more time. Qadir, assuming she was about to cast a spell, ducked out of the way. Seconds later a bright green flash filled the cave and when Qadir glanced over his shoulder, he discovered that the exit behind them had been sealed.

'No more light, no more twinkling stars to help you now, only darkness,' screamed the Spindle and she began to laugh hysterically.

Asmund was now very weak and he slumped to the floor of the cave, no longer able to stand.

'I can't feel my legs any more Qadir. She has done something to me,' whispered Asmund.

'Don't worry Asmund, I've rescued you from dark places before and I'll do it again. I promise I'll get you out of here,' whispered Qadir. Although he didn't want to say it to his brother, secretly he was worried. The Spindle seemed so much stronger than before and now that he was trapped inside a dark cave, he had no way of looking to the stars. Each time he had overcome the witch in the past, he had always turned to the stars.

'If I am the Prince of Stars, surely I can summon their light no matter where I am?' thought Qadir. The Spindle was now dangerously close, although she had trapped both princes, she was nevertheless apprehensive for she knew they were powerful sorcerers, particularly Qadir. She hadn't forgotten the terrible pain she felt the first time she tried to imprison Qadir deep in the heart of the Belwald wood. It had taken her many years to recover.

'Well boy, it seems like you'll be staying for dinner after all. I'd like to talk with you for a while before I kill you for you do interest me. As for your pathetic brother, he isn't anywhere near as powerful as you. I'm bored with him now, he's too weak. Look at him lying on the floor in a pitiful state? I can't bear to see it. Shall I put him out of his misery? Just the tinniest of spells would snap him in two,' sneered the Spindle.

'Leave him alone, I am warning you now. Back off or you will regret it,' shouted Qadir.

The Spindle began to scream with laughter as she floated around the cave. Suddenly her long, wispy hair turned into hundreds of hissing snakes which began to spit more venom.

Dion,' shouted Qadir. He managed to create a protection shield just in time to separate both him and his brother from the shower of poison that began to rain down inside the cave.

'You are afraid now young Prince, I can tell. I can hear your little heart go pumpety-pump, thumpety-thump. Oh, how I'd love to squeeze it tight and then swallow it whole,' screeched the Spindle. A long, fork-like tongue shot out from her mouth in an attempt to lick her lips.

'I'd like to see you try. If you come any closer I'll show you what pain feels like,' shouted Qadir.

The Spindle was actually quite impressed with Qadir's bravery. Never before had she encountered a human who didn't collapse with fear at the very sight of her.

'Oh, what will you do to me boy? Sprinkle me with fairy dust?' screamed the Spindle and she began to cackle with laughter again.

Asmund began to stir on the ground at Qadir's feet. He was desperately thirsty and weak.

'Qadir, I don't feel so good. I need water and fresh air,' whispered

Asmund.

'Hang on Asmund. We will be out of here very soon,' said Qadir.

The Spindle watched with interest as Qadir knelt down and helped his brother to sit upright.

'Oh, is the poor little boy sick? Perhaps he'd like to come back down inside and sit by the fire? I'll make him nice and warm,' sneered the Spindle.

Qadir ignored her and continued to support his younger brother who was now struggling to breathe.

The Spindle did not like to be ignored and suddenly the expression on her skeleton-like face turned to anger.

'Why don't I put him out of his misery once and for all, or even better, why don't you do it? Yes, that's a good idea. Why don't you snuff out his pathetic life and then we can throw him on the fire?' screamed the Spindle.

'You are mad as well as evil and if anyone deserves to have their life snuffed out it is you for all you do is bring pain and suffering,' shouted Qadir.

'Yes, you are right. That is exactly what I do and I am very good at it too. I love pain and suffering. The sound of screaming is like music to my old ears. Oh, how I danced around the fire when I killed the other two. They made such sweet music as they pleaded for their lives and begged for mercy but then one of them spoiled it and started to cry. There is nothing more pathetic than seeing a grown man cry,' sneered the Spindle.

'And so you killed them? You killed two innocent people? What gives you the right?' roared Qadir. It was the Prince of Stars who was angry now.

'And so I killed them … snap, snap. I crushed them so easily. They didn't even put up a fight,' spat the Spindle. She made a tight first with her bony hand as she spoke. 'They were so pathetic, just like your brother,' said the Spindle.

'Well, let's just see how pathetic you look when you are begging for mercy,' said Qadir. The young Prince stood up and pointed at the Spindle.

'Solas sìorraidh gun dealraich air,' shouted Qadir. The brightest of lights shot out from Qadir's hand and filled the entire cave. The Spindle screamed louder than ever and had to turn away from the bright light for it made her feel pain.

'Does this make you feel like dancing?' shouted Qadir. He then lifted up his other hand and pointed it towards the Spindle, more of the same light came shooting out. Qadir watched on as the Spindle began to literally burn in front of his eyes. Her scream was now so loud, it caused Asmund to pass out and large cracks began to appear on the walls around them.

'You've had your last dance witch,' shouted Qadir.

The Spindle collapsed onto the floor of the cave. Qadir watched as she continued to melt until all that remained of the age-old witch was a smouldering, venomous puddle on the ground.

Suddenly Qadir became aware of a bright light behind him and when he turned round he saw that the exit out of the cave had reappeared. He carefully picked up his brother and made his way towards it.

'I promised I'd get you out of here Asmund. Now, let's get you home,' whispered Qadir.

Chapter 20: Meet Hildegard Otrava the High Witch

It had been over half an hour since Luna left the company of her father and grandmother. Although her absence had been noted, Queen Valda wasn't concerned at first. She assumed that her granddaughter had simply grown bored with adult company and had gone upstairs to her bedroom.

'I'll check on Luna, then I'll head outside for some fresh air,' said Queen Valda.

'You aren't still planning to travel into the Wolfhaven are you? Please Mum, that really would be madness,' said Adair.

'Let me just check on your daughter first for she has been gone quite a while. Fingers crossed she is upstairs in her bedroom, otherwise we may have no choice but to cross over into the Wolfhaven,' said Queen Valda.

'Do you know something Mum? Why wouldn't Luna be upstairs?' asked Adair.

'Well, you know what your daughter is like. It wouldn't be the first time she sneaked off without telling us and put herself in danger,' replied Queen Valda.

It took less than five minutes before Queen Valda returned with the disappointing news that Luna was nowhere to be seen and that her coat was missing.

'Hopefully she won't have gone far. I had hoped she'd learned her lesson after the last time she ran off without telling anyone,' said Adair.

'One would hope, although she did express to me an interest in visiting the Wolfhaven and I don't think she was very happy when I told her that it was out of the question,' said Queen Valda.

Adair and Queen Valda quickly pulled on their winter coats and rushed outside. They approached the soldiers who were standing guard and asked if they had seen Luna, but no one had.

'There is only one thing for it, I will have to head east to try and find her. You should wait here in case she turns up,' said Queen Valda.

'Mum, why don't I go and you wait here? That would make more sense,' said Adair.

Suddenly their conversation was interrupted when an exceptionally large tawny owl swooped overhead and landed on the ground in front of them. It was of course Harailt, the owl who had carried Luna over the Black Mountains and into the Wolfhaven.

'Tuweet, tuwoo. Good Evening, I am looking for Her Royal Majesty, Queen Valda of Ordania, tuweet, tuwoo,' said Harailt. His large eyes blinked up at them.

'Well, you're in luck for you have found her. I am Queen Valda. I must say, you are rather large for an owl,' said the Queen.

'Tuweet, tuwoo. My name is Harailt Your Majesty. I bring news of your granddaughter, Princess Luna,' hooted Harailt.

Queen Valda and Adair looked at each other nervously.

'What do you know about my daughter? Is she okay?' asked Adair.

'She has crossed over into the Wolfhaven. I tried to convince her to come back but she would not listen to me and so I came back to fetch you. Hopefully you will have more luck than I,' hooted Harailt.

'How do you know this Harailt?' asked Queen Valda.

'She asked me to take her there. She used her magic to make me bigger and then she flew on my back but she never mentioned anything about staying there. We were only supposed to have a quick look and then come straight back. I really am sorry,' hooted Harailt.

'There is no need for you to apologise. You did the right thing by coming back and telling us. Tell me, what did you see when you crossed over?' asked Queen Valda.

'Oh, Your Majesty, we discovered a terrible army of monsters, spread across the land as far as the eye could see. There were many more eis jätte as well as giant werewolves, ghoulish vampires and thousands of huge raganosi warriors. They looked as if they were preparing for battle. Princess Luna convinced me to land on the ground. I only agreed because she made us both invisible but nevertheless I was still terrified. Tuweet, tuwoo,' hooted Harailt.

'Harailt, can you take me there now? Don't worry, you will be quite safe with me. We can travel under another invisibility spell if it will put you at ease?' asked Queen Valda.

'Yes, of course Your Majesty. I will take you there immediately.'

Harailt then allowed Queen Valda to climb onto his back.

'I will follow closely behind but first I need to arrange my own transport,' said Adair.

'Let's just hope she hasn't gotten herself into more trouble. As if we don't have enough on our plates already,' sighed Queen Valda.

'Do-fhaicsinneach,' whispered the Queen as Harailt the owl took to the night sky once again, this time with the Queen of Ordania on his back. No one saw the giant owl as he gracefully lifted up off the ground, for Queen Valda's invisibility spell had already taken effect.

By the time Harailt and Queen Valda were passing over the top of the Black Mountains, they began to hear the howl of landga wolves, echoed by the roar of the raganosi. More flame lit torches could be seen on the ground below and the loud thump of their war drums meant that an attack was imminent.

'I should have known better than to believe that stupid story about climate change causing the eis jätte to awaken. It is obvious that a far greater force has been behind it all but who could be strong enough to build and lead an army of this size?' thought Queen Valda. She was indeed shocked when she first caught sight of the enormous army spread out across the ground below.

'I can only hope that Qadir arrives soon with the mammohofs otherwise we will struggle to keep such a large army from entering Westerlyn,' thought Queen Valda.

She had hoped the War of the Wolves would be the last battle she'd ever have to witness and she had seen many over the years. However, despite the celebrations up and down the land following the last victory, the Queen's gut instinct told her that all was not won. She had often thought that a more powerful evil had been gathering strength in secret and plotting an attack from an unknown hiding place. She had hoped that by the time this evil force made itself known, all of her grandchildren would be fully grown and able to protect themselves, never mind protect the land and its people.

'Well, I suppose if I try hard enough I can find the strength to fight one last time but it will be my last,' thought Queen Valda. She scanned the ground below for any sign of her granddaughter but it was impossible to see clearly in the dark. Assuming that Luna might also still be invisible, Queen Valda decided that the only way to find her granddaughter would be to get down on the ground herself and so she asked Harailt to land in a small clearing.

Queen Valda was clever enough to realise that an invisibility spell wasn't enough to allow her to walk beside the terrible army. She knew that landga wolves and raganosi had a very keen sense of smell and would be able to pick out a human easily. She only hoped that her granddaughter had realised that before she set foot on the ground.

'*Boltrach,*' whispered Queen Valda just before she stepped off Harailt's back.

'You can fly back now Harailt. You might see Prince Adair on the way but if not, if he still hasn't found transport by the time you arrive back in Iara, please bring him here,' whispered Queen Valda.

'Yes, of course your Majesty. I told your granddaughter to call for me when she wanted to leave and I would come back for her. Likewise your Majesty, if you need me to return, please send a message,' hooted Harailt.

'Yes, Harailt. If I need your help to get back to Iara I will send a message to you some way. Now, safe journey back and thank you,' whispered Queen Valda.

'Please take care your Majesty,' replied Harailt and then he took off again into the night sky and headed back towards the Black Mountains.

Once on the ground Queen Valda found the noise coming from the army truly deafening. The numbers of raganosi warriors, grotta ghoul and landga wolves had almost trebled and each and every monster was psyched up for a fight. As the Queen made her way through the giant army, she looked out for any sign of their leader. If they had discovered Luna, they would more than likely have taken her to him.

After twenty minutes of what felt like aimless wandering, the Queen's attention was drawn to two landga wolves. She overhead a conversation between them which confirmed her worst fear, her granddaughter had indeed been caught.

'According to Officer Morticus a human has been caught inside his Lordship's tent. It was a young girl. Apparently she sneaked in unseen,' growled a landga wolf by the name of Modovar.

'Really? How in all of Wolfhaven could a child get past thousands of raganosi without being eaten? It doesn't make sense. What is she even doing here?' growled a second landga wolf called Bloodfang.

'Apparently she's one of those pesky sorcerer kids from Ordania. She must have been using magic to make herself invisible. She's got some nerve spying on his Lordship like that. He'll be furious,' growled Modovar.

'She's certainly brave, I'll give her that. I wonder what he'll do with her?' said Bloodfang.

'He'll probably use her as bait to lure the rest of them over here. He wants them all dead, so I reckon she'll live for now,' growled Modovar.

As Queen Valda listened carefully to the conversation between the landga wolves, she suddenly had an idea. She knew that she needed to find her granddaughter and thought what better way than to ask these landga wolves to show her. Of course, she had no intention of revealing her true identity for that would be folly. Queen Valda decided to adopt a new identity which would not only fool the hair brained landga wolves into leading her straight to the one whom they referred to as *his Lordship*, but more importantly they would lead her to Luna.

'Aimh-riochd,' whispered Queen Valda. She waited a few seconds before clicking her fingers and then she whispered the words *'Seall do làthaireachd.'*

Suddenly both landga wolves found themselves staring at a cruel-looking witch. With the exception of her pale skin which appeared almost luminous under the darkened sky, everything about her was black; her long hair, her lips, even the velvet cloak draped over her shoulders and down her back. Anyone who saw her would agree that most unsettling of all were her eyes, for when she opened them to look around, they too were completely black. She stared down at the landga wolves menacingly. At first both wolves were stunned and speechless when she suddenly appeared in front of them. However, eventually they found their tongues and began to question her.

'Who in all of Wolfhaven are you and how did you get here?' growled Modovar.

'She looks like a witch and a wicked one at that,' laughed Bloodfang.

'Have some manners,' snapped the tall witch. 'The next time you address me you had better do so appropriately, otherwise I will be forced to teach you a lesson.'

Both wolves stared back at her and began to laugh.

'Teach us a lesson? I'd like to see you try,' sneered Modovar.

'You had better us tell us who you are, otherwise we'll be forced to report you. We are under strict instructions to let his Lordship know of any strangers in the area. What is your name and which coven are you from?' growled Bloodfang.

'If you must know, my name is Hildegard Otrava. I am the High Witch therefore I am not a member of any coven. I am the head of all witches. I have come to speak with your leader for I bring him important news,' said Hildegard.

'What news do you bring and how do we know you are the head of all witches? I've never heard of a High Witch called Hildegard,' growled Modovar.

'The news I bring is no business of yours and you'll soon realise I am the High Witch when I skin your hide and make it into a coat,' said Hildegard.

Modovar was enraged when he heard her say this. He was not used to being spoken to in such a way. The large landga wolf bared his teeth and growled before pouncing through the air towards the witch.

However, Modovar did not get far for as soon as his giant paws lifted off the ground, Hildegard Otrava raised her hand and shouted something in a language which the landga wolves did not understand. All of a sudden Modovar found himself suspended in mid-air and unable to move.

'It would seem that I will have to teach you some manners after all,' shouted Hildegard. She lifted her hand once again and shouted more words in the unfamiliar tongue. The werewolf was lifted higher into the air and then began to spin round.

'You will keep spinning until you learn some manners. Let me know when you want to stop,' shouted Hildegard.

Bloodfang looked up in horror at his friend Modovar as he spun round in circles in the air above him.

'Are you going to take me to your Lordship or would you like to join your friend?' said Hildegard to Bloodfang as he continued to stare at Modovar.

'Yes, of course High Witch. I will take you to his Lordship,' growled Bloodfang. Although the landga wolf did not want to appear afraid of the witch, he certainly did not want to be humiliated in the same way as Modovar therefore taking her to his Lordship seemed like the best option

Modovar was beginning to feel quite ill from the constant spinning and just as Bloodfang and Hildegard began to head off, he begged the High Witch to make the spinning stop.

'Please High Witch, no more,' howled Modovar.

Hildegard stopped and looked back at the landga wolf.

'Since you asked nicely,' said Hildegard and then she snapped her fingers. The great landga wolf stopped spinning instantly and crashed to the ground.

'Remember, I expect manners at all times otherwise there will be more punishments,' snapped Hildegard.

The High Witch turned and continued to follow Bloodfang however no sooner had she turned her back than Modovar tried to attack her again. He felt humiliated and angry at being treated in such an undignified way. The landga wolf jumped at Hildegard from behind, bared his terrible teeth and prepared to bite the witch in the neck. However, before he got the chance and just as he was about to snap shut his jaws, Modovar felt a searing pain in his body. Hildegard Otrava spun round and dealt the werewolf a terrible blow. He fell to the ground and when he looked back up at the witch, he found her staring down at him with terrible rage in her eyes.

'Didn't you hear what I said? If you can't show me good manners then you must be punished. Let this serve as a warning to any beast or man who dares to attack the High Witch,' screamed Hildegard. She pointed at Modovar as he lay on the ground and then what resembled a bolt of lighting, shot out from her middle finger and struck him. The landga wolf howled in pain for several minutes and then fell silent.

As Bloodfang stared in horror at the body of his friend Modovar, he began to tremble. If there had been any doubt in his mind as to whether or not this tall, dark lady was indeed the High Witch, this doubt was now removed. Whoever she was one thing was sure, she was not to be reckoned with for she was both powerful and deadly.

'Now, show me to the one whom you refer to as *Lordship* immediately and no tricks, otherwise you will be dealt the same punishment as your friend,' screamed Hildegard and she pointed at Bloodfang threateningly.

'Of course High Witch, I will take you to him. You can count on me and there is no need for any more spells and magic,' said Bloodfang. He turned and began to head off in the direction of the camp where the Lord of the Wolfhaven was based.

As Hildegard made her way through the army of monsters, she received quite a few looks. The landga wolves and raganosi were surprised to see a tall witch walking amongst them. In general, witches were not well liked. Despite the fact that they had a lot in common with witches (in other words they were all evil), the raganosi and landga wolves did not trust them. They were afraid of the fact that they could cast spells at any minute, something which they could not.

'Look, there's a witch walking behind Bloodfang. What's he doing with a witch?' snarled another landga wolf.

'I hate witches. I've a good mind to clobber her with my club,' roared an oversized raganos warrior.

'Be my guest, but if you know what's good for you, you'll stay away from her. She looks nasty,' said the landga wolf.

It took less than ten minutes for Bloodfang and Hildegard to reach the camp. In the middle stood the same marquee tent where Luna had been caught. Its flag of black, grey and white flapped furiously in the brisk breeze. It was the flag of Wolfhaven; the grey outline of a lone landga wolf staring at a black night sky and with large white circles to represent full moons.

'Have we arrived?' snapped Hildegard.

'Yes, High Witch. This is his Lordship's camp. Wait one moment while I go and see if he is inside,' snarled Bloodfang.

However, Bloodfang did not need to go inside for their approach had been heard and seconds later Officer Morticus appeared outside the tent entrance.

'Lieutenant Bloodfang, why are you not at your post?' snarled Officer Morticus.

'I have brought with me the Highest of witches who would like to speak with his Lordship,' replied Bloodfang.

'A witch? Why would a witch want to speak to his Lordship? He is very busy at the moment,' growled Officer Morticus.

'I have urgent news and must speak with him immediately,' shouted Hildegard.

Officer Morticus narrowed his eyes as he stared at her. He, just like many other landga wolves, did not trust witches.

'There is no place for a witch here therefore I suggest you leave. Witches are not welcome in these parts,' snarled Officer Morticus.

'Is that so? Well, I'm afraid I won't be going anywhere until I have spoken with him,' shouted Hildegard. The High Witch lifted her hand in the air and began to mutter more strange words. Bloodfang who had already witnessed her power began to tremble. He watched as green light shot out from her fingers and struck the large tent, causing it to burst into flames. Officer Morticus had to run for cover and only narrowly missed having his tail singed.

Hildegard watched as the tent quickly disintegrated in front of her, large pieces of burning canvas lifted up into the atmosphere and were scattered across the camp. Seconds later, what had been a large marquee tent was now no more than a pile of smouldering ash. However, much to Hildegard's disappointment there was no sign of the one whom the landga wolves referred to as his Lordship.

'Where is he? Tell me before I set you on fire?' screamed Hildegard and she pointed threateningly at Officer Morticus.

'His Lordship has had to leave on urgent business. If you must know, he has had to return to Whitewitch Mountain,' snarled the Officer.

'In that case I will head there immediately and you will be my transport,' said Hildegard and she pointed at Bloodfang.

'I don't think that is wise. His Lordship will not want to be disturbed. What is this news that you say is so urgent?' growled Officer Morticus.

'That I can't tell you, but you can rest assured that once your Lordship hears my news, he will be *most* interested,' said Hildegard. The High Witch walked over towards Bloodfang and told him to crouch down.

'Why? What are you going to do?' snarled Bloodfang suspiciously.

'I thought that was obvious. I need you to crouch down so that I can climb onto your back,' snapped Hildegard.

The landga wolf hated the thought of the witch riding on his back for it would be humiliating however he knew that he did not have much choice. The image of what happened to Modovar was still fresh in his mind.

'If you must,' growled Bloodfang. The landga wolf crouched down on all fours, allowing Hildegard to climb up onto his back. It wasn't long before the witch was seated comfortably and holding on to Bloodfang's thick mane.

'Right, let's get moving,' shouted Hildegard and she kicked Bloodfang in the ribs. The landga wolf growled for he was angry. He was tempted to throw her off but he decided against it; moments later they departed.

By the time they started to head out across the vast, desolate landscape the sky overhead had turned a light grey, suggesting that dawn was just around the corner.

'Come on, surely you can run faster than this?' screamed Hildegard and she tugged hard on Bloodfang's mane. The landga wolf felt he had no choice other than to try and pick up speed and soon his great claws were tearing up the earth as he sprinted against a bitterly cold, northeast wind. Several half-starved and casteless landga wolves who had been scavenging out on the plains, suddenly lifted their heads in surprise as Bloodfang whizzed past with the tall witch on his back; her long, black cloak flying in the wind.

By the time they reached Whitewitch Mountain, it was broad daylight. Bloodfang was exhausted as Hildegard had refused to let the landga wolf stop for a rest.

'Thank you. You are now free to go,' said Hildegard as she stepped down off Bloodfang's back and looked up at the fortress perched on top of the steep rock. Bloodfang could not believe his ears when the witch told him that he was free to go. He was afraid there would be a catch. He thought she might do something to him as soon as he turned his back to leave and so he walked backwards ever so slowly and kept his eyes on the witch. However, Hildegard was no longer interested in the landga wolf, she was too preoccupied with the enormous fortress that towered overhead. It had been many years since she had last visited Whitewitch Mountain and when she looked up at the cold, dark fortress, painful memories came flooding back.

Just as Bloodfang was about to turn and run away, the strangest of things happened. Hildegard Otrava the High Witch suddenly transformed into a majestic, old woman with striking blue eyes and silvery white hair that sparkled beneath the hood of her cloak. The landga wolf watched as the old lady began to climb the hundreds of steps that led up the mountainside towards the door of the fortress.

'She'll get what's coming to her when she meets his Lordship. I bet she's pretending to be an old lady so that his Lordship will think her weak and then she'll try and attack him. He won't be fooled that easily. The stupid witch obviously has no idea how powerful his Lordship is,' thought Bloodfang. After that the landga wolf turned and ran off, pleased with the thought that the witch was unlikely to ever make it back out of Whitewitch Mountain alive.

Chapter 21: A Welcome Arrival from the Past

Qadir carried his brother until he reached outside the cave. As soon as he stepped outside, he stopped to breathe in the fresh air. He decided to rest briefly and sat Asmund upright with his back against a flat rock. He removed his coat, folded it and placed it carefully behind his brother's head. Now that they were outside, even thought it was dark, Qadir noticed how cold and pale Asmund looked.

Just as Qadir began to wonder how he would get back to Northdale, he heard the voice of Oswald.

'Young Prince, you made it back outside, well done. Now you must move back towards the fire and then I can help you get back,' squealed Osvald.

'Where is the fire? I can't see it,' said Qadir.

'Look above you,' shouted Osvald.

Qadir lifted his head and was surprised to see what can only be described as a ball of fire floating in the air above him.

'Okay, I see it now but I am not entirely sure what I am supposed to do,' shouted Qadir.

'Move forwards until you are standing directly beneath it. I will do the rest,' shouted Osvald.

Qadir lifted his brother from his resting place and carried him until they were both standing directly beneath the ball of fire that hovered in the air.

'Okay Osvald. I'm here, what should I do now?' shouted Qadir.

No sooner had Qadir spoken than the ball of fire exploded and both Qadir and Asmund were engulfed in the cool flames. When Qadir opened his eyes again, he found himself back inside Osvald's sitting room, standing in front of the fireplace, Asmund was slumped at his feet.

'You made it back young Prince and you found your brother I see but quick, we must help him. He is not out of danger yet,' shouted Oswald and he ran to fetch his teapot.

'I have made some very special tea which both of you must drink immediately. It will help you to recover from the evil to which you have been exposed,' said Oswald.

'Really? A cup of tea will do that?' said Qadir.

'This is no ordinary tea. I have helped the people of Northdale recover from witch attacks in the past. Although I can't protect them from her, I have worked hard to devise this special brew which really does help those who encounter her and manage to survive. Unless treated, her victims will usually end up dying from shock afterwards,' said Oswald.

Qadir looked over at his brother and was concerned to see how pale he was in the light of day.

'I suppose at the very least a hot drink can't hurt and then I need to get Asmund home. My Grandmother Lucinda is a healer, she will be able to help him but she lives quite far away. I hope that you can make him well enough so that he can survive the journey,' said Qadir.

'Yes, of course. I cannot guarantee a cure but the more help he gets, the better. When you were away the mammohof called Iglis came to look for you. He said that the army of mammohofs are ready to depart as soon as you are ready. In fact, they are waiting downstairs as we speak,' said Oswald.

'Okay, let's give Asmund some of your special tea and then we'll get going,' said Qadir.

'You must drink some too,' said Osvald.

'I'm fine. I don't think the Spindle had any effect on me,' said Qadir.

'You might think you are fine now, but trust me you can't underestimate her power. She poisons your mind but it doesn't always take effect immediately. It's better to be safe than sorry,' said Osvald.

Qadir quickly held a cup of the strange tea to his brother's lips. Asmund was only semi-conscious and it wasn't easy to get him to take it. Eventually, once Qadir had managed to get the last drop down his brother's throat, he quickly drank his own cup.

'Wow, that does taste and feel good,' said Qadir sounding surprised. When he looked down at his brother, he was pleased to see that his face now appeared less pale and he had begun to stir.

'Q ... Qadir, I f ... feel so c ... cold,' whispered Asmund. His voice was weak at first but it was a positive sign that he was even talking.

'Don't worry Asmund. We will be heading home shortly. It won't be long before you are back in Castle Draccwyne,' said Qadir.

'Oh, tha ... that would b ... be gr ... great. I h ... hope I g ... get to s ... see Castle Dr ... Draccwyne again,' whispered Asmund.

'Of course you'll see Castle Draccwyne again. Now, let's get moving,' said Qadir and he helped his brother to his feet.

'Oswald, I don't suppose there's any chance we could have some of your special tea for the journey?' said Qadir.

'Yes, why of course. The only problem is, it has to be made by me. As soon as I make it, you have to drink it immediately otherwise it will lose its effect,' said Osvald.

'Oh, that's a pity,' said Qadir looking rather disappointed.

'Well, I have a suggestion. I don't know if you will agree but I was thinking of travelling with you and the mammohofs as far as Iara. I could take care of your brother on the way. Although I can't cure him, I can keep him comfortable and my special tea will certainly stop his condition from worsening. There is no medicine that can cure him as such. It is only a mother's love that can help him now,' said Osvald.

'Oswald that would be amazing. Would you really do that for us? Will you come with us?' said Qadir.

'Why, of course. I have been around for almost as long as the witch and I have helped and nursed many people over the years who have succumbed to her poisonous evil. It would be an honour to help the Princes of Ordania,' said Osvald.

'Qadir felt so relieved when he heard that Osvald the Medicine man would be there to care for his brother on their journey south. There would be a lot of snow and ice to cross before they reached the rest of the family. Qadir knew how weak his brother was and he was worried he might not make it. However, with someone as experienced as Osvald on hand, the prospect of Asmund reaching Iara alive now seemed much more likely.

By the time Qadir and Oswald had carried Asmund down the steps and outside the white tower, several mammohofs had gathered. Once outside, Qadir quickly explained to Iglis what had happened and it was agreed that Qadir, Asmund and Oswald would each be carried separately on the backs of the mammohofs. Iglis was keen to depart as much time had already been lost. As soon as they were outside, Asmund was quickly wrapped in warm furs and then carefully strapped to Iglis' back.

'Right young Prince, we'd better get moving. Your brother looks like he needs help, I think it's best we don't delay any more. Once we are out on the ice plains, we can really pick up speed. We can stop occasionally to allow the medicine man to attend to your brother but apart from that we will keep going until we reach Iara,' said Iglis.

Once they reached the main city gates of Northdale, Qadir was astounded to see the huge army of mammohofs that had gathered outside. They trumpeted loudly as soon as Iglis and the other mammohofs arrived. Shortly after their arrival, Qadir was helped up onto the back of Glasis and Oswald was placed onto the back of another mammohof called Rastor.

'Right, I think we are ready to go. You hang on in there Prince Asmund, we'll get you back to your parents in no time,' said Iglis. Qadir looked over and was reassured to see his younger brother wrapped up cosily and safely on the back of the mighty mammohof. Just as they set off, Qadir was sure that Asmund opened his eyes for a brief moment and looked around. 'This must be a sign that he is feeling better,' thought Qadir.

Soon the city of Northdale was left behind as the great army of mammohofs led by Iglis and Glasis, headed out over the frozen lands. Once they had reached a certain distance from the city, the land began to flatten and the air grew colder.

'Right, on my trumpet we'll pick up speed,' shouted Glasis. Suddenly the giant mammohof trumpeted loudly, signalling to the army that it was now time to sprint. As soon as his trumpet was heard, the army of mammohofs trumpeted back in response almost deafening Oswald and Qadir as they bounced up and down on the backs of the mammohofs. Before long, the icy wind was whistling past Qadir's face as they began their high speed race across the ice. The Prince was surprised at just how much ground they could cover in a relatively short time.

'Are you alright back there young Prince?' shouted Glasis.

''Yes, Glsis. I'm fine thank you. We'll be there in no time at this speed,' replied Qadir.

They travelled for several hours and made good time, only stopping once or twice so that Oswald could tend to Asmund. Qadir watched with interest as the little old medicine man withdrew a variety of strange ingredients from his backpack, mixed them together in an old teapot and then whispered a spell in a language which he had never heard before. As soon as the concoction in the teapot began to give off steam, Oswald poured it into a small cup. He then lifted Asmund's head and encouraged him to drink. Once the Prince's complexion had change from a ghastly grey to more of a pale pink, Oswald gave Iglis and Glasis the green light to continue the journey.

Although the journey only took half the time, thanks to the mammohofs, it felt incredibly long for Qadir. He had barely taken his eyes off his brother throughout the journey and when finally the small town of Iara came into view, he breathed a sigh of relief.

'There is the town of Iara straight ahead and by the looks of things, they are getting ready for war,' shouted Glasis and he trumpeted loudly. As always, his trumpet was echoed by many more and suddenly the great army that had already gathered outside Iara were drawn to the sound of the mammohofs.

'Look over there, if I'm not mistaken there is an army of mammohofs heading our way,' shouted an Ordanian soldier called Torcuil.

'I cannot believe what I am seeing. It's like a re-enactment from a history book, don't they look the part,' shouted another soldier called Niall.

'Do you think they might join us? Wouldn't that be great? If they are half as strong as the real Iglis and Glasis were, then I think we've as good as won this war before it even starts,' shouted Torcuil.

The great army of snee menesker and Ordanian soldiers stood

gasping at the formidable army of shaggy, red hair that suddenly appeared on the horizon, trumpeting loudly and carry huge bows and arrows on their backs. For many of the soldiers, stories of Iglis and Glasis had been their bedtime favourites when they were children. It was a welcome surprise for the soldiers on such a cold evening, as they waited for the war to commence. Of course, none of them knew that it was in fact the real Glasis and Iglis, brought by magic from one thousand years in the past.

As Qadir looked out over the army, he recognised the familiar face of Lord Finhildur. He was sitting on the back of a large snee yak.

'Greetings young Prince Qadir. We were very worried that you might not make it back at all, let alone with such a huge army. Tell me, is it true? Are you the real Iglis and Glasis?' said Lord Finhildur as he looked up at the huge mammohofs who towered over him.

'Yes, I am Iglis and that's Glasis. We came because we heard that you've been having a few problems with eis jätte,' said Iglis.

The crowd of soldiers gasped loudly for they could not believe what they were hearing.

'How can you possibly be the real Iglis and Glasis? They must have died centuries ago,' shouted a soldier called Raghnall.

'Do I look dead to you?' roared Glasis, then he stamped his foot and trumpeted loudly.

'Hello everyone. I am Prince Qadir Rosencratz from Ordania and I swear on my family's life that they are the real Iglis and Glasis. If you have ever read about them in history books, you will know that it was always a mystery what became of them. They, along with their huge army set out on the ice plains from home one day and were never seen again,' said Qadir.

'I read that the snee hex got them and ate them one by one,' shouted

Raghnall.

'A witch? Do you think I'd let a daft, wee witch eat me? I'd stamp her into the ground if she came came close enough,' roared Glasis and he shook his fist angrily in the air.

'Well, he certainly fits the description of the bad tempered Glasis,' whispered Torcuil.

'Go on Prince Qadir, please continue your story,' said Lord Finhildur.

'Well, they certainly weren't eaten by the witch or snee hex as you call her, but they were under one of her spells which left the City of Northdale and all of its inhabitants hidden under thick ice for one thousand years. I returned several days ago to break the spell and now they are here,' said Qadir.

'What? They've been frozen in ice for a thousand years and now they are able to walk about as if it was only yesterday? How can this be true?' shouted Raghnall.

'Now, let's mind our manners. We are in the presence of Ordanian royalty and we also don't want to be upsetting Iglis and Glasis. I understand why you find this hard to believe, I too find it hard to believe but that is because we are non-magical people. However, over the past few years I have learned that when magic is involved, be it good magic or bad, absolutely anything is possible. For that reason I believe the story,' said Lord Finhildur.

'Wise decision! Now, are we going to get the sick laddie some help or are we going to just stand here all night talking?' roared Glasis. Neither Qadir, nor Iglis got the chance to answer for no sooner had Glasis spoken, than Qadir's mother pushed her way through the wall of soldiers and ran over to where her son was now standing.

'Qadir, you made it? I heard you were back. I too only arrived a short time ago. Oh, you've no idea how glad I am to see you,' said Isabella and she hugged her son.

'Where is your brother?' said Isabella.

Qadir did not speak, instead he pointed over to where Osvald was tending to Asmund as he lay wrapped in thick furs to keep him warm.

Isabella threw her hand over her mouth and ran over to where Asmund was, Qadir followed.

'Has he been injured? What happened to him?' said Isabella and she placed her hand on her son's pale forehead.

'Your Royal Highness, your son has been poisoned by the one they call the snee hex or the Spindle as I believe she is known in Ordania. Your son was trapped inside her lair and when he tried to escape, she poisoned him. Fortunately Qadir managed to rescue him,' explained Osvald.

'Mum, this is Osvald. He is highly skilled in treating those who have been attacked by the Spindle and so he offered to come with us just so he could look after Asmund,' said Qadir.

'Oh, thank you Oswald. Can you cure him?' said Isabella.

'No, unfortunately I cannot cure him completely. I can only stop his symptoms from worsening. The cure lies with you, for you are his mother. I am sure that with much love and the proper care, you will heal him back to full health. There is nothing more powerful than a mother's love for her child, powerful enough to overcome the evil witches' poison,' said Osvald.

'What must I do?' said Isabella.

'All you need to do is care for him, nurse him as if he were a small child again and love him as you already do. The more time you spend with him, the quicker the poison will leave his system,' explained Osvald.

'I must get him inside immediately so that I can care for him. Lord Finhildur, I must care for my son. I am afraid that I won't be around to help with this fight,' said Isabella.

'Princess Isabella, the life of your son must take priority. Please take care of him and let me know if there is anything I can do. As for your help with the war, I think now that we have Glasis and Iglis, plus their formidable army we just might be okay,' said Lord Finhildur. Shortly after, they arranged for two soldiers to carry Prince Asmund to the inn where he was placed on a warm, comfortable bed. Qadir stayed by his brother's bedside for a while and chatted to his mum.

'Where are Dad, Gran and Luna?' said Qadir, suddenly realising that he hadn't seen them.

'I was wondering when you might ask me that. They weren't here when I arrived, but the soldiers have informed me that your father left for the Wolfhaven only a short while ago,' said Isabella.

'The Wolfhaven? Why would Dad want to go there?' said Qadir.

'Apparently he went to find your grandmother,' added Isabella.

'Gran has gone to the Wolfhaven as well? Are they mad? Why would they go?' asked Qadir.

'They went to find Luna. Apparently she wandered off last night by herself and convinced an owl to carry her over the Black Mountains,' said Isabella.

'Oh, not again. I've already had to rescue her from sixteenth century Edinburgh. Now she needs rescued again. Luna is such a liability,' said Qadir.

'I only hope she's okay. I've not heard from your father or from your

Gran,' sighed Isabella.

'I should head over there to see if they need my help,' said Qadir.

'No Qadir, you mustn't. I have enough to worry about without you disappearing off again and anyway, as much as I hate to say it you might be needed here to help in the war. Whatever happened to our quiet family holiday on the Isle of Lewis?' sighed Isabella.

'It's always like this Mum and I don't think things will ever change,' said Qadir.

'Why don't you go downstairs and get something to eat. You must be starving and you'll need all your strength if you are to fight in the war. I'll stay here with your brother for a while,' said Isabella and then she kissed Qadir on the forehead.

Chapter 22: Lord and Lady of Whitewitch Mountain

By the time Queen Valda had reached the last step and stood outside the entrance to the fortress, she was feeling rather tired and impatient. Under normal circumstances the Queen would have knocked on the door and waited for someone to answer however on this occasion she wanted her arrival to come as a surprise. With a simple spell, the Queen forced open the great doors and soon she was able to make her way inside the long, dark hallway that would lead her deep into the cold heart of Whitewitch Mountain.

'What a terribly sad and depressing place,' thought Queen Valda as she walked down the long hallway. She looked up at the high ceiling overhead and thought that its huge arches resembled great bones. She imagined herself walking inside the long neck of a huge, sleeping dragon; every step forward bringing her closer to its stomach. Unlike the great hallways in Castle Draccwyne which were full of natural light, this hallway had no windows. However, there was some light from an unknown source, albeit dim which allowed Queen Valda to take in her surroundings.

'A castle with so much space and grandeur, but no love or happiness to be found. It should have happy memories tucked away in its bricks and walls but instead there is a suffocating silence; it's almost as if the memories are too terrifying to recall. What a dreary home indeed,' thought Queen Valda as she continued to make her way deeper into Whitewitch Mountain. When she reached the end of the hallway, she finally spotted something which interrupted the monotony of the slate-grey walls. On the wall to the right was the portrait of a young soldier dressed in full body armour. In order to study the painting more carefully, Queen Valda used some magic to create more light. Soon an enormous bright glow on the end of her fingertip filled the hallway, allowing her to study the painting more closely. She recognised the armour immediately. It represented typical armour worn by Ordanian soldiers of high ranking around one hundred to one hundred and fifty years previously. When she lifted the light higher to get a better look at the soldier's face, the Queen got a shock for it was someone whom she recognised; it was her own father as a young man.

'Oh, Daddy? Now, why would there be a painting of you in this horrible place?' thought Queen Valda.

Suddenly Queen Valda's concentration was interrupted when she heard a young girl scream from further inside the castle.

'Luna, whatever are they doing to you? I'm on my way,' shouted Queen Valda. Her granddaughter's scream served as a quick reminder why she had come to Whitewitch Mountain in the first place. She would have to forget about the painting for the time being but once she had rescued her granddaughter, Queen Valda fully intended to return and try to find answers to the many questions which were now swirling around in her mind.

Queen Valda began to race down the many corridors in the general direction of the scream. Soon she was moving so fast, her feet barely touched the floor.

'Luna can you hear me? It's your grandmother. I have come to rescue you, please hold on my dear,' said Queen Valda. As she whizzed along the many dark and dreary corridors of the castle, Queen Valda tried to use an old trick which she had successfully used in the past in order to communicate with her granddaughter. Queen Valda tried to speak to Luna using a form of mental telepathy.

'Luna my love, can you hear me? Let me know where you are? I'm here to rescue you' said Queen Valda. She waited for a response but none came and so she tried again and again. Although Luna did not respond to her grandmother, suddenly another scream could be heard and this time it was much closer.

'Hang on in there Luna. I'm almost there,' said Queen Valda. The long dark corridor along which Queen Valda had been running came to an abrupt end and she found herself standing in front of two enormous doors that were shut tight. There were no handles that she could see therefore she placed her hand against one of the doors to see if it could be pushed open. As soon as the Queen made contact with the door, something terrible happened. Many faces appeared on each of the wooden panels and they began to scream loudly. As soon as her fingertips made contact with the wood, Queen Valda felt immense pain and grief surge through her body causing her to stagger backwards, lose her footing and fall onto the floor.

When Queen Valda looked back up at the door, the faces had gone and the screaming stopped. It took her a few moments to recompose herself and recover from the terrible pain and suffering that she had just experienced.

'Now I know why this place is so depressing. So many people have suffered in this cold, dark castle. Those poor souls have had the most terrible ordeal, if only I could help them,' thought the Queen.

Eventually, Queen Valda found her feet again and decided to make one final attempt to open the great doors however this time she would avoid making any physical contact.

'Fosgail farsaing!' shouted Queen Valda.

It took less than ten seconds before a shimmer appeared on the enormous doors then there was a loud rumble as they began to pull open. Eventually the rumbling stopped, the doors stood wide open revealing an eerie black void that seemed to whisper 'enter if you dare'.

'Solas,' shouted Queen Valda. As she spoke she threw her hand forwards sending an enormous ball of light into the pitch black. Once inside, the ball of light revealed the interior of the chamber. Although the effect only lasted several seconds, it was just enough time for the Queen to catch a glimpse of the enormous chamber with high, arched ceilings. However, there was something at the far end of the room that she didn't have time to study for the light had extinguished much quicker than expected.

'*Solas*,' shouted Queen Valda again. This time the ball of light remained in the palm of her hand as she took a few steps forward into the mysterious chamber.

'My, this is a grand room or at least it was at some point,' thought Queen Valda as she stared around in awe at the enormous stone pillars that ran from the floor up to the ceiling. She reckoned that each pillar must have stood two hundred feet tall and there were at least a dozen of them. By the time she had reached the centre of the chamber, she caught sight of three huge thrones on the far side. Each one was made from stone and although she could not quite make out the detail, they saw that they were covered in various carvings. The throne in the middle was the largest and most striking. Each of its armrests had been carved into the heads of landga wolves. On each side of the largest throne sat two smaller thrones and when the Queen used her light to inspect them more carefully, she was surprised to discover a dark, robed figure seated in one of them. The Queen stopped still in her tracks and peered across at the figure, unsure what to do. It was impossible to see a face for the hood hung low and whoever they were, they appeared to be slouched forwards. Eventually, it was Queen Valda who decided to break the unearthly silence.

'Are you the Lord of the Wolfhaven? My name is Valda Rosencratz, Queen of Ordania and I have come for my granddaughter,' said Queen Valda. She paused for a few seconds before continuing to see if the figure would respond however the silence continued and so she tried again.

'I have come to take Princess Luna of Ordania back home and I will not be leaving without her,' said Queen Valda. Her voice was now much stronger and as she spoke her words reverberated around the enormous chamber.

Suddenly there was a loud noise from behind. The Queen jumped round in time to see the doors through which she had entered, slam tight shut.

It was then for the first time Queen Valda heard someone speak, but whoever it was the voice did not appear to be coming from the robed figure seated on one of the thrones. It was the voice of a man and it was cold and harsh, it seemed to be coming from the darkness on the far side of the great chamber.

'Welcome Queen of Ordania. It has been a very long time since you last walked under this roof. We are honoured to welcome you again,' boomed the deep, harsh voice.

'Thank you. Yes, it has been a long time indeed. If you truly mean what you say then surely the honourable thing would be to present yourself to your guest and not hide in the shadows,' said Queen Valda.

'I said you were welcome, I did not say you were a guest for I did not invite you,' boomed the voice.

'No, that is true. I came to fetch my granddaughter and take her home. Please tell me where she is,' said Queen Valda.

'I am afraid that you have arrived too late. Princess Luna is no longer with us,' boomed the voice.

'What do you mean? What have you done to her?' shouted Queen Valda.

'All in good time Queen of Ordania, all in good time. Why don't you take a seat and rest and then we can talk some more,' said the voice.

'I am afraid I have no time to waste. You must show me where my granddaughter is immediately, otherwise I will have to use force,' said

Queen Valda. Her voice remained confident and calm. Years of experience had taught her that losing one's temper too quickly was not the cleverest thing to do.

'Will you indeed? I must remind you Valda that in these lands you are not Queen and that means no one needs to bow to your demands,' said the voice.

'Yes, you are correct. Queen I may not be however I am still a grandmother. I know that you have my granddaughter,' said Queen Valda.

'*Seall do làthaireachd,*' roared Queen Valda and she threw the ball of light that she had been holding into the darkest part of the chamber.

'*Solas an latha,*' shouted Queen Valda again. Moments after she spoke the air around her lit up so brightly, it was as if the sun itself had risen indoors and was now shining down on the great chamber, revealing everything and everyone in it including Queen Valda, the three thrones with the dark, robed figure slouched in one of them and now also a second dark figure which until now had remained out of sight. It was obvious to the Queen that the stranger was indeed a man but what was even more obvious to her was the fact that this individual had incredible power.

Once they are within close proximity to one another, sorcerers can sense each other's presence and can gauge the strength of the other's magical power. Queen Valda hadn't expected the Lord of the Wolfhaven to be as powerful as this. Although she had known for some time that the mysterious, evil lord of the Wolfhaven was a sorcerer, there was never any indication that he would have this much strength.

'The stars above Starrydell did not predict this, unless all this time I have been misinterpreting what they were telling me. Had I known, I would have brought some extra help along with me,' thought Queen

Valda.

'I have told you my name, now tell me yours,' said Queen Valda. She stared hard at the tall man. Hoping to catch a glimpse of the face hidden beneath the cloak.

'I am Lord Varvarski, Lord of Darkness, Ruler of the Wolfhaven. You have entered my territory Queen of Ordania and I am afraid that you will never leave again. You must obey my command now, if you want to survive,' said Lord Varvarski.

'I obey no one and do not try and detain me here for you will not succeed. I have come for my granddaughter and once I have found her, I will take her home. Now, for the last time where is she? I know that you brought her here,' said Queen Valda.

Lord Varvarski paused temporarily before responding. He was impressed by the elderly Queen's courage and also her commitment to rescuing her granddaughter. He had never before experienced another living being who would go to so much trouble in order to save the life of another.

'I am afraid it is too late. Your granddaughter has forsaken you and your family and instead, she has chosen to be powerful, she has chosen to be stronger, she has chosen to be immortal,' said Lord Varvarski. As he spoke, Queen Valda noticed his head turn momentarily towards the other cloaked figure seated on one of the thrones.

The Queen had the sudden realisation that the other cloaked figure who had remained silent and motionless could be her granddaughter.

'Luna? Is that you over there?' shouted Queen Valda and she ran over towards the throne where the figure was sitting.

'I wouldn't do that if I were you, she is in the middle of her transformation. If you disturb her now she may attack you,' said Lord

Varvarski.

'Attack me? What nonsense. You obviously don't understand anything about families. Luna would never attack me,' said Queen Valda. She reached forwards and pulled down the hood to reveal the face. Queen Valda breathed a sigh of relief as soon as she saw that it was her granddaughter and that she appeared to be breathing.

'What have you done to her? Is she under some sort of spell?' said Queen Valda. As she spoke, the Queen turned her head back towards Lord Varvarski and as she did so, she failed to notice Luna open her eyes.

'Why don't you ask her yourself? You have awoken her and disturbed her transformation. I did warn you,' said Lord Varvarski.

When Queen Valda turned back to look at her granddaughter, she was surprised to find her standing upright and staring forwards. What shocked the Queen most of all were her granddaughter's eyes; they were not the usual bright, shiny and mischievous eyes that she knew, instead they were cold, cruel and full of hatred.

'Luna my darling, it's me, your grandmother. I have come to rescue you from this evil place and take you home,' said Queen Valda.

'Luna? Are you speaking to me old lady? My name is Prevara Mirtis and I have no grandmother. My Lord told you not to disturb me but you ignored him and interrupted my beautiful transformation.'

'This is madness. Your name is Luna Rosencratz of Ordania, Princess of the Woods and you are now under an evil spell. You must listen to me, you will return home to your family. They need your help,' shouted Queen Valda. However, it was no use. The granddaughter whom Queen Valda knew and loved had gone and in her place was the evil spirit of sorceress Prevara Mirtis who had haunted the lonely, dark corridors of Whitewitch Mountain for centuries. She had finally found a youthful body to possess and not just any old body, the body of a powerful sorceress princess.

'Family? What family do you speak of?' shouted Prevara and she pointed her finger at Queen Valda. A bright red light shot out and struck the Queen full force in the chest, sending her flying backwards through the air before crashing down onto the cold floor of the chamber.

'Lady Prevara, it has been a long time since you have killed someone. Now is your chance, kill the old lady and you can absorb her power,' said Lord Varvarski.

'Yes, you are right Dark Lord. It has indeed been a long time since I last killed. This old lady is indeed powerful and I could put her powers to much better use,' said Prevara. The evil sorceress stepped down from the throne and made her way over to where Queen Valda was lying on the floor. Queen Valda was still conscious and when she looked up, she discovered Prevara standing over her with a look of evil in her eyes.

'This is the end for you old lady. You have something that I want and I am going to take it … now!' said Prevara and she raised her hand in the air above Queen Valda.

Lord Varvarski watched on from the side of the room. He could not quite believe his luck; two members of the Ordanian Royal Family had as good as sacrificed themselves by entering his land. He knew that it was only a matter of time before more of the family came to look for them.

'I don't need to do anything other than wait for them to come to me and when they do arrive, Prevara will see to them one by one. With every kill she will be able to absorb their power and become so much stronger. Prevara and I will then rule these lands as King and Queen and we will go down in history as the most powerful sorcerers that ever lived,' thought Lord Varvarski. 'The boy remains the biggest obstacle but once we get rid of him there will be no stopping us. With any luck, he'll come running to fetch his grandmother,' smiled Lord Varvarski.

Chapter 23: The War of Westerlyn

It was late afternoon when the war horn signaled that the War of Westerlyn was finally underway. Officer Morticus led the army of eis jätte, raganosi, landga wolves and grotta ghoul over the Black Mountains and down into Westerlyn. Fortunately, Lord Finhildur had been forewarned and he had prepared his soldiers accordingly. Thanks to the information shared by Harailt the owl, the ambush led by Officer Morticus was not quite the surprise that he'd hoped it would be. When he and his army of monsters finally reached the foot of the Black Mountains, it was they who were caught by surprise when they were met by an equally large army of snee menesker, Ordanian soldiers and of course the giant army of mammohofs led by the infamous Iglis and Glasis. Soon the peace and quiet of sleepy Iara town was shattered by the roar of battle. Never before had the small town experienced the terrible sound of teeth and claws clashing with steel.

Qadir and Isabella had been sitting by Asmund's bedside. His condition had improved quite a bit since his arrival in Iara. However, the sudden sound of the war horn seemed to unsettle him and he began to stir from his heavy sleep.

'I must speak to gran. I must tell her before it's too late,' muttered Asmund.

'What do you want to tell Gran? Are you having a bad dream Asmund?' said Isabella.

Suddenly, Asmund opened his eyes and looked up at his mum and brother.

'Mum, I need to tell Gran what I saw. Uncle Espen didn't die on the battlefield. He was kidnapped by an evil shape shifter,' muttered Asmund.

'Darling, I think you have been dreaming. Please try not to stress,' said Isabella. As she spoke she stroked her son's hair.

'No Mum, it wasn't a dream. I saw it with my own eyes when I time travelled. I wanted to tell Gran in person but I never got the chance,' whispered Asmund.

'Is this true Asmund? I'd be really surprised if such a secret could have been kept from Gran all these years,' said Qadir.

'I promise it's true. He never made it onto the battlefield. I watched as a strange, black mist encircled him, then he collapsed onto the ground before being picked up and carried away over the Esterway Mountains,' said Asmund.

'Wasn't that what happened to Eden when you were both in Fair Forrest and she was kidnapped? Do you think he was taken to Whitewitch Mountain and imprisoned as well?' said Qadir.

'I think it's a strong possibility. Do you remember Eden said that her captor claimed to be our Uncle? Perhaps Uncle Espen has been alive all this time and living in Whitewitch Mountain,' said Asmund.

'I don't understand. Why would he stay there all this time? Surely if he was as powerful as they say he was, he would have eventually managed to break free in the same way Eden did?' said Qadir.

'Your gran refused to believe that story when Eden first told her, although I think she has been haunted by it ever since. Eden's captor was evil and hideously deformed; you can therefore understand why your gran found it too upsetting,' said Isabella.

'I understand that it must be hard, but wouldn't she want to know the truth? Surely it is better knowing one way or another?' said Asmund.

'Yes, I think she will want to know but it can't be easy finding out that your son has turned to evil. I know that as a mother, I would find that impossible,' said Isabella.

'Well, I suppose Gran might find out for herself when she is in the Wolfhaven. I hope she and Luna are safe,' said Qadir.

'I hope so too. Your father will hopefully have found them both by now,' said Isabella.

Their conversation was suddenly interrupted when the war horn sounded again. Qadir decided that he would head outside to see if he could help in any way.

'I need to give you something before you go, I brought some of your belongings with me from Castle Draccwynne. I had a feeling that you might need them again,' said Isabella. She walked over to the corner of the room and withdrew a large sword hidden in its gilded sheath, along with a cloth bag containing a cylindrical object which Qadir soon realised was the glass ball containing part of ancient King Narù's star. Then from her pocket, she withdrew a beautiful ring boasting a large ethereal stone.

'You brought Grandad's gifts? Mum, that's brilliant. I am sure they will all come in very useful with so much evil around. I will definitely need Morning Light,' said Qadir. He took the sword which he had named Morning Light from his mother' hand, then he withdrew the blade and marvelled at its shininess.

'Every warrior needs his own sword when he goes to battle,' said Isabella.

'I wish I could help in the battle,' said Asmund.

'You need to rest for the time being. Although you have improved a lot, there is still a long road to recovery. Now that you are a bit stronger, I will take you home to Castle Draccwyne this evening where you can recover properly. Osvald has already agreed to come with us. When we get home, your grandmother Lucinda will meet us there. She will then use her powers to heal you,' said Isabella.

'Good luck Qadir and thanks for rescuing me. That's two I owe you,' said Asmund.

Qadir said goodbye to his brother, kissed his mother goodbye and then headed outside to join in the battle. Before long he found himself surrounded by all kinds of monster but they were no match for the sorcerer Prince. Other soldiers watched in wonder as Qadir flew around the battlefield wielding his sword and slaying every evil creature who dared cross his path.

'Look at young Prince Qadir go! There's a King in the making if ever I saw one. He makes it all look too easy,' said an Ordanian soldier who stopped what he was doing to watch the starry Prince take on two eis jätte, one landga wolf and a raganos warrior all at the same time.

It had been a while since Qadir had last fought in a battle like this one but he took to it like a duck to water. He, along with Iglis and Glasis were beginning to make Officer Morticus and his army of monsters slightly concerned; they certainly hadn't anticipated that the people of Westerlyn and the Ordanians would put up such a fight. The giant mammohofs were unstoppable, destroying everything in their path. As they made their way across the battlefield, they left behind a huge trail of dead eis jätte and raganosi.

When the landga wolves saw Qadir holding his sword called Morning Light, they began to feel afraid. They had heard of this powerful, deadly sword and how it had killed their former leader, Abnocta Mirus. In the Wolfhaven, Qadir's sword was referred as the Wolf Slayer. However, there was one landga wolf who wasn't afraid, quite the opposite in fact. As soon as he spotted Qadir wielding his sword of power, his eyes narrowed with hatred and he began to growl. He had hated Prince Qadir ever since he had slain his former master and saw this as his opportunity for revenge. The giant landga wolf ran at top speed towards Qadir, leapt through the air and landed on the Prince's back, pinning him to the ground with his giant paws.

'Now, let's see how powerful you really are Prince of Stars,' growled Officer Morticus. The landga wolf pushed down harder on Qadir's back, crushing him into the ground.

'You're not really that strong after all, are you boy?' growled Officer Morticus. Drool dripped from his monstrous mouth and landed on Qadir's neck. The Prince kicked hard in an attempt to free himself but it was no use, the landga wolf was simply too heavy.

'If only I could free one hand, I'd blast him into pieces,' thought Qadir.

His face was being pushed deeper into the mud and since he was lying on top of his sword, he could feel the handle and blade digging into his chest and stomach. He tried desperately to reach for the handle of the sword in order to pull it away but it was impossible.

'Do you have any last minute requests before I end your life Starry Prince?' growled Officer Morticus. Qadir wanted to use magic but the landga wolf was now crushing him so much, he could barely breathe let alone mutter the words of a simple spell.

'Oh, the poor little Prince is lost for words. In that case let me say something to mark this memorable occasion; today will go down in history as the day the sorcerer Prince of Ordania was shown for what he really is, a mere pathetic little boy who thought that he could take on the world. He thought that he could defeat the powerful landga wolves and crush the mighty Lord Varvarski. Well, it looks like you and your family were wrong. It takes more than a few magic tricks to become a powerful leader. This is for Lord Mirus,' roared Officer Morticus.

He threw his head back and howled into the wind, then prepared to bite Qadir. Jaws dripping with drool, Officer Morticus opened wide around the Prince's neck. It was then that Officer Morticus howled again, although Qadir thought that it sounded more like a scream this time. Instead of feeling the monster's teeth on his neck, Qadir suddenly felt even more weight push down on him. The giant landga wolf had suddenly fallen silent and had collapsed on top of Qadir. It was several moments before the weight began to lift and Qadir was finally able to breathe again. Eventually, he managed to pull himself up off the ground and turned round to see what had happened. When he did, he was most surprised to see the body of Officer Morticus lying beside him with an enormous arrow in his back and standing over him, dressed in battle armour was a very familiar face, it was Qadir's younger sister, Eden.

'Well? How was my shot? Did I get him?' smiled Eden.

'Wow! Eden, when did you get here and how did you manage to do that with no eyesight?' Qadir stood up and brushed himself down, then he gave his little sister a hug.

'I just trust my instincts, that's all,' smiled Eden. There was little time for them to stop and catch up, for shortly afterwards more raganosi charged at them, swinging their giant clubs in the air.

'Does Mum know you're here?' shouted Qadir as he swung his sword over his head and then brought it down onto a raganos warrior who was trying to spear him.

'Yes, I spoke to her briefly. She said she's taking Asmund home to Draccwyne. He looks like he's been through a lot,' said Eden. Just after she spoke she spun round in a circle and fired several arrows. Her arms moved so fast they appeared blurred to onlookers. Seconds later three raganosi, one landga wolf and one grotta ghoul lay dead at her feet, each one with an arrow in their head.

'When did you learn to shoot a bow and arrow like that?' asked Qadir.

'Oh, I had a few lessons while I was staying in Westercourt,' replied Eden.

The War of Westerlyn raged on throughout the afternoon and into the evening. By sunset, most of the evil army had been defeated and the few remaining landga wolves and raganosi began to retreat to the Black Mountains. Without a leader, they felt lost and vulnerable. Officer Morticus had assured the evil army that victory would be easy and had promised the raganosi and landga wolves that once they set foot in Westerlyn and Ordania, they could eat whatever and whomever they liked. However, Officer Morticus had made poor judgment and as a result they had lost the battle.

The Dark Lord of the Wolfhaven, Lord Varvarski had been too preoccupied to attend the battle scene. He had left it up to Officer Morticus to ensure that a pathway was cleared from the Wolfhaven to Ordania via Westerlyn. Lord Varvarski had then planned to make his way unhindered from the Wolfhaven and into Ordania where he would then challenge and kill the Ordanian Royal Family, or at least that was his plan. However, it now seemed that the Ordanian Royal Family were coming to him, therefore the War of Westerlyn was no longer of such importance and he quickly lost interest.

'I just need to get the boy to come to Whitewitch Mountain and I think I have the perfect plan,' thought Lord Varvarski.

'Prevara, don't kill the old woman just yet for we will need her. I want you to pretend that you are her and send a message to the boy. Let him know that she is in danger and desperately needs his help. I know he'll come running, just wait and see,' said Lord Varvarski.

'Yes my lord. She isn't completely dead yet but I have managed to take most of her power. How does this sound?' said Prevara and she cleared her throat and began to impersonate the voice of Queen Valda.

'Oh, my dearest Qadir. Please come quickly. Luna and I need your help. We are being held against our will in Whitewitch Mountain. Only you can save us with the power of the stars. Please hurry, before it's too late,' said Prevara.

Lord Varvarski was very impressed for Prevara sounded exactly like Queen Valda.

'Excellent work Prevara, do you think he will have heard you?' said Lord Vavarski.

Prevara closed her eyes and tried once more, this time she used only her mind to communicate with Qadir.

Meanwhile back in the valley that lay between the foot of the Black Mountains and the town of Iara, Qadir and Eden were finishing off the few remaining raganosi and landga wolves who had been brave enough to hang around, despite the fact that most of their army were either now dead or had fled east.

Suddenly Qadir stopped what he was doing and looked over at Eden.

'Hey, did you hear that?' said Qadir.

'Did I hear what?' said Eden.

'I am sure I just heard Gran's voice. I think she was calling for help,' said Qadir.

'I didn't hear anything. Are you sure it was Gran you heard?' said Eden.

'Yes, I am sure. I would recognise her voice anywhere,' said Qadir.

The next time he heard the voice, it was crystal clear. Qadir closed his eyes and listened carefully before replying.

'Yes Gran, I can hear you and I will be there as soon as possible,' said Qadir.

'Who are you talking to?' asked Eden.

'Gran has just spoken to me. She and Luna are in grave danger. I need to go to Whitewitch Mountain immediately,' said Qadir.

'Whitewitch Mountain? Wait, is that wise? Shouldn't you try and find Dad first? He has already gone to the Wolfhaven to look for them. Perhaps he has already reached Whitewitch Mountain,' said Eden.

'I don't think so. Gran would have said. The situation must really be desperate for her to contact me. Usually Gran would never do that, she never wants to put us in danger. I must go to her immediately, but please don't tell Mum. She has enough to worry about with Asmund,' said Qadir.

'I can come with you if you like,' said Eden.

'I think it's better if you stayed here. Dad might come back and he'll wonder where everyone is. I'll be absolutely fine, don't worry about me,' said Qadir.

Chapter 24: Secret in the Shadows.

Darkness had fallen by the time Lord Finhildur declared that the war was over for now and that the people of Westerlyn and Ordania had been victorious. By the time Qadir was preparing to leave for the Wolfhaven, celebration was already underway in and around the town of Iara. Qadir's concerns over how he would travel to Whitewitch mountain were soon allayed when he discovered that his shapeshifter friend Nelson had arrived earlier that day from Ordania, along with several other shapeshifters; Athelea, Kaimono and Marete. Kaimono had been called upon to carry Prince Asmund back to Castle Draccwyne, Marete had offered to carry Princess Isabella. Nelson and Athelea had simply come along to see if they could be of assistance to the Royal Family whom they had served for years. Qadir was overjoyed to see his old friend and quickly engaged him in private conversation.

'Nelson, this is perfect timing. I really do need your help as does Gran and Luna. They are being held prisoner in Whitewitch Mountain and I need to go and rescue them. Can you help me?' said Qadir.

'This is terrible news. Of course we will go and help you rescue Her Majesty and Her Highness Princess Luna immediately. How did this happen? It could not have been easy to take a sorceress as powerful as your Grandmother prisoner,' said Nelson.

'Thanks Nelson. I am keen to go as soon as possible,' said Qadir.

'Yes, of course. However, if we are to rescue Queen Valda and Princess Luna, I will need some extra support. I don't think I could carry three people on my back at once. I'll ask Athelea to join us, after all she is Princess Luna's watcher,' said Nelson

Soon it was agreed that Nelson and Athelea the shapeshifters or tàcharan as they are known in Ordania, would accompany Qadir on his journey northeast to Whitewitch Mountain. Marete and Kaimono would travel back southwest over the Esterway Mountains to Castle Draccwyne as planned whilst Eden would remain in Iara with Lord Finhildur, awaiting news from her father.

By the time Nelson and Athelea had changed into beautiful winged horses and took off into the sky, the stars were shining across the land of Westerlyn. As Qadir sat on Nelson's back, he looked up at the stars and was reassured to see the star of his late grandfather twinkling brightly. Suddenly the voice of King Andris could be heard coming from the sky above him.

'Qadir, you are immensely brave and I am proud of you. Your grandmother does need your help as does your sister but beware; not all is as it seems. There will be others who seek to trick and harm you. Your grandmother would never draw you towards danger but she does need your help. I will be with you all the time Qadir. Please use the gifts I gave you for they will prove to be most useful where you are heading; it is indeed the darkest of all places. Be careful Qadir,' said the voice of King Andris.

'Yes Grandad, I will and thank you. I will make sure that both Gran and Luna come home, that I can promise,' said Qadir as he stared back at his grandfather's star.

As Qadir continued his journey east, he thought carefully about everything his Grandfather had said. He also thought about his younger brother Asmund and what he had said about their Uncle Espen.

'Surely Uncle Espen can't still be alive and living in Whitewitch Mountain? He can't have been a prisoner all these years? I wish I had asked Grandad if he knew anything about this,' thought Qadir. He looked up to the sky again to see if his grandfather's star was still visible however they were now flying over the Wolfhaven where no stars ever shone.

'We'll be arriving shortly your Highness. Perhaps you could try and communicate with your grandmother again, tell her that we are almost there,' suggested Nelson.

'That's a good idea Nelson. I have never done it before but it's worth try,' said Qadir. He then closed his eyes and concentrated hard.

'Gran, this is Qadir. Can you hear me? I am on my way to get you and Luna. Please hold on, I'm almost there,' said Qadir.

At first there was no response however just as he was about to try again, he heard the voice of his Grandmother in his head. This time it was the real Queen Valda whom he heard and not the evil sorceress Prevara. She sounded very weak and was barely audible.

'Qadir, you must stay away from here. It's too dangerous. Please turn back before it's too late,' came the voice of Queen Valda.

'I don't understand Gran, you asked me to come. Don't you and Luna need rescued?' said Qadir. Despite several more attempts to communicate with his grandmother and Luna, there was no response. Shortly after, Nelson announced that they were beginning their descent towards Whitewitch Mountain.

'What is the plan of action when we arrive?' asked Nelson.

'To be honest, I don't really have a plan. This all happened so fast, I had no time to prepare. I intend to find Gran and Luna as quickly as possible and then head home, it's really as simple as that,' said Qadir.

'Do you think it will be that straight forward?' said Nelson.

'No, but there's no harm in hoping,' said Qadir.

As they approached Whitewitch Mountain, Qadir could just about make out the tall, dark fortress perched on the edge of the mountain. The light from one of the moons was reflected against its south side allowing Nelson and Athelea enough visibility to find a suitable landing spot near to the entrance. Several minutes later, Qadir set foot on Whitewitch Mountain for the first time. As soon as the sole of his shoe touched the cold, bare rock Qadir began to feel the evil that surrounded the place.

'This mountain has seen a lot of pain and suffering over the years. I can feel it seeping up through the rock and into my body. What a horrible place. Let's find Gran and Luna and get out of here,' said Qadir. He made his way over to the main entrance and was surprised to find that one of the doors was already open.

'Why don't you both wait out here? I know that you don't like being inside castles at the best of times,' said Qadir to Nelson and Athelea. They had assumed their human form and he watched as they both glanced up nervously at the towering fortress.

'No, we insist on coming in with you. You don't know what you will find in there Your Royal Highness,' said Athelea.

'Okay, if you insist. I'm not going to argue with that,' said Qadir. Although he didn't say it, he was secretly pleased to have some company as he entered the cold, dark fortress.

'The entire place appears to be in darkness; there doesn't seem to be anyone here,' said Nelson as he stared up at the dark windows.

'No, someone is definitely here. I can sense their presence and whoever they are, they are highly skilled in the art of sorcery,' said Qadir.

'Well, your Gran and Luna are both supposed to be here, perhaps it is them who you are sensing,' suggested Athelea

'No Athelea, this is an evil sorcerer. In fact, I think there might be two of them. I can sense a male and a female. I have never felt such wickedness and cruelty in a living being before, it even feels more evil than the Spindle and she takes some beating,' said Qadir.

Qadir was the first to enter the open door that led inside, Nelson and Athelea followed closely behind. Once they passed through the entrance they were surprised to find burning torches on the wall all the way along the hallway.

'Well, at least we'll be able to see where we are going,' whispered Nelson. However, as soon as all three had stepped inside, the door behind them suddenly slammed shut, the burning torches extinguished themselves and they found themselves standing in complete darkness.

'I spoke too soon,' whispered Nelson.

'*Soillsich,*' whispered Qadir. A large sphere of light appeared in the palm of his hand and he held it in front of him in order to light up the way ahead.

'Nelson was only kidding about not being able to see, we tàcharan are used to living in the dark forests and once our eyes adjust, we can actually see quite well in the dark,' said Athelea. As soon as Athelea had spoken, a bloodcurdling scream could be heard further down the hallway.

Suddenly they felt an icy cold breeze blow down the corridor, Qadir's magical light went out and they found themselves standing once again in the pitch dark. As they stood shivering, Qadir had the sudden realisation that they were no longer alone. At the far end of the hallway, an eerie light appeared. It was quite faint at first and it flashed on and off. Qadir stared hard, trying to work out who or what was behind it. After several minutes, it was obvious that the light was moving towards them.

'What shall we do Prince Qadir? Do you think this is one of the evil sorcerers whom you mentioned earlier?' whispered Athelea.

'I have no idea, but I intend to find out,' replied Qadir.

'Please tell me who you are before you come any closer,' said Qadir. As he spoke his voice echoed down the long hallway. There was no reply and since the light continued to move towards them, Qadir tried one more time.

'If you continue to hold your tongue and refrain from telling me who you are, I will take it as a threat. I don't take too kindly to threats,' said Qadir.

The light had just about reached them and Qadir lifted his hand, ready to strike. He whispered to Nelson and Athelea to get behind him.

'Who are you? This is your last chance. Come no further, I'm warning you,' said Qadir.

'Psst, Qadir. It's me. You need to keep your voice down in case he hears you,' said a voice that came from behind the light.

'Luna? Is that you?' whispered Qadir.

'Yes it's me,' said the voice. Qadir looked more closely and saw that the strange light was a lantern and sure enough, he could just make out a pale face which did indeed resemble his youngest sister, Luna.

'Thank goodness we've found you. Why aren't you using magic to light up the hallway? It would be more effective than that strange lantern you have in your hand. We had no idea what was coming towards us,' said Qadir.

'I can't use magic. If I use magic he will find me. That is why I extinguished your light earlier. He will know that you have entered his home if you use magic,' whispered Luna.

'Okay, well the sooner we get Gran, the sooner we all get out of this creepy place. Where is Gran?' whispered Qadir.

'If you follow me I'll take you to her. She's in bad way and I will need you to help me carry her. Come this way, but please be quiet,' whispered Luna.

'Luna, who are you taking about? Who is *he* that you keep referring to?' whispered Qadir as he began to follow his youngest sister deeper into the dark fortress.

'He is Lord Varvarski of the Wolfhaven, an incredibly powerful sorcerer. He does not take kindly to trespassers. He caught me when I entered the Wolfhaven and I was arrested and brought here for punishment. He put me in a cell, but I managed to escape. I heard you earlier when you tried to communicate with me but I was too afraid to respond in case he heard me. As soon as I knew you were coming I planned my escape. I am so glad you are here Qadir,' whispered Luna.

'Aren't you going to say hello to Nelson and Athelea? You do realise that they are behind me,' said Qadir.

'Oh, yes of course. Hello Athelea and Nelson. Sorry, I am a bit distracted at the moment,' whispered Luna.

'Yes, you don't seem yourself at all,' whispered Qadir. He looked back at Nelson and Athelea apologetically.

'Don't worry Prince Qadir. It's really not an issue given the circumstances. She has a lot on her mind,' said Nelson.

'I know, but it was as if she didn't recognise either of you. Athelea has looked after Luna since she was a baby. I find her behaviour odd,' whispered Qadir.

Luna had marched on and by the time they caught up with her, they had reached the end of the hallway and were being shown into a large chamber.

'Quick, come inside. I need to close the door behind me,' whispered Luna.

'Why do you need to close the door? Surely it makes more sense to leave it open?' whispered Qadir.

Just as Qadir spoke he looked at his sister's face and saw a look of anger spread across it. At first he thought that it was all down to the poor light but then he noticed that her face looked much older than normal. She seemed to have lost her childish looks and her eyes seemed distant and dark.

'Luna, are you sure you are alright?' whispered Qadir. He reached forwards and placed his hand on his sister's shoulder but as soon as he touched her, Luna turned on Qadir like a cornered wild animal. Her entire demeanour changed including her voice. She looked at Qadir with hatred.

'Don't you dare touch me,' snarled Luna, although Qadir now realised that although she did look like Luna, this was most definitely not his sister speaking.

'Who are you and what have you done with my sister? Tell me now of your own free will otherwise I will take the information from you by force,' shouted Qadir.

'You are not the only powerful sorcerer here young prince. My name is Prevara and I am afraid you have now met your match or at least you are about to. Let me introduce you to *the* most powerful sorcerer ever to have lived,' snarled Prevara. She made a gesture with her hand and suddenly the door behind Qadir began to close.

'Quick Nelson, Athelea get out before the door closes,' shouted Qadir.

As soon as he spoke both tàcharan jumped back through the narrow space into the hallway. Of course they had assumed Qadir would follow and were most shocked when the door closed tightly behind them leaving Qadir locked inside the great chamber along with the evil sorceress who had possessed Luna's body. However, Qadir and

Prevara were not the only sorcerers in the great chamber. Prevara had led Qadir there on purpose for hidden in the shadows was Lord Varvarski.

He had longed for the day when he would meet the boy whom everyone referred to as the prophecy, the only one who was as equally strong or potentially stronger than he. Now that he had him trapped, Lord Varvarski felt as if he had already won. He had fulfilled a lifelong dream to remove any potential threat that might stop him from taking what was rightfully his; the throne of Ordania. He wasn't worried about the rest of Qadir's family, whether they died tonight or not was now irrelevant to Lord Varvarski. He had all he needed right in front of him.

'Prevara, this is the moment that we have been waiting for. When I give you my signal, you will kill him and then you can absorb all of his power. After that, you can join me as my Queen. We will be equally strong and every living creature in these lands will fear us, they will tremble at the mere thought of us. We will be the most powerful King and Queen ever to have lived and we will live forever,' roared Lord Varvarski.

'Oh, my Dark Lord. You are so good to me. I have haunted the empty rooms and corridors of this fortress for years waiting for this opportunity. I cannot believe that it has finally happened,' screamed Prevara.

'Hello, am I missing something? There is just one slight problem that might spoil your plans. In case you haven't realised, I am still alive,' shouted Qadir. Suddenly, the moment of euphoria between two of the most evil beings ever to have lived and breathed was interrupted and they were none too pleased.

'How dare you address us in this way! You are nothing but a pathetic child. Before I kill you, I will make sure that you suffer for your rudeness,' snarled Prevara.

'I've heard all this before. You are not the first witch that I've met who has threatened to kill me. In fact you remind me of the last one,' said Qadir.

With a terrible rage in her eyes, Prevara lifted her hand to attack Qadir but he was too quick for her and managed to block her attack by creating a defence shield around him. Prevara was enraged further when her own spell bounced back and struck her hard, knocking her to the floor.

'By the power of the Great Spirits, I demand you leave my sister's body for I know that she can be saved,' screamed Qadir.

'Never, never, never,' screamed Prevara and she spat at the Prince.

'*Slàraig,*' shouted Qadir and he pointed at Prevara. The evil sorceress screamed in pain and began to thrash around on the floor of the great chamber.

'My Lord, you must help me. Stop him from hurting me,' screamed Prevara.

Why Lord Varvarski did not intervene quicker, nobody knows but Qadir did not stop until eventually the evil spirit of Prevara left Luna's body. Qadir watched as a white ghost-like apparition floated out of Luna's body and lifted up towards the ceiling. The terrible screaming and wailing continued until eventually the spirit of Prevara disappeared out of the room.

Meanwhile, on the floor in front of Qadir, Luna opened her eyes momentarily. She was dazed at first and when she tried to speak, she found that she couldn't.

'Welcome back Luna. You can rest there for a bit while I take care of this. Don't worry, you'll be going home soon,' said Qadir.

'You haven't destroyed Prevara you know. Neither you nor anyone else can kill her. She won't stop until she finds a new body in which she can live. You have humiliated her but she'll be back, that I can assure you,' said Lord Varvarski.

'Well, if she does come back I can assure you she won't be possessing my sister's body again,' said Qadir.

'You think you are clever don't you? But do you think you are strong enough to take on me? I could have easily killed you by now. I was going to let Prevara kill you as a special treat. She hasn't been able to kill in a very long time and I know she was very much looking forward to doing it, but since that hasn't worked out I suppose I will have to do it. What you don't understand is that I have been around a lot longer than you and that means I am wiser and I have had so much more time to develop my power. In fact, my power is so strong, no one has ever been able to match it,' said Lord Varvarski.

'If that's the case then why are you hiding in this lonely fortress? If you are so powerful, then why haven't you already taken over the Ordanian throne? Why have your plans to take over these lands failed time and time again?' said Qadir.

The Dark Lord was angry when Qadir said this but he made no response, instead he lifted his finger and pointed at him. A single bolt of lightning from the tip of his finger zigzagged across the room towards Qadir. The Prince created another defence shield to block the attack, only this time it did not work. The Dark Lord's magic was able to penetrate it, something which had never happened before. Suddenly, Qadir felt a searing pain pass through his body as he was thrown across to the far side of the room where he hit the floor hard. He was temporarily winded and it took several moments before he could breathe properly again.

'I don't often do this but I am going to give you a choice; you can either choose to become my apprentice and let me teach you how to use your magic properly or you can die. Together, we would make a great team and I dare say we could rule side by side as Uncle and nephew,' said Lord Varvarski.

'What do you mean as Uncle and nephew? What are you saying?' shouted Qadir. He had recovered from the assault and was finally able to speak again.

'I mean what I said, we could rule these lands together; two of the most powerful sorcerers ever to have been born. I was going to offer the job to Prevara but since we are family I thought I'd give you the opportunity. You see, by rights the throne of Ordania should be mine. After your grandfather's death, I should have been made King. The prophecy says that the next King will be the most powerful sorcerer in the land and that is me. However, I am willing to share the limelight. Do you accept?' said Lord Varvarski.

'Never, I will never accept. Do you honestly think you could make me evil just like you and your maniac of a girlfriend? You cannot possibly be my Uncle for he died a long time ago and I am going to prove that you are lying,' shouted Qadir. He pointed at Lord Vavarski and shouted, *'neo-sgàilich'*.

Qadir's spell made Lord Varvarski's hood fall to the floor revealing his face for the first time. It was a hideously tortured, half skeleton face, exactly as Eden had described several years previously when she had been kidnapped and imprisoned in Whitewitch Mountain.

'How dare you,' screamed Lord Varvarski and he pointed at Qadir again sending more bolts of lightning from his fingertip. Qadir had only just found his feet but was sent crashing to the floor again. This time he found himself lying beside another body which he hadn't noticed before as it was still quite dark in the chamber. Whoever it was, they were draped in a long, black cloak making them practically invisible.

'Who is that?' thought Qadir. He reached out and gently pulled away the hood revealing the pale face of his grandmother.

'Gran, what have they done to you?' shouted Qadir. He looked back at Lord Varvarski with hate and disgust. 'If you really are my Uncle, if you are who you say you are, then why have you done this to her? Why have you done this to your own mother?' screamed Qadir. Tears began to roll down his cheeks and splash onto the floor.

'She stopped being my mother many years ago. Neither she nor my father came to look for me. I was immediately ignored and forgotten. That was a choice she made,' replied Lord Varvarski calmly.

'You talk as if she abandoned you but that isn't true. She thought you were dead, she always believed that you had been killed on the battlefield and she never got over it,' shouted Qadir.

'That's what she told you but it is lies, all lies. If you won't join me, then it's time for you to die,' said Lord Varvarski.

'Why are you being like this? I have told you the truth and you are choosing not to believe me. If you really are my Uncle Espen, then I don't believe you are evil,' said Qadir.

'Do not mention that name again,' screamed Lord Varvarski. His voice was no longer calm. A terrible rage began to build inside him causing Whitewitch Mountain to tremble.

'But why not? That is your real name isn't it? If you are my Uncle like you said, then you must be Uncle Espen, Prince Espen of Ordania,' said Qadir.

Qadir was not quite prepared for what happened next for Lord Varvarski screamed so loudly, the walls and ceiling around the great chamber began to crack.

'You will never say that name again,' and he pointed once more at Qadir and struck him hard. This time it was Qadir who was screaming. At one point the pain was so bad he thought he would pass out. Just as he began to close his eyes, he heard the voice of his grandfather whisper in his ear. 'Don't give up my lad. You are stronger than him but you need to believe in yourself. Keep calm and clear your mind. Remember your training with Adamaris,' said King Andris.

As he lay on the floor in terrible pain, Qadir managed to force open his eyes. He slowly lifted up one arm and pointed at the Dark Lord.

'*Slàraig*,' screamed Qadir. A bolt of white lightening shot out from his fingers and struck the Dark Lord causing him to stagger backwards. Qadir wasted no time in sending more of the same until Lord Varvarski fell down. However, neither of them stayed down long and within minutes both sorcerers had found their feet and were attacking each other.

'Great Spirits of the Starry, Great Spirits of the Mountains High, Great Spirits of the Woods and Trees, Great Spirits of Deep Blue Seas, I invoke thee,' roared Qadir.

'Ha Ha, there are no stars to help you in this part of the world,' laughed Lord Varvarski.

'Well, it's a good job I came prepared then,' said Qadir. He placed his hand inside his pocket and withdrew the blue ethereal ring that his grandfather had given him. It was already glowing brightly when he took it out which it always did whenever it was near evil. Qadir slipped the ring onto his middle finger and pointed it at Lord Varvarski. An enormous beam of blue shot out from the ring and struck the Dark Lord. Qadir watched as the evil sorcerer tried to move away only to find that he couldn't, the power of the ring had him imprisoned. With his other hand and without taking his eyes off the Dark Lord, Qadir reached into his backpack and withdrew another bright object from his bag; it was the star of King Narù. As soon as the glass sphere was free from the backpack, it began to glow even brighter until a beam of starlight shot up into the ceiling and right through the roof. For the first time in many years the dark skies above the Wolhaven were brightly lit. It seemed as if the star of King Narù had called out to other stars, for soon after the beam of light burst across the night sky, other stars began to appear. Qadir recognised the first few stars immediately; they were the stars of all his family, including his own star shining more brightly than ever.

'Great Spirits of the Starry Sky, join me now and help to banish this evil,' roared Qadir. Next there was an enormous flash, brighter than any Qadir had seen before and both he and Lord Varvarski fell backwards.

Qadir quickly jumped back up onto his feet, but when he looked over at the Dark Lord, he noticed that he was still lying down and appeared not to be moving.

'It can't have been that easy,' thought Qadir. He approached the Dark Lord carefully, expecting him to spring up at any moment and attack him again, but he didn't. Soon Qadir was standing over the top of Lord Varvarski. When he looked down, he was shocked to see that the Dark Lord no longer had the hideously disfigured face, instead it was the face of a man. The man's face was familiar to Qadir for it resembled that of his own father and indeed his younger brother, Asmund.

'So, you are my Uncle after all,' said Qadir.

Espen opened his eyes and looked up at Qadir.

'No, I was your Uncle once but that was a long time ago,' came the reply.

Qadir noticed instantly that his voice has changed and he felt as if a huge, dark cloud had lifted.

'Uncle Espen,' whispered Qadir. He hesitated before saying it but it was a test that he needed to carry out. Fortunately, there was no angry reaction this time. The sorcerer lay on the ground exhausted and broken.

'Aren't you going to speak to me?' asked Qadir.

'Why haven't you killed me?' said Espen.

'I haven't killed you because you are my Uncle and I know that deep down you are not evil. What I don't understand is what drove you to be so cruel all these years?' said Qadir.

'It wasn't me, I was possessed by an evil sorcerer and now you have made him leave my body, something which I could never do. For years he has taken control of me. For years he has searched relentlessly for another sorceress whom his evil girlfriend could possess. His plan was that they would then rule together as King and Queen. That is why I or should I say he kidnapped Eden and then Luna,' said Espen.

'Who is he?' said Qadir.

'His name was or is Lord Zadicus, a former rival of Abnocta Mirus. I have been his slave and puppet for all these years. I am afraid that I am not the powerful sorcerer everyone thought I was,' said Espen.

'Well, I don't know about that, but at least you are free from him now. He has left your body and you can be Prince Espen again,' said Qadir.

'Can I, Can I really? I'm not so sure. I have had evil inside me for most of my life now and I don't think I can ever be the same again,' said Espen.

'You can be cured of evil, I know that for sure. If there is good in you which there is, then you can definitely be cured,' said Qadir.

'Although he has left my body, there are still too many scars and I can still feel traces of his putrid evil lurking somewhere inside me. Although it isn't anywhere near as strong as before, it is still there. I don't think I can be cured,' said Espen.

'Then let me cure it for you, I can take away the evil,' said a faint, weak voice from the other side of the chamber.

Both Qadir and Espen looked round in the direction of the voice and saw that it was Queen Valda. Although incredibly weak and barely able to lift her head off the ground, she was alive and she had heard everything.

'Come over here son so that I can see you,' said Queen Valda.

Espen made his way over to where his mother was lying and looked at her.

'I'm sorry Mum. Look what I have done to you, to my own mother. I am so sorry,' said Espen and he began to weep.

'You will be free of him now that Qadir has called upon the stars for help. Had we known sooner, we would have come for you. It is I who should say sorry; I am sorry for leaving you trapped here all these years,' said Queen Valda.

'Lord Zadicus talked me into thinking that you didn't want me and that was why nobody came to look for me. In fact he said that you had arranged for me to be kidnapped. He brought me here and told me that I was a powerful sorcerer and that he would teach me how to use my powers. As a young man I was angry with the world and I wanted to show everyone that I could be someone. In the end I believed everything he told me, I was naïve and I trusted hm. By doing that, I let my guard down and then he possessed me. His plan was to travel to Castle Dracwynne disguised as me, but then I somehow managed to resist. I was stronger back then and I was able to put up a fight. Eventually I gave in through sheer exhaustion and he won however the struggle seemed to have changed my appearance. I no longer looked like mysef, but the horrible, tortured soul that was Zadicus. This of course meant that his plan to return to

Castle Draccwyne would no longer work. The next obstacle was of course Qadir's protection spell which put an end to his next plan and he was furious,' said Espen.

'You were always such a good person and I know that you could never turn bad. You were so young at the time Espen and you must have felt terribly hurt and abandoned; please know that I have always loved you. When it was first suggested to me that you might be Lord of the Wolfhaven, I didn't believe it and it would seem I was right; Zadicus was behind everything. I thought that your father and I had destroyed him years ago but as is the case with the dark power, it often reshapes and returns. Now, I will help you remove any last traces of evil from your body so that you can begin to feel normal again,' said Queen Valda.

'How will you do that Mum?' said Espen.

'I will do it by loving you the way any mother loves her son,' said Queen Valda. She placed her hand on her son's forehead and closed her eyes.

Leig le Espen falbh ann an sìth,' whispered Queen Valda. Before Espen and Qadir realised what was happening, a greenish-looking mist passed from Espen's forehead and up Queen Valda's arm. As soon as it dawned on Espen what his mother was doing, he tried to pull away only to find that he couldn't.

Moments later, Queen Valda lay her head down on the floor again and closed her eyes.

'Is she okay? What just happened?' said Qadir.

'I didn't know she was going to do that, if I had I wouldn't have let her do it. She has withdrawn all evil from my body but now it is inside her,' said Espen.

'What does that mean? Is she going to be alright?' said Qadir.

'I'm not sure. Normally it wouldn't be such a problem, but she is already very weak. We need to find a healer or someone who is knowledgeable about medicines which combat evil,' said Espen.

'I know people who can help, but they are quite far away,' said Qadir.

'How far away? She is no longer strong enough to deal with evil in her body. If we don't get help, then she will die,' said Espen.

Their conversation was interrupted when the sound of someone moaning came from the other side of the room. When Qadir looked round, he saw that it was coming from Luna. Suddenly she sat upright, rubbed her eyes and looked around the room.

'Qadir, is that you? What's going on? I feel as if I have been drugged,' said Luna.

'You'll be fine Luna, I let you rest for a while. Athelea is waiting outside to take you home to Castle Draccwyne. Do you think you can stand up?' said Qadir.

'Yes, I think so. I really have no clue where we are,' said Luna.

'Don't worry, I'll fill you in on the way home,' said Qadir.

When Luna and Qadir looked up through the enormous hole in the roof, they could see the brightly shining moons surrounded by many twinkling stars. Suddenly, two large shadows passed overhead. Concerned that it might be the evil spirits of Lord Zadicus and Prevara seeking revenge, Qadir prepared himself for another assault however moments later he breathed a sigh of relief when he saw two flying horses; it was Nelson and Athelea. Both tàcharan flew down through the hole in the roof and gently landed on the floor of the great chamber.

'We will take you home now your Majesty and your Royal Highnesses,' neighed Nelson.

'We have a slight problem, there is now one extra passenger,' said Qadir and he looked over at his Uncle Espen.

'Don't mind me. I won't be travelling back with you. The main thing is to get your grandmother home as quickly as possible so that she can get the help she needs,' said Espen.

'Well, she can't fly by herself. She is too weak to hold on. Someone will have to fly with her,' said Qadir.

'Okay, I will accompany her back to Castle Draccwyne but I won't stay. I will leave as soon she gets the help that she needs,' said Espen.

'But Castle Draccwyne is your home and your family will be there. Why wouldn't you stay? Once I explain to everyone what has happened, they will be over the moon to see you. Of course Mum and Dad will be shocked at first, who can blame them but it will be even more of a reason to celebrate,' said Qadir.

'You might be right but in the meantime we need to hold back on the celebrations until we get your grandmother some help,' said Espen.

It was agreed that Nelson would carry Queen Valda back to Castle Draccwyne and Espen would ride with them, so that he could support his mother during the long flight. Athelea offered to take Qadir and Luna although she did say that she might need to stop and rest every so often. She wasn't really designed to carry two passengers. Just as Athelea knelt down to allow Qadir and Luna onto her back, another flying creature passed overhead and began to circle the open roof. Qadir looked up and saw that it was a giant bird.

'Oh, it's Harailt. He has come to look for me,' said Luna.

'Tuweet Tuwoo, is that yooohou down there Princess Luna?' hooted Harailt.

'Yes, Harailt. What perfect timing and thank you for not forgetting about me,' said Luna. She then turned and smiled at Athelea.

'It looks like you won't have to carry two passengers after all. Why don't you take Qadir on your back and I'll take the owl,' said Luna.

'I'm not even going to ask,' said Qadir. 'Okay everyone, let's get Gran home!'

Shortly after Qadir spoke, two winged horses could be seen lifting up into the moonlit sky, followed by a large tawny owl, each one bearing passengers. It would be a long journey back and they were worried about Queen Valda but at least this time they were heading home.

Chapter 25: Winds of Change

As the last rays of golden sun filtered through the thick, green leaves of the bacari tree outside Queen Valda's bedroom; its fruit maturing in the warmth, Queen Valda lay propped up in bed, staring out through the open window. A swarm of mygga flies caught her attention as they did their ritualistic dance in the late sunshine. Never before had she paid so much attention to the small, busibodied creatures and she suddenly found them interesting. The Queen loved the smell of a mature Ordanian summer and she inhaled deeply when a sudden breeze blew in through the bedroom window, bringing with it a single white feather. The Queen watched as the feather gently floated across the room and settled at the foot of her bed.

Since her return, the Queen had not spoken one word. Although she was content to be at home with her family, there was now a new concern that troubled her as she lay in bed and stared out the window. The return of Prince Espen and the victory over Lord Zadicus should have been more than enough reason to celebrate and rejoice, however a feeling of sadness hung over Castle Draccwyne. No one had seen or heard from Prince Adair since the War of Westerlyn. He had gone to the Wolfhaven to look for his daughter and Mother and then vanished from sight.

The Queen had found her youngest son after many years of believing he was dead and then at the same time, her eldest son had gone missing. The family could not be happy until they knew what had become of Prince Adair. They tried everything they could possibly think of to help uncover the mystery; magical spyglasses, locator spells, they even turned to Starrydell for answers but each time they uncovered nothing.

Several weeks had passed since the family had returned home to Castle Draccwyne and with each passing day the landscape around Castle Draccwyne began to change. Soon the trees across Ordania had outgrown their summer clothes and one by one they started to

undress, carpeting the land with reds, golds and browns. By the time
the trees at the foot of Elfview Mountain were completely naked,
there was still no word from Prince Adair.

A gentle knock on the bedroom door made the Queen turn away
from the dancing myyga flies temporarily. She hoped that whoever it
was, they would bring news of her eldest son. Seconds later the
familiar face of her lifelong friend, Ailsa Carmichael popped her head
round the door.

'Good evening Vronnie, How is my patient?' said Ailsa. Queen Valda
smiled over at her friend. It was reassuring to see Ailsa and she was
really pleased that she had offered to come back and live in Castle
Draccwyne again. During each visit, Ailsa made sure the Queen was
kept up to date with everything that was happening. On this
particular evening, she had some very peculiar and interesting news
to share.

'You'll never guess what happened to me this afternoon. I was out
walking with Luna and Auld Annie when we stumbled across a group
of Varken Mensen. As soon as they saw us, they stopped and asked
for some advice. According to what one of them said, they
discovered two old ladies wandering in the woods several weeks ago.
At the time both ladies were completely disorientated and incoherent,
unable to explain who they were or where they came from. The
varken mensen have been looking after them all this time. Anyway,
they said that finally the old ladies had found their tongues and were
able to tell them where they were from. You'll never guess what the
answer was?' said Ailsa. She paused momentarily for the Queen to
answer and then realised that she was no longer able to speak. Queen
Valda was staring back at her friend with her eyebrows raised, she
was indeed most intrigued to know the next part of the story.

'They told the varken mensen they were from a place called Uig
which of course they'd never heard of. At this point I asked the
varken mensen if they didn't mind taking me to their home so that I

could meet them for myself and they did.

Vronnie, I can honestly tell you that I have never been as shocked in all my life and that's saying a lot from a non-magical person born and raised on Lewis who is now best friends with a sorceress Queen. When I arrived outside their home in the Belwald wood, sitting outside with their feet up and enjoying a cup of Ordanian tea were none other than Brighid MacLeod and Ealasaid Mackenzie from Uig on Lewis. Never in a million years would I have expected to see them. Back home they are known as the local newspapers for they know absolutely everything that is going on but I have absolutely no idea how they came to be in Ordania. It looks like you might need to share your secret spell with Princess Isabella, so that she can erase their memories and send them back. Can you imagine if they go home talking about a magical land with people who live in the woods and resemble pigs? They'd get carted off and locked up.

The Queen shook her head in dismay. Although she was surprised to hear this news, straight away she had a good idea how it had happened.

Queen Valda wasn't the only one who spent most of her time staring out of a window. From the moment the sun rose in the sky and until it set in the evening Princess Isabella also found herself looking outside, hoping to catch sight of her husband.

'Will we ever see Dad again?' asked Eden.

'I hope so Darling, I hope so. Your Dad is strong and if he is alive which I believe he is, then he will get home eventually,' said Isabella. As she spoke she continued to look out the window.

'But what's keeping him? If Dad is alive, why haven't we heard from him after all this time?' asked Asmund.

'I only wish I knew the answer but one thing is for sure, we must never give up hope,' said Isabella.

'I take it we will be staying here permanently from now on?' said Qadir.

'No, not quite. Your Aunt Eva has said that she will look after you when you return to school. I will need to stay here for the time being and await news from your father,' said Isabella.

She noticed the look of disappointment on her son's face when she said this.

'It won't be for much longer. If you finish this year at school, then you can move to Ordania permanently next year,' added Isabella.

'Really? Do you mean it?' said Qadir. Suddenly he looked excited again.

'What about Gran? Shouldn't we stay here and help look after her?' said Asmund

'Your Gran is already being very well looked after. She has her own personal nurses; Nanny Carmichael and her new apprentice; Auld Annie. Nanny Carmichael brought her to Ordania and she seems to be quite happy here.

'Who couldn't love being here in Ordania? I just wish we knew where Dad was then we really could be one happy family again,' said Qadir.

'I am sure we will but until that happens, your dad would want you to go back to school and most important of all, he would want you look after each other,' said Isabella.

'Don't we always?' smiled Qadir.

The following day Ailsa Carmichael took Isabella into the Belwald and introduced her to Ealasaid and Brighid.

'Good afternoon ladies. It's time for you both to go home,' said Isabella.

'Oh yes, I suppose we do need to get back. Our families will be terribly worried about us but we do like it here. I've never felt so young and full of energy,' said Ealasaid.

'Aye, it will be a shame to leave this beautiful forest. I've never seen a forest more beautiful than this one. It's magical,' said Brighid.

'How will we get home? Is there a bus that will take us there?' asked Ealasaid.

'No, there is no bus but the journey will be very quick. When you do get back, I'm afraid that you won't really remember Ordania. It will seem like you had a strange dream. I need you to drink one final cup of ordanian tea. This one is very special and made by the Queen's own secret recipe,' said Isabella.

Once both ladies had swallowed every last drop of the special brew and commented on how delicious it was, Isabella invited them both to stand up and join her where she stood in the glade. Rays of sun came streaming down through the trees and when both ladies looked up, a firebird began to sing. Its fiery feathers of red made a striking contrast against the autumn leaves.

'Oh, what a bonnie wee bird. I've never seen anything like it,' said Brighid.

As both ladies stood and stared up at the firebird, they failed to notice the brightly glowing ring that suddenly appeard around their feet on the floor of the forest.

'*Till nad dheann, till gu slàn*', *till nad dheann, till gu slàn*', *till nad dheann, till gu slàn*', *till nad dheann, till gu slàn,*' chanted Isabella.

As soon as Ealasaid and Brighid heard Gaelic being spoken, they both looked away from the firebird and stared at Isabella.

'*A bheil Gàidhlig agaibh?*' asked Ealasaid. Isabella never got the chance to answer for as soon as Elasaid asked the question, both she and

Brighid vanished.

A short while later both ladies found themselves standing at the side of the road, just down from the bus stop at Timsgarry on the Isle of Lewis. Several days had now passed on earth since the disappearance of the two local ladies and the suggestion of a possible alien abduction had attracted media attention from right across the globe. A police enquiry unit had been set up across the road from the bus stop as this was the area where both ladies had last been seen. It wasn't long before both Ealasaid and Brighid were spotted, standing beside the road and looking around them with a look of complete bewilderment on their faces.

'Good evening ladies, are you Ms Macleod and Ms Mackenzie from Brenish here on Lewis?' asked a police officer.

'Yes, indeed we are,' replied Brighid.

'My goodness ladies. Whatever happened to you? We have been searching for you for several days now. You have made news headlines,' said the police officer.

'Several days? That can't be right. We only went for a walk,' said Ealasaid.

'Have you both been hiding in the thicket over there? Surely you can't have slept outdoors overnight? The past few nights have been a bit chilly. It's almost late October,' said the police officer.

'Of course we haven't been sleeping outside. You must have made a mistake officer. We were on the number 4 bus earlier today and stepped off a few stops early to catch some fresh air,' said Ealasaid.

'Well, I can assure you that you have been missing since last Tuesday and it's now Sunday. However, the main thing is that you both appear to be okay. Your families have been very worried about you. Let's get you over into the police hut and I'll give you some warm tea, then we'll get you both checked out by a doctor. I have a few important phone calls to make,' said the police officer.

By the following day, Ealasaid and Brighid had become global celebrities. Reporters from all over the world arrived on the Isle of Lewis and gathered outside their crofts. They were intrigued by the story of how the ladies had miraculously reappeared after having been missing, assumed abducted by aliens, for up to five days. At first both ladies were startled by the huge media interest and could not understand why they were being bombarded with requests for interviews. However, it didn't take them too long to warm to their new celebrity status. When asked in an interview what had happened, although she did say that it felt more like a dream, Ealasaid was able to recall waking up in a strange place and being interrogated by people who she said resembled pigs. Whether they were believed or not, the story was well received and the more Ealasaid told the story, the more interesting and detailed it became.

'If you ask me, I think they've been spending time with Ailsa Carmichael and were probably hiding in her house the whole time. I wouldn't be surprised if whisky was involved as well. You would think at their age they would know better,' said Mrs McNeil, the lady who ran the local post office in Aird Uig.

Meanwhile back in Castle Draccwyne, Luna, Asmund and Qadir were saying goodbye to their mother, grandmother and Uncle Espen for they were to return to Scotland in time for the new school term. Eden would remain in Ordania with her mother and grandmother. Since she lost her eyesight, Eden had become completely dependent on her magical powers to act as eyes therefore it was no longer possible for her to return to earth and pretend to be non-magical. Although Qadir, Asmund and Luna usually only got to visit Ordania during school holidays, their mother had promised that they could return every weekend from now on. This reassured the children and made them feel less anxious about leaving without any news of their father.

'Goodbye Gran. I would say that it won't be too long until we see you again but it will feel longer for you than it will for us. Mum says we can come back every weekend but that will seem more like every four months to you,' said Asmund.

One by one the children kissed their grandmother goodbye. Although no words left her lips, the children could tell by the sadness in her eyes that she would miss them. Qadir was the last to leave the room and just before he walked out of the bedroom door, he turned one last time to look at his grandmother. He caught sight of a lone tear sparkling like a tiny diamond in the corner of her eye. It was then that she spoke to her eldest grandson, although no words passed her lips. The Queen communicated with Qadir using her mind.

'Goodbye for now Qadir. I have no strength to talk through my mouth any more but I needed to tell you a few things before you go. First of all, words could never describe how immensely proud I am of you. I want to thank you for rescuing Luna and I and bringing us home again. I also want to thank you for finding your Uncle Espen and returning him to me. I only wish your father were here to share the good news. Please take care of your brother and sister. Keep a careful eye on Luna. She appears okay on the surface but inside she is still struggling to come to terms with everything that happened. Just make sure Asmund doesn't tease her too much. If you have any concerns, please let me or your Mother know immediately. Like your Uncle Espen, she too was touched by terrible evil. Hopefully it was not in her body long enough to cause any long term harm but you never know. If ever you do need guidance Qadir, always look to the stars, even the stars that shine in the skies above earth will listen to you. Goodbye for now Prince of the Starry Sky.

Qadir smiled back at his grandmother. 'I will see you again soon Gran. Please take care and be a good patient for Nanny Carmichael. Goodbye for now Queen of Ordania,' said Qadir.

It was almost dark when Qadir, Asmund and Luna stood outside in the castle gardens waiting for their transport home. There would be a blue moon that evening which meant they could travel back to earth by moonbeam.

'Remember to be on your best behaviour for Aunt Eva. She will be waiting for you in the house when you get back to Ravenswood Drive. Asmund, please don't fight with your sister and Qadir, as the eldest I expect you to set a good example and help to look after your brother and sister. I have also asked your watchers to travel back to earth with you. Nelson, Athelea and Kaimono will stay throughout your time on earth so I am sure you will all be quite safe,' said Isabella.

Soon three glum-looking children were zooming across the night sky of Ordania and heading for one of the moons. As they began their journey back to earth, the children stared down at their family home for as long as they could until it disappeared out of sight. By the time they were passing over the moon and had begun to float around inside the protective moon bubble, they started to feel their magical powers being switched off.

When they finally landed in the back garden of Number 32 Ravenswood Drive, the bubble popped and Quentin, Aaron and Anna Bartholomew found themselves back where they started.

'Do you think we win first prize for the most bizarre October break ever?' said Aaron.

'I think we would be in with a fair chance. No more adventures for a while though, I'm exhausted. I never thought I'd say this but I'm going back to school for a rest,' said Quentin.

'What, no more adventures ever? That's not like you?' said Aaron.

'I said no adventures for a while. How many weeks until the Christmas holidays? That should be enough of a break,' smiled Quentin.

'Nine more weeks, not that I'm counting,' sighed Anna.

Meanwhile next door in Number 33 Ravenswood Drive, the curtains twitched from an upstairs window and the familiar face of Angus Macpherson appeared. As soon as he saw Anna in the garden he quickly threw open his bedroom window and shouted down to her.

'Hey Anna. Where have you been? I've been trying to contact you. Did you miss me?' said Angus.

Anna got a fright when she suddenly heard her name being shouted out in the middle of the night.

'Shhhh Angus, don't shout. You'll wake everyone up,' said Anna. If it hadn't been so dark, Quentin and Aaron would have noticed that her face was now very red.

'Have you had a good holiday? What did you get up to?' said Angus.

Anna was getting more embarrassed by the minute. It was now so late she really needed to get indoors and her Aunt Eva had now appeared at the window.

'I have to go Angus. It's late and I need to get some sleep. If you want, we can walk to school together tomorrow and I'll tell you all about my week then,' said Anna.

'Okay Anna. That would be great,' said Angus.

'Goodnight then Angus,' said Anna.

'Goodnight Anna,' said Angus and then he paused again before adding; 'I've missed you.'

By the time all three children tumbled into the familiar kitchen at the back of Number 32 Ravenswood Drive, Aaron could no longer hold in his laughter.

'It sounds as if someone has been broken hearted without you,' sniggered Aaron.

'Leave it Aaron,' said Quentin.

'So Anna, when will you and loverboy be getting married?' said Aaron and he made kissing noises with his lips.

'Drop it Aaron,' warned Quentin. He could see his youngest sister starting to get really annoyed.

'Aaron, have you forgotten what happened the last time someone annoyed her?' said Quentin.

Aaron paused and thought about it for a minute. 'Ah, that's a fair point. Time for bed I think!'

THE END

Other titles in this series

Ordania

ISBN-13: 978-1534999855

ISBN-10: 153499985X

18147938R00159

Printed in Great Britain
by Amazon